Praise for

SEAL TEAM SIX: HUNT THE WOLF

"*Hunt the Wolf* comes alive as members of SEAL Team Six chase terrorists from one port to another with consummate skill and grit. You're sure to get caught up in the suspense and danger, unable to look away for even a second. This new SEAL Team Six series will become addictive—and I'm already looking forward to the next installment."

—Margaret Marr, NightsAndWeekends.com

"Action galore."

—John Harrington, *The Oklahoman*

"*Hunt the Wolf* was a rocket-fast read, and is true to its promise of entertaining the readers of Vince Flynn and Brad Thor. By the end, I wanted more, more guns, more explosions, and more dead terrorists. I want more and so will you."

—C. J. Edwards, *Grift Magazine*

"Mann's sparse prose keeps the story crackling, and he imbues the novel with authenticity thanks to his thirty years of service. His is a new voice in the genre that I'm sure we'll hear from again."

—David Ingram, *Suspense Magazine*

"*Hunt the Wolf* roars out of the most authentic inspirations in the blood and bayonets commando saga genre, and for lovers of military action fiction, this is a read to have."

—James Grady, author of *Six Days of the Condor*

"Don Mann writes like a soldier talks—straight to the point. And he packs a mean punch."

—Chris Ryan, author of *Strike Back*

"A steady stream of action makes this a worthy entry into the burgeoning SEAL thriller genre."

—*Publishers Weekly*

"A lot of slam-bang action."

—Robert Conroy, *Library Journal*

"SEAL aficionados and action addicts will find...engaging hours of reading here."

—*Kirkus Reviews*

SEAL TEAM SIX:
HUNT THE WOLF

ALSO BY DON MANN WITH RALPH PEZZULLO

Inside SEAL Team Six

SEAL TEAM SIX:

HUNT THE WOLF

DON MANN

WITH RALPH PEZZULLO

MULHOLLAND BOOKS

LITTLE, BROWN AND COMPANY

NEW YORK BOSTON LONDON

The characters and events in this book are fictitious. Any similarity to real persons, living or dead, is coincidental and not intended by the author.

Mulholland Books / Little, Brown and Company
Hachette Book Group
237 Park Avenue
New York, NY 10017
mulhollandbooks.com

Printed in the United States of America

Originally published as *Hunt the Wolf* in hardcover by Mulholland Books, June 2012
First Mulholland Books mass market edition, November 2012

10 9 8 7 6 5 4 3 2

"We sleep safe in our beds because rough men stand ready in the night to visit violence on those who would do us harm."

—George Orwell

This book is dedicated to those rough men and women, and especially the Navy SEALs.

SEAL TEAM SIX:
HUNT THE WOLF

PROLOGUE

It is a principle of human nature to hate those whom you have injured.

—Tacitus

AS MARINE Staff Sergeant Nancy Cisneros bounded from the main building of the U.S. embassy in Rabat, Morocco, the space around her seemed to light up with her energy. She was armed with an M4 automatic rifle and M9A1 sidearm, and wore a lightweight helmet with a MARPAT desert cover and an outer tactical vest with two bullet- and heat-resistant Kevlar plates.

Despite her formidable appearance, Sergeant Cisneros was in a good mood because she'd just finished Skyping her fiancé back in the States. In less than two weeks, they were planning to get married in San Diego during her annual leave.

Last Saturday, the leader of the embassy guards—a tall Berber tribesman named Jalil—had escorted her to a stall on the covered Rue Souk as Sabbat, where Cisneros picked out matching filigreed gold wedding bands.

As she crossed the driveway to Post One, the sergeant

flashed a thumbs-up to Jalil, who stood outside Post Two dressed in a black Royal Gendarmerie uniform with an MP5 slung over his shoulder. Despite their cultural and religious differences, she and her Moroccan counterpart had become friends. Several months ago, Nancy and some other Americans had attended an elaborate ceremony in Jalil's family compound near the Rif Mountains to celebrate the birth of the Moroccan's first son. Together, she and Jalil had raised thousands of dollars for a fund that provided soccer balls, nets, and uniforms to needy local children.

The two fortified guard posts at the U.S. embassy entrance stood approximately fifty feet apart. Post One, to Cisneros's right, monitored vehicular traffic in and out of the main gate. The smaller Post Two, where Jalil was standing, was responsible for checking people who were trying to gain access to the embassy compound on foot.

Every workday morning, hundreds of local Moroccan visa applicants lined up along the high concrete wall that surrounded the embassy compound, waiting to be checked and patted down before a marine guard waved them through the body scanner. If the red light didn't flash, the applicants would then be escorted through a metal door and along a path to the U.S. consular office, which was housed on the ground floor of the main building.

Before entering Post One, Sergeant Nancy Cisneros looked up to see the sun burning its way through the morning haze. Inside the six-sided reinforced-concrete structure, two Moroccan security agents and another marine stood watching the front gates through a Plexiglas window. A State Department security officer named Havlichek sat before a console of six monitors that broadcast pictures of the traffic on nearby Avenue Mohamed El Fassi and the access street to the main gate.

"All clear?" Sergeant Cisneros asked the American at the console.

"Except for that white pickup," Havlichek answered. "It's been parked there about ten minutes doing jack shit."

Sergeant Cisneros noticed that the Toyota truck appeared to be carrying a heavy load in its back cargo bay, which was covered with a canvas tarp.

"Driver probably stopped to drink some *na'na,*" she offered, referring to the popular local mint tea.

"Or smoke some kif, more likely."

"I'll send one of the gendarmes to check it out."

Sergeant Cisneros exited Post One and took two steps toward the front gate with the intention of giving orders to one of the four Moroccan security officers stationed there, when she heard a vehicle honk behind her. Turning, she saw the big white water truck that had arrived to deliver fifteen hundred gallons of potable water to the embassy backing toward the gate.

"What the hell's he backing up for?" Cisneros asked into the helmet headset that connected her to Post One.

"Because he's a typical Moroccan driver," answered Havlichek.

"Open the inner gate," Sergeant Cisneros barked.

Then she held up her arms to stop the driver of the water truck and yelled, *"Arrêtez!"*

But the driver, who had his radio blaring, didn't hear her. Cisneros had to jump on the truck's running board and shout through the side window before the driver applied the brakes and stopped.

Sergeant Cisneros was trying to figure out how to tell

the driver in French that he should reverse course, proceed farther down the driveway, and turn around, when she heard one of the Moroccan guards shout. She turned to her right to see a white pickup speeding toward the open gate. It looked to be the same one she had viewed on the monitor only half a minute earlier.

She jumped off the running board and ran toward the gate yelling, "Halt! Halt! Tell that son of a bitch to stop!"

The Toyota screeched to a halt in front of the Delta barrier, a steel structure that came up from the ground with a flap that faced the driver. As smoke rose from the pickup's tires, a young scrawny man got out of the passenger side, pointed to the barrier, and started screaming in Arabic.

"What's he saying? What the hell does he want?" Sergeant Cisneros shouted to Jalil, who had joined her at the gate. Both of them held their weapons ready.

"He wants you to lower the barrier," Jalil replied in English.

The young man on the other side of the barrier was dressed head to toe in white. His dark eyes were popping out of his head, and he was gesturing wildly.

"Tell him to get back in the truck and back it the fuck out of here before I blow him and his friend away!"

As Jalil started shouting instructions in Arabic, Sergeant Cisneros remembered that Arab men who were preparing for martyrdom often wore white. Feeling an enormous surge of fear and adrenaline, she screamed, "Jalil, take cover!" Then, "Tell the driver to get out of the vehicle and hug the ground!"

The man in white turned suddenly and started running away from the pickup toward Avenue Mohamed El Fassi.

Sergeant Cisneros lowered one knee to the pavement and opened fire on the Toyota driver.

Seeing a flash from the barrel of the American's M4, the driver of the pickup pushed a button that detonated the seven hundred pounds of explosives in the truck. The last thing Sergeant Nancy Cisneros saw was an enormous white flash. The power of the blast completely pulverized her body and threw her head a hundred yards.

Jalil, Havlichek, the driver of the water truck, the other marines, and all the Moroccan guards were killed immediately. The visa applicants standing in line were either killed outright or horribly wounded. All that remained of the water truck was a shredded chassis. What had been the pickup became a twelve-foot wide, six-foot-deep crater.

The blast destroyed the front of the embassy building, killing thirty-three Americans and twenty-four local employees. Flying metal, glass, and debris seriously injured another seventy people inside the building, including the U.S. ambassador, who suffered facial lacerations and a concussion. Windows were blown out in neighboring buildings, including the Belgian embassy and a preschool, injuring hundreds of others.

Less than an hour after the attack, as rescuers fought through smoke and the nauseating smell of burnt human flesh to search for victims, the president of the United States and the king of Morocco issued a joint statement calling it a "heinous and cowardly crime" against both of their countries and promising to cooperate fully to find the perpetrators and bring them to justice.

The *Washington Post* called it the worst terrorist attack against Americans since 9/11/2001.

CHAPTER ONE

Don't raise more demons than you can lay down.

—Old English proverb

TWO WEEKS later, U.S. Navy Chief Warrant Officer Tom Crocker and three of his SEAL Team Six teammates, all dressed as civilians, were flying at 32,000 feet over Mount Erciyes in central Turkey when the Emirates Airlines Boeing 777 they were in hit an air pocket. Akil (full name Akil Okasha El-Daly, aka Akil Daly), who was standing in the aisle, lost his balance and landed in Crocker's lap.

"Do I look like Santa Claus?" Crocker asked.

"Sorry, boss," the handsome Egyptian American said, smiling, trying to pull himself up.

Crocker, the assault leader of Blue Team of U.S. Navy SEAL Team Six, aka the U.S. Naval Special Warfare Development Group—the premier antiterrorism arm of the U.S. military—lifted the 220-pound former marine sergeant up and set him back in the aisle like he was a little boy.

Then he pulled off his earphones. Dave Brubeck's "Take Five" seeped into the drone of the engines. The forty-two-year-old team leader had recently discovered that fifties jazz put him in a mellow groove. Something about the 5/4 rhythm and the cool precision of the melody. Gentle, economical, restrained.

"You're one strong mother," Akil said, looking down at the manila folder on the middle seat. "Don't you ever take a break?" Pushing back his bristly black hair, smoothing the sky blue Nike polo over his muscular torso.

Take a break from what? Crocker wanted to ask. Working out? Studying? Preparing for the mission? Listening to music? Trying to relax?

Crocker didn't answer. Akil held on to Crocker's headrest and leaned over, flashing his pearly whites like he was performing for the other passengers. "You pumped?"

A fifteen-year veteran of the Navy SEALs and dozens of top-secret ops to Afghanistan, Iraq, Pakistan, Yemen, Somalia, and other hot spots around the world, Crocker was too disciplined to talk about a mission with foreigners within earshot. So he said, "You're referring to the climb, right?"

"That's right, boss," Akil answered. "The climb."

The climb was the team's cover. Hours after the U.S. embassy bombing in Rabat, CIA officers had picked up the trail of the man who ran away from the pickup before it exploded in front of the gate. They learned that his name was Mohammed Saddiq and he had managed to survive, even though the blast had blown him off his feet and forward, leaving lacerations and cuts from the back of his head to his ankles. Bleeding through his clothes and feverish, Saddiq had managed to board a flight to Rome.

CIA operatives found him in the Italian city two days after the bombing, hiding in an airport bathroom.

Crocker looked up at Akil and said, "It's a training climb to give you guys a feel for what it's gonna be like when we really do attempt to summit K2."

"Yeah. Yeah. Piece of cake."

"We'll see." In addition to being the assault leader of Blue Team, Crocker was ST-6's lead climber. SEAL stands for Sea, Air, and Land, and Crocker was determined to prepare the men on his team for any contingency, including dealing with the most treacherous terrain on the planet.

Previously, he had led his men on ascents of Denali, Mount Whitney, and winter ascents on Grand Teton and Mount Washington (the latter featured unimaginably bad weather, with gusts up to 230 miles an hour). Physical challenges were his bread and butter, his manna. He lived for them.

Leering, Akil said, "I hear Edyta might be there."

Edyta Potocka. Early forties. Legendary climber. Third woman to summit Mount Everest. "Yeah. What about her?"

She and Crocker had spent a night together eighteen years before in a tent in the Himalayas. This was before he'd married his current wife. Neither had bathed for days. He remembered it as an odd mixture of wrestling and sex, with no words spoken. Seeking warmth and relief in each other's bodies as frigid winds roared outside.

"Hot, huh?"

"Kind of attractive in a gritty Eastern European way."

"I'm looking forward to meeting her."

"I bet you are." Crocker stroked his strong chin. He knew that anything with a pair of tits under the age of sixty was prey to the single Omar Sharif look-alike, who consistently claimed to have bedded over three hundred women.

Akil lowered his voice like he was passing a secret. "You read the file on AZ?"

Crocker nodded, picked the folder off the middle seat, and pushed it into the backpack on the floor in front of him. He'd practically committed all twenty-some pages to memory. Crimes ranging from bombings, to torture, to kidnapping and murder.

"What'd you think?"

"It's light on visuals."

A couple of blurry security-camera stills of a man with a black beard. A profile from a meeting with Pashtun warlords in eastern Afghanistan.

"How's your stomach?" Akil asked.

"My stomach?" In the Ankara airport, Crocker had consumed a chicken kebab smothered in dill-accented yogurt. Pushed the pita and rice aside. Leading up to a climb, he watched what he ate. Leaned heavily on the protein and fresh vegetables. Eased up on the carbs, especially those that quickly converted into sugar.

"It's in a good mood. Why?"

"Move over."

Crocker slid into the middle seat. A third member of the team—indefatigable, smart Davis—was snoring lightly by the window, the shade down, his blond surfer hair smushed into a little blue pillow. The fourth, Mancini—a former college football star with an encyclopedic knowledge of practically everything relating to science, history, and technology—was two rows back, reading a technical treatise on cell-phone hacking. The fifth—Crocker's next-door neighbor and workout buddy, and a former navy firefighter, Ritchie—was waiting for them in Karachi, Pakistan.

No sooner had Akil settled beside Crocker than he reached into his pocket and stuck a thumbnail drive into the port on the side of Crocker's laptop.

"Don't mess up my iTunes."

"I'm not touching anything, you pussy. Watch."

Akil slapped some keys and a video appeared on the screen. Murky at first. Then dark shadows moving against a gray background. Someone screaming in Arabic.

Akil quickly toggled down the sound, then turned the thirteen-inch screen so it wasn't visible to passengers in the aisle.

Crocker put on his reading glasses and leaned forward. "What am I watching?"

A bright light illuminated a face in the foreground. White, sandy haired, blindfolded, tied to a metal chair.

Crocker knew immediately what this was. Felt a ball of rage gathering in his stomach.

"Steve Vogelman, right?"

"The *Washington Post* reporter."

Tom Crocker had shared a transatlantic flight with Steve and a wiseass journalist from CNN, drinking single malt scotch and playing blackjack. The two of them prodding him to reveal things that they knew he couldn't, like a couple of naughty kids.

Before passing out, a drunken Steve had shown him pictures of his wife and two little girls, sighing, love in his eyes, so that Crocker would understand what he really valued.

But he hadn't appreciated the danger he'd flirted with,

that had caught him in its teeth. On the screen, Crocker counted four armed men on either side of Steve Vogelman, shouting in his ears, spitting, slapping, punching. All with black masks covering their faces.

Fucking cowards...

Crocker's strong dislike of bullies and sadists dated back to when he was a kid growing up just north of Boston. Racing motorcycles, riding wheelies, with a group of hell-raising teenagers—most with one foot in the grave. Proudly became the only non-Italian member of the Mongrels. Black leather jackets; Levi's with leather belts with big buckles—good for fighting; black T-shirts; bandanas worn on their heads. Beating up drug dealers, stealing their money. Taking no shit from anyone.

"Where'd you get this?"

"A friend of mine downloaded it from a jihadist website."

During that flight a year and a half ago, two hours short of Dulles, Vogelman had started lecturing him about what he called Crocker's narrow-minded, military conception of Sunni radicalism. Explaining that it was espoused by men with strong beliefs, who needed to be understood in the context of a religious-historical struggle over hegemony of the Middle East and Europe.

"They're the products of a unique cultural experience," Vogelman had said. "They feel threatened by the West. With good reason."

"So what?"

"They want what we want. Power. That commonality is important and misunderstood. Political leaders on both sides play up the fear."

"What's your point?"

"Guys like you, Crocker, who see things in black and white, are a big part of the problem."

Crocker, who hadn't graduated from college and didn't like being talked down to, had heard enough. "You're right, Vogelman, I do evaluate people more in terms of black and white than you do. And I can tell you right now, you're talking like a fucking sheep."

"What the hell does that mean?"

"Sheep and wolves, buddy. The wolves are the threat—the evil motherfuckers who live among us. Whatever they call themselves, jihadists, Nazis, murderers... they're basically aggressive sociopaths. They prey on people who are too trusting, or buy their bullshit. Sheep like you. Like the woman walking through a dimly lit parking lot alone at two a.m. and not hesitating when a strange man approaches."

"Then what are you?"

"I'm a sheepdog whose job is to protect sheep like you, which means I'm a ruthless motherfucker who spends a good deal of time in the heart of darkness."

On the laptop screen perched on the fold-down tray, the *Washington Post* reporter was facing a steady stream of insults in Arabic. Accusations of being a Zionist, a Mossad secret agent, an infidel crusader. White-faced Vogelman denied it all in rudimentary Arabic, sobbing, pleading to return to his wife, his young children, promising that he had, and always would, fairly represent Islam's point of view.

That's when a fifth man entered from the direction of the camera and grabbed Vogelman by the hair. Pulled his head up.

The armed men shouted a prayer of some kind. Crocker's Arabic wasn't good.

"What are they saying?"

"They're explaining to Allah that this man is an infidel who has to be killed," Akil muttered.

Crocker, his blue-hazel eyes burning, focused on the screen, where a sixth man stepped forward. Dressed all in black like an executioner. Thick black whiskers obscured his face.

He held a knife, which he raised and brought down violently along the side of Vogelman's head. The journalist's ear came off in a spurt of blood.

"Fucking savages!" Crocker exclaimed, bile rising like he'd been kicked in the stomach.

The man in black hacked off Vogelman's other ear, then sliced off his tongue.

Crocker wanted to punch something. Anything. The bastards!

"Look," Akil said.

The bearded man was holding Vogelman's severed tongue and shaking it at the camera, his eyes red with hatred, rage.

"That's AZ."

"Zaman?"

"Abu Rasul Zaman, yes. Number three man in al-Qaeda. The so-called Protector of Islam."

As Zaman started gouging Vogelman's left eye out, Crocker groaned, "Turn it off."

Akil hit a key and the screen went dark.

Soon after Mohammed Saddiq was captured in Italy, he confessed to his role in the U.S. embassy bombing. He said the attack had been planned and ordered by Abu Rasul Zaman.

Crocker growled. "I want that motherfucker . . . bad!"

"Ssh..."

A passing flight attendant shot Crocker a wary look. He seemed like a friendly, fit man. Had a long, narrow face with prominent cheekbones and chin, big teeth, a salt-and-pepper mustache, short graying hair, a warm smile. He was an outdoorsman of some sort, or maybe a businessman. Now he looked like he wanted to kill someone.

He did.

Karachi's Jinnah International Airport was insane, as usual. Bag handlers, businessmen, hustlers, Pakistani soldiers cradling AK-47s, women sobbing, ticket agents screaming in Urdu and English, flight announcements smooth and seductive over the PA.

The four men walked down the sleek beige stone corridor, each carrying several bags packed with gear—double plastic climbing boots with liners, insulated overboots, gaiters, synthetic socks, liner socks, polypro underwear, down parkas, down pants, balaclavas, bandanas, nose guards, ski goggles, gloves, expedition mitts.

Crocker led the group. Dressed in sports clothes, they looked more like members of a rugby team than scrawny climbers. Pakistani officials picked through their gear thoroughly.

Two days earlier, on a sleepy Sunday afternoon, Crocker had been driving his teenage daughter to a local movie complex when he'd received a text message from the commander of ST-6. He dropped his daughter off at the theater, then gunned the engine of his SUV to ST-6 headquarters in Little Creek, Virginia.

His CO, Captain Alan Sutter, sat waiting for him with

two senior officials from the CIA. His orders: Put a small team together. You're going into Pakistan completely black, under the cover of sports enthusiasts, climbers. The agency has a location on Zaman in Karachi. This is coming straight from the White House. The president wants us to hit him, fast.

This wasn't the first time Crocker and his men had been sent on a special mission for the CIA. Twelve hours later, they were on a flight to London. Slam bang.

Now Pakistani officials were picking through the team's gear.

"You gentlemen headed north?" one of the Pakistanis asked in accented English.

"Yes, sir. A day and a half here, then we're flying to Islamabad."

"For what purpose?"

"We're climbing."

"Karakoram?"

"Past there into the Baltoro Glacier."

"Very difficult terrain, sir. Good luck."

Their translator and driver, Wasir, stood waiting on the other side of customs. Short, skinny, early thirties. A wannabe businessman, Crocker thought.

"Mr. C. It's good to see you again."

"Good to see you again, too. How's your family?"

"Very good. Thank you."

"I'm glad." Crocker wasn't much for small talk.

"Mr. Maguire is waiting at the hotel." That would be Ritchie, the fifth member of Crocker's team.

"Good."

The Ramada Plaza Karachi was a long punt from the airport, nestled in an industrial zone. A standard semi-modern structure inside concrete barriers manned by police.

The sky was turning dark by the time they arrived. The city of twenty million glowed in the distance like a murky orange dream, a polyglot of glass-and-steel business towers, colonial monuments, mosques, neo-Gothic cathedrals, Sikh and Hindu temples.

While the other guys checked in, Crocker went directly to the room he was sharing with Ritchie. He found him watching BBC World News and sipping from a can of Coke. The air conditioner groaned under the burden of the humid ninety-degree-plus August heat.

"What's going on?"

Ritchie was a cool customer. Six feet tall, fit, straight dark hair, fierce black eyes, high cheekbones from the Cherokee blood on his mother's side. He was a meticulous explosives expert and breacher who had a wild side that he kept well concealed. Mostly.

A couple of years ago he'd been arrested for murdering a biker who pulled a knife on him in a bar, a big dude with a beard and a skull and crossbones tattooed on his bald head. Ritchie had stopped there after work, to have a beer and flirt with the blond bartender, when this big biker and a couple of his buddies started giving Ritchie shit about a turquoise amulet he wore around his neck. Some kind of tribal thing that had been passed down from his grandfather.

The biker called it "faggot's necklace" and tried to rip it off. Ritchie slapped the biker's hand away and said he'd heard he liked to suck cock.

Whereupon the biker pulled a knife and lunged at Ritchie's throat. Ritchie, who was fast and a lot stronger than he looked, redirected the force behind the blade back into the biker's chest, under his ribs, into his heart. The biker died on the spot.

He was thrown in jail, but was later exonerated and promoted to master chief. His SEAL teammates thought it was funny in a can-you-believe-it kind of way. Ritchie? Easygoing Ritchie?

But Crocker knew. He ran with Ritchie three mornings a week through the forested lowlands near where they lived. Ritchie seemed like a laid-back guy until you challenged him. Then watch out.

Now he smiled at Crocker and shut off the TV.

"I've got all our climbing gear waiting in Islamabad," Ritchie said. "Ice axes, climbing helmets, harnesses, ascenders, carabiners, trekking poles."

"You get the carabiners I asked you for?" Crocker started rearranging the furniture. Desk by the window. Bed turned so that it faced the door.

"Locking and nonlocking."

"Good."

Unpacking, he laid out a black T-shirt and pants on the chair. He had multiples of each, exactly the same.

"The weather might be more difficult than we—"

The soft-spoken team leader stopped him. "I thought we'd get a clear window through September."

"Just got a weather update from the German team that's there. There's a chance of high winds and freezing temperatures at base camp."

"The weather hopefully won't stop us."

Ritchie got up and threw the bolt on the door. Then he punched on the TV again and cranked up the sound.

Crocker, who had stripped down to his underwear,

noted the all-business look in the explosive expert's dark eyes. "What you got?"

Ritchie pulled a large envelope out of one of the dresser drawers and threw it on the bed. Then pointed to a series of surveillance photos of a three-story apartment building.

Crocker stopped. "Where are we?" he asked.

"Kemari. The port area of Karachi. Near the railroad tracks."

He knew the general vicinity. "Good."

Crocker noted that the primitive concrete structure stood on a corner next to what looked like a car repair lot. Behind it stood an abandoned field littered with junk.

"What's here?" Crocker asked, pointing to the opposite side of the street.

"A warehouse. It's mainly a pretty rundown commercial area."

Crocker nodded. "Okay. Call Akil. Tell him to meet us by the pool."

The three men sat at a round metal table and drank from bottles of local Murree Classic beer, which was available only to non-Muslims after the ban by President Ali Bhutto in '77. Broad-shouldered, tattooed Mancini swam laps in the pool. A couple of kids were trying to do cannonballs off the diving board. Davis—the most talented athlete on the team—was showing them how.

Crocker thought back to his wife and daughter in Virginia Beach. Both complained that he was away too much. Jenny, sixteen, had been having trouble adjusting to her new high school.

Akil cleared his throat and started. "You hear the one

about the guy who took his blond girlfriend to her first football game? They're sitting right behind their team's bench. After the game he asks her how she liked it. 'It was great,' she says. 'Especially the tight pants and big muscles. But I couldn't understand why they were killing one another over a quarter.' 'What?' the guy asks. 'What are you talking about?' She says, 'Well, they flipped a coin, one team got it, and then for the rest of the game, they all kept screaming Get the quarter back! Get the quarter back! I'm like... Hellooo? It's only twenty-five cents!' "

They laughed. Then Crocker got up. "Let's walk..."

They strolled past a row of jasmine trees to the patio. Crocker waited for two men to drift away—one British, one Pakistani, discussing cars and heroin. Nearing the rectangular aqua pool, he watched the two light cigarettes. Smoke wafted into the yellow artificial light.

Then he turned to Ritchie, who had stuck his hands in the pockets of his khaki shorts. "You think you can get your hands on ten fifty-gallon barrels of diesel fuel and enough ammonium nitrate to mix a good batch of ANFO?"

"The diesel fuel is easy. I can buy that at the port."

"What about the ammonium nitrate?"

"I know a local contractor who can get anything for a price."

"You got cash?"

Ritchie patted his pocket. "Many rupees, yes."

"Akil, Ritchie's going to give you a map. I want you to eyeball the site. Make sure we can drive a car bomb into the place without causing too much collateral damage."

"A car bomb?"

"Yeah, a car bomb," Crocker answered. Then he

looked at Ritchie. "You think you can put one together in less than a day?"

"No problem."

Akil asked: "When do you want me to surveil the site?"

"Tonight."

"All right."

"Before you go I want you to talk to Wasir. Tell him to rent a van first thing in the morning. Park it in back, then give the keys to Ritchie. Ritchie will take it from there."

Ritchie grinned so that his eyes were almost hidden. "Boss, I like the way you think."

"We'll meet out here tomorrow 0700 hours to go over the plan." In the morning, he'd get input from his men, then incorporate that into a PLO (patrol leader's order). They'd discuss insertion, fire positions, concealment, what to do with prisoners, what to do in case of an emergency, and other contingencies.

He said: "Akil, check with Mancini now. Make sure he gets his hands on everything we need from our contact at the Agency. Glocks, AKs, comms, NVGs, maps, GPS units."

"Got it."

"Go."

Akil crossed to the pool, which left Crocker and Ritchie standing together.

The explosives expert lowered his voice. "So we're going in with one van packed with a VBIED and one SUV?"

By VBIED he meant vehicle-borne improvised explosive device.

"That's correct."

"Sweet."

Crocker put a hand on Ritchie's shoulder. "How many fucking truck bombs has Zaman sent our way?"

"One too many."

"I want that baby packed tight. As much as you can fit. Let's give that bastard a taste of his own medicine."

CHAPTER TWO

It was a blonde. A blonde to make a bishop kick a hole in a stained glass window.

—Raymond Chandler

STEPPING OUT of the shower, she remembered seeing his face through the front-hall curtains, dark and curious, somewhat exotic, looking up from the road past the chestnut tree. Then she shivered. A strange rumble that rose from her toes, like crows taking flight. Was it excitement? Expectation? She wasn't really sure.

Not surprising, because Malie Tingvoll had just turned eighteen.

Pausing before the full-length mirror, she let the coarse white towel slip away and studied the glow of her body and how it offset the cool Oslo light. Already in late August the tan she had worked on during the summer was starting to fade. Holding her breath, she watched the color rise in her face and crawl down her neck to her breasts.

They stood full and proud. Nipples pink and taut. Her stomach smooth. Her hair long and light, like two pale yellow curtains that accented her light blue eyes and the sharpness of her high cheekbones, inherited from her mother. She also had her mother's high waist and long legs. Narrow hips.

Better for dancing, she'd been told. If only her feet weren't so clumsy and her chest so large, she might have had a chance of dancing professionally. Her dreams of twirling on the big stage got her through the long dull days cleaning in the Residence Kristinelund. Dreams of being eighteen and the toast of London. Rehearsals by day. Performances at night. Limousine drives through the countryside. Handsome young men sitting across from her at dinner, charming her with clever stories. She changed sheets to Tchaikovsky on the radio. Cleaned bathrooms to Schubert playing in her head.

It wasn't too much to ask, she thought. She'd work hard for everything, of course. And she'd be humble, appreciative, the way she'd been raised by her parents, who had retired to Kristiansand on the south coast.

The phone rang in her tiny room. At a quarter to five the afternoon sun was already starting to sink, casting a band of gold across her wrist.

"Hello? Cyrus... It's Malie, yes."

He was calling already. They had met just forty minutes earlier. A brief conversation in the lobby. He said he was the friend of an Italian cyclist Malie had met in Lyon last summer when she was volunteering for the Tour de France.

Cyrus was speaking quickly, excitedly, about a friend of his in Malta who was opening a restaurant housed in a fancy hotel.

Malta. "Nice..."

She didn't catch all the details as he rattled on in heavily accented English. Enough to hear that this friend was looking for a hostess for his new restaurant. Someone young and beautiful. And, more importantly, someone who liked people, could put them at ease with her lovely smile.

Cyrus said that even though they'd talked earlier for only a few minutes, he had a feeling that she was the one. He had called his friend, who said that Malie sounded perfect.

"That's so sweet."

Something opened in her chest. A feeling of hope. Then the tremor came again and she remembered she was naked. Wrapped the coarse towel tight.

It was a chance to escape the Residence Kristinelund and the narrow confines of Norway, the cruel winter that made her feel sad and heavy. She imagined sunshine, new friends, money to spend, days at the beach.

"Do you know if they have a ballet school in Malta?" she asked. "It's important to me."

"They have everything there," Cyrus answered. "Absolutely everything, you know. But I'll find out."

"I'd love to meet your friend."

"He's in the south of France now."

"Oh..."

"He's leaving tomorrow for New York."

"I see..." More disappointment. Hope slipping away.

But Cyrus's voice remained bright, with a funny accent that she would ask about at the right time. He said, "Maybe we can meet later and Skype."

"What do you mean, Skype?"

"You don't know what Skype is? I guess you don't have a computer."

"Not my own. No. Not yet." Her parents were frugal. Things had to be earned.

"Skype is a computer program where you can see the person you're talking to on the computer screen," Cyrus offered. "Maybe we can arrange to do one with Michael tonight before he leaves for New York City."

"Michael is the name of your friend?"

"Michael Mannus. He's a great guy. Very successful. You'll like him. Everybody does."

"I like his name."

"You know where the Café Con Bar is, yes?"

"Of course." Café Con Bar was a café/hangout/restaurant/music club near the Spektrum, downtown. Ten minutes away by metro. Get off at Grønland.

"Why don't we meet there at ten."

"At the bar?"

"We can meet there, and I'll take you after."

"Where?"

"To the Internet place."

"Yes. But I have to be back here at midnight." Her employers were strict.

"No problem. We should be able to do this whole thing in an hour."

"Good."

"I'll see you at Café Con Bar, then, at ten."

"I'll be there. Thank you."

"Ha det."

She dressed carefully. Tight Diesel jeans, a blue V-neck top that highlighted her blue eyes and showed a hint of cleavage, red heels that added two inches to her five-foot-eight height. She struggled with whether to let her hair hang or pull it back. Loose, she thought, made her look younger and sexier. Pulled back, she saw herself as older and more professional.

She chose to wear it down, with little mascara and lipstick. Very subtle. Butterflies spun in her stomach as she entered the metro.

The *click-click-click* of her heels across the Brugata sidewalk like the beating of her heart.

The club was big. Crowded dark rooms with long sofas. She ordered a White Russian and checked her watch. The numbers glowed 10:05. She stood by the door and looked out, wondering if Cyrus would show.

She felt men's eyes measuring her. She was comfortable with her body. Nudity at the beach wasn't a problem. She wasn't embarrassed to admit that she liked sex, as long as it was with the right person. She even figured one day she'd marry and have children. Saw herself living in another country, maybe in California. But that was at least ten years away. Ten years to dance, explore the world, have fun, learn.

Malie felt a tap on her shoulder and turned abruptly into Cyrus's big smile.

"Hey!"

Warm kisses on both cheeks.

He said quickly: "I was waiting inside. I have a table."

"I didn't know."

She followed him. A checked pink shirt, unbuttoned over a brilliant white tee. Shredded black jeans. Tan boots, worn at the heel. A brown leather blazer with a stain on the sleeve. Dark hair slicked back. A funny hitch in his stride. A hint of lime cologne. She thought he looked older than she remembered. Like he'd been around.

He smiled a lot. Dark eyes. A dark complexion.

"Where are you from?" she asked.

"My father is French. My mother, Lebanese."

"How do you know Tulio?"

"I spent some time in Rome. We raced together."

"Bicycles?"

"No, no. Motorbikes. Cross-country."

"Oh."

He looked down at his watch, then pulled a cell phone from his pocket and punched in a text.

"Is there a problem?"

"That was Michael. He's ready. As soon as you finish your drink, we'll go."

"You found an Internet café already?"

"Yes. No hurry. It's not far away. We can drive."

She took a last sip of her White Russian and said, "Okay."

He stood and pushed back his hair. "You look very beautiful."

"Thank you." She wanted to like him. He seemed confident, worldly, energetic, a little nervous, the way he kept touching his face, his hair, something in his front pocket.

"My car's in back."

"You have a car?"

"It's a delivery van, actually. That I borrowed from a friend."

Clumsy feet, always getting in the way. She carefully lifted them across the carpeted back room, down the stairs. Her back straight, her chin up, imagining she was already a hostess at a glamorous restaurant. A famous model.

The alley was dark. She had to step around a puddle.

"If you want to wait here, I'll get the car."

"That's okay. I can walk." She wanted to stay positive and friendly, so she could make the best impression on Michael.

The *click-click-click* of her heels again. He offered his arm and smiled. "I think you'll like him." His teeth were big and white. She caught him glancing down at her breasts, then quickly away.

The van was parked close to the side of a store. Gray with a white roof. Japanese make, Danish plates.

"I've been helping a friend move his business," Cyrus remarked as he unlocked the passenger door. "Electronics. Flat-screens. Stereos. I can set you up with a good price."

There was something dark on the passenger seat. A coat, maybe. A blanket. He bent in ahead of her to move it.

That's when she felt rough hands grab her from behind.

"Hey!"

A hand with a cloth over her mouth. A strange smell that reminded her of a hospital. Strong arms lifted her off her feet. Then Cyrus spun and threw the dark blanket he had been holding in his hands.

"No!"

Two men, maybe three, pushed her violently into the back of the van. Malie tried to get her high-heeled feet under her and fell. The back of her head hit the floor hard.

She came to several minutes later. The taste of blood in her mouth. A dull throb at the back of her head. Her mouth had been taped shut, her hands and arms bound together, too. She lay on a thin mattress and tried to kick herself free, until her jeans chafed her thighs.

They were parked somewhere. Vigeland? Slottsparken? Ekeberg? The wind was blowing. Branches scraped the top of the van.

She heard a car door shut and men's voices speaking a strange language. The smell of cigarette smoke.

Feeling like she was five years old and lost in a forest, she started to pray for help.

The van door slid open. A sharp light hit her eyes. Behind it, dark dull faces. Strangers. One with a beard. Another wearing a green ski mask. A third, shorter man holding a knife.

"No, please..." she tried to say through the tape.

When they leaned over her, she shut her eyes and prayed silently to her grandmother in heaven, her mother and father, who all seemed so far away.

Something cold touched her stomach. She shivered, then realized they were cutting away her sweater. They pulled it off her roughly. Then ripped her bra.

She heard one man sigh with appreciation. Another seemed to scold him with a guttural sound like he was clearing his throat.

Someone squeezed a nipple. She winced and tried to lift herself up. Strong hands held her down and slapped her. Another squeeze, then someone spit. "*Putain!*" Saliva landed on her face.

Oh, God!

Something in Malie shut down, as though she knew what was coming. A feeling of panic gripped her stomach and threatened to turn it inside out.

Please don't be sick.

They handled her roughly, pulling off her jeans. Her heart-patterned panties. Praying to God that they wouldn't hurt her. Cold sweat oozed down the insides of her thighs.

One of the men shouted in accented English: "Open your eyes, you bitch!"

She did for a moment, and saw the knife. Cold, jagged sparks ran up and down her spine as it passed over her tender stomach. Rough hands pulled her legs apart.

Please don't hurt me!

She clenched with all her might, expecting something to enter. It had happened half a dozen times before with boys her age. Fumbling efforts.

I'm not an expert, not nearly. If that's what they think.

Instead the van door banged open violently. She opened her eyes.

Cyrus held a pistol in one hand and grabbed the backs of the men's shoulders with the other. "You fucking idiots!" he screamed.

The men mumbled protests and backed away. Cyrus threw the blanket over her. *"Imbéciles. Je vous ai dit. Le cheik veut qu'elle sera intacte!"* (Imbeciles. I told you. The sheik wants her untouched!)

CHAPTER THREE

Gamble everything for love, if you're a true human being. If not, leave…

—Rumi

CROCKER WAS usually soft-spoken and relaxed, but at midnight the following night, he sat on the edge of the hotel room bed dressed head to toe in black, stroking his mustache and nervously tapping his foot. He was talking to his daughter Jenny on the phone. She hadn't made the First Colonial soccer team and was bummed.

"Sweetheart, I can't tell you how many times I've failed at something the first time I tried," he said gently. "The point is to regroup, work on your weaknesses, focus harder."

Only a year earlier, Jenny and Crocker had moved in with his new wife, Holly. His first marriage hadn't worked.

"Yeah."

"Get mad."

"Dad—"

"Show those girls what you're made of."

"I don't know if I'm that into soccer anymore," Jenny said. "I think I'll—"

"Don't say it, honey."

The word he didn't want to hear was "quit."

She said it.

"Come on, sweetheart. Come on."

Soccer he could take or leave. What worried him was her apparent lack of determination. Grit.

He told her how great she was. Reminded her of times she'd been outstanding in a number of other sports. Told her that he'd run specific drills with her when he got back.

He was a man who had had to fight for everything. Built himself up from a skinny kid from the poor side of town into a leader of the toughest unit in the U.S. military. Got there with the help of intense physical and mental discipline. Studied hard, and trained like a beast. Lifted weights incessantly. Ran thirty-six marathons in three years. Competed in over a thousand endurance competitions before turning thirty-five, including Ironman Triathlons, Double Iron Triathlons, the grueling Raid Gauloises ("the world's most challenging human endurance competition"). He always set his goal high, and often won.

As the assault team leader of ST-6's Blue Team, he'd led dozens of physically arduous missions in Pakistan, Afghanistan, Panama, El Salvador, Colombia, Iraq, Iran, Somalia, Yemen. Hostage rescues, assassinations, drug raids, weapons recovery, surveillance. Over forty in the past year. All highly classified. Some for the navy, some for the CIA, some for the White House. In and out.

Throw a challenge in front of him and he'd chew it up, or die trying.

It was all about will. Fire in the gut. The determination to push yourself beyond the barriers of fear.

The way his dad had taught him—a U.S. Marine hero who was shot in the leg by a Japanese sniper on the last day of World War II.

Some people had determination. Some didn't. Crocker thought of it as the vital ingredient that lifted an individual above others. Made achievers. Created heroes. He rated it ahead of intelligence and physical ability.

And here was his daughter, threatening to quit.

He sat, forehead furrowed, feeling like he'd failed somewhere as he listened to himself talk. Words into a wire that bounced across oceans and deserts to his daughter's room in suburban Virginia. He pictured her sitting in front of her iMac, surrounded by photos of the actors from *Twilight*. Vampires with six-packs. Kids who had never faced real physical danger in their lives.

He'd killed people. Witnessed drownings, decapitations, bombings, brutal hand-to-hand combat. The worst. Was that the life he wanted for his daughter? Hell, no!

He stopped. Did a mental one-eighty. "Sweetheart, I just want you to be happy. You decide what you want to do, I'll support you one hundred percent. I love you more than life itself. You're a wonderful girl."

A moment of stunned silence from Jenny on the other end. When she finally spoke, she sounded more like herself. "That means a lot to me, Dad."

"We'll talk more about soccer when I get home. Sound good?"

"Yeah. Thanks."

He felt something opening in his chest when Ritchie walked in and pointed at the glowing LED numbers on the clock. Dark eyes burning. Jaw clenched.

It was 12:14. Time to hump.

"I gotta go, sweetheart. I love you. Be your best."

"Get home safe, Dad. We miss you."

He bit his bottom lip and hung up. Looked at Ritchie standing there like Johnny Blaze from *Ghost Rider*. Black 5-11 pants. Black shirt with cargo pockets. Black belt. Half expected flames to start shooting out of his head.

"You get the things we talked about? We set to launch?"

"It's all teed up for you, Tiger."

"Tiger? Where the hell did that come from? You know I don't play golf."

Crocker checked his Suunto GPS watch, which featured separate fields that measured altitude and barometric pressure. It also had a 3-D compass, a bottom timer for diving, and a route planner.

Ritchie led the way to the service stairs, Cherokee cheekbones reflecting the fluorescent light. Black military boots echoing off the cinder block walls, then outside.

No one could mistake them for tourists now.

Beyond his shoulder a low hiss rose from the city, which threw off an eerie orange glow.

Crocker could practically smell the adrenaline pouring out of them as they crowded into the black Suburban. Davis, Ritchie, Mancini, Akil in a cloud of musk, always anticipating a chance to bump into an attractive female, even on an op.

Bull-necked Mancini, already starting to sweat, rechecked that every man was fully equipped—.45

Glocks in carbon holsters fitted with attached pistol lights and loaded with hollow-points, three mags, AK-47s with collapsible stocks with twenty-eight 7.62 x 39 rounds in each of the eight mags, knives, emergency medical gear, comms with earphones and throat mikes, GPS units, nylon black belts with heavy-duty belt rigs for rappelling.

He'd cleaned and inspected everything himself. Probably half a dozen times. No wonder he drove his wife crazy.

Crocker went over the plan again as Ritchie started the engine. "Target: Abu Rasul Zaman, aka AZ, forty-nine. Expect him to be accompanied by Islamic guards from Yemen. These guys will be ferocious. There's a high probability that we'll run into women and children, too. If the women aren't armed, we don't shoot. If they engage in aggressive action, do what you've gotta do. Our orders are to take AZ alive."

Akil, as they pulled out of the parking lot: "I know his background. The guy's a sadist, boss."

"The Agency wants him alive, if possible." They were on assignment to the CIA, which they had been doing often, especially since 9/11.

"Fuck the Agency."

"Orders, Akil. No stepping out of line."

"All right."

Tires squealing, Crocker asked Ritchie, "You know where we're going?"

"Is the pope Catholic?"

Davis shook his blond surfer hair and laughed. Ritchie amused him. Davis, like Ritchie, seemed like the most easygoing guy in the world, until he got into a fight.

Crocker handed out maps and the latest surveillance

photos. He said: "AZ Central is a three-story concrete structure. First floor houses some kind of store. We think the second floor is being used for meeting rooms, offices. AZ and his men live on three."

"Any intel on the interior?" Mancini asked.

"I'm expecting an interior stairway."

"Maybe an elevator?"

"Three floors. Cheaply constructed. No visible motor on the roof."

Mancini: "The motor might be housed in the basement."

"The building doesn't have a basement," Akil countered.

Crocker continued. "Keep an eye out for booby traps. We might have to breach through security doors between floors."

Each man had a specialty. Mancini handled equipment and weapons; Davis ran the comms; Akil, maps and logistics; Crocker had been trained as a corpsman (the navy's version of a medic); Ritchie was the explosives expert and breacher. They were all the best in the world at what they did.

Ritchie asked, "Who's driving the van with the explosives?"

Akil raised his hand. "I got that."

Ritchie continued: "All right. Then drive her right up on the curb. I'll set it off. Give you sixty seconds to seek cover."

Akil frowned. "Don't you think they're gonna hear us? I mean, we're pulling up right under their noses."

"No, but—"

Crocker cut Ritchie off. "Akil's right. Let's do this one

the old-fashioned way." He pointed to the map. "Come up this perpendicular street. Tie a brick to the pedal. Keep that sucker in gear. You jump out here. What's that, approximately?"

Mancini: "A hundred and fifty feet."

Crocker: "That gives you approximately fifteen seconds to duck behind Warehouse One. Here."

"No problem."

"We'll all deploy from Warehouse One."

Akil nodded. "That works."

Each man knew his assignment when they hit the target—who would insert where, who would cover left, who would cover right, fire positions, the appropriate hand and arm signals. They'd committed the basic layout of the building and street to memory.

Crocker, as the corpsman, carried specialized medical equipment on his back that enabled him to perform a cricothyrotomy, put in a chest tube, or do a cut-down to clear an airway, if needed. In addition, each man had a blowout patch in his pocket—a four-by-four-inch battle dressing to control major bleeding.

"Any more questions?" he asked.

No one answered.

"Let's go."

They'd taken the Shahrah-e-Faisal and had entered central Karachi over the Napier Mole Bridge, gunning by the port and passing sleeping heroin addicts, barking pye-dogs, roaming bands of toughs looking for an unguarded car to jack. The choking stench of kerosene heaters and burning garbage from squatter camps seeped in through the ventilation.

They rode in silence, individual thoughts and emotions filling the vehicle with tension.

To Crocker's right, billboards hawked Wonder Super Slim cigarettes and a movie called *Rocket Singh: Salesman of the Year*. Whatever that was.

It appeared that nothing had been left untouched by human hands. Even the air was crowded with smoke and the stink of oil and rotting fish and garbage from the nearby port.

Ritchie pointed through the windshield down a potholed street that ran parallel to the train tracks. "She's parked down there."

"Who?"

"The van, Manny. Who do you think?"

The glow of the dim yellow streetlight barely reached the back bumper of the battered gray Econoline van. Mancini, who read Arabic, pointed out jidahist graffiti sprayed on one side that translated roughly to "All infidels will be vanquished."

"Nice touch."

Crocker checked his watch. At fifteen minutes shy of three the temp felt like it had already pushed past ninety again. Putrid air clung to his skin like a warm wet towel.

They did a final gear and commo check, then loaded and press-checked their weapons. Ritchie found a chunk of concrete to fix to the pedal. Mancini produced a roll of duct tape to hold it in place.

The SUV went in first. Cut the lights three blocks away. Pulled into the dirt parking lot at the back of what they had designated Warehouse One. True to the surveillance photos, it was a raw concrete structure with most of the windows punched out.

They parked next to the carcass of an old yellow bus sitting in one corner with weeds thriving around it.

Warehouse One was directly across the street from AZ Central, the apartment building that, according to the latest intel, housed Zaman and his thugs.

It took Davis twenty seconds to pick the lock to Warehouse One.

The inside was crowded with old refrigerators and parts: stacks of condensers, fan motors, thermostats, water valves, copper tubing. Davis kneeled to read the label on one of the steel drums.

"What is it?" Crocker asked.

"Acetone," Davis answered.

Mancini spoke up. "A solvent. Auto-ignites at around eight hundred and seventy degrees Fahrenheit. When mixed with oxygen, danger of explosion or flash fire."

Count on Mancini to know shit like that.

Mancini: "This place is an accident waiting to happen."

Davis: "Thanks, professor."

Crocker: "We can't launch from here. Someone needs to surveil the place down the street."

That would usually be Akil's job, but he was in the van. Davis volunteered.

The blond-haired SEAL ran off and soon was back, breathing hard. "Filled with scrap metal, boss," he reported. "No chemical drums. Nothing flammable. Looks like it hasn't been used in months."

"Radio Akil. Tell him we'll deploy from the back of Warehouse Two. Tell him: Roll left. Make sure he knows his left from his right."

Davis smiled, readied his radio. "He might need help with that."

"Move out."

Back into the SUV. Lights out across the broken-up street.

The SEALs surveyed the scene from the back wall of Warehouse Two. This one was lower and shabbier. A slab concrete roof. No windows in the rear. Crocker concluded there was minimal danger of anything falling on their heads.

"We're good."

"Yo."

"Remember, keep an eye out for civilians. We're trying to take AZ alive."

"Roger that."

Ritchie ran in a crouch to the far corner to recon the target approximately two hundred feet and forty-five degrees to the right.

"Light on the third floor. Some movement," he reported back.

"Give Akil the signal."

"Romeo, this is Def Jam One..."

Half a minute later, the van sailed past, groaning slightly. They watched Akil roll out. One somersault and he was on his feet and running, his smile catching the half-moon light. Like an actor winking at his audience. Smooth.

Crocker couldn't help but laugh inside.

"You see that, boss?"

"Fucking show-off. Cover your ears! Hit the ground!"

Fourteen seconds. Fifteen. The van's tires hit the curb and the back fishtailed right. For a second it looked like the Econoline was going to flip over on its side, but the rear panel smacked the corner of the building with a crash.

Ritchie pushed the digital signal that activated the detonator. A fraction of a second later a huge explosion split the air and propelled out like an angry god spreading his arms. The force lifted all five men half a foot off the ground. A hot, churning wind blew past their faces. Chunks of concrete and shards of metal pelted everything around them.

Then a moment of silence, punctuated by a woman's scream from the apartment house.

Crocker whispered urgently into his headset: *"Now!"*

They rose up as one and deployed as planned. Davis and Mancini approached the front. Ritchie ran left along the side street. Crocker and Akil crossed to cover the right of the building and the back.

The three-story apartment looked like a layer cake that had collapsed on one side—the left front. The charred wreckage of the van was barely visible past what had been the roof. The right side, particularly the rear of the structure, was more or less intact. Which meant survivors. Stunned, no doubt.

Crocker heard someone screaming in Arabic as he crossed the street. Dust and smoke rolling out in thick waves.

He motioned to Akil to circle around back, while he stopped at a side door that had shifted so that the top leaned forward. One kick from his boot smashed it in.

Angry flames shot out. He jumped back.

That's when he heard a peal of automatic-weapon fire from his right, reverberating off the wall.

Akil's voice in his earbud: "Shooter back of Z Central. Second floor."

The firing immediately picked up. Lead splattered and ricocheted off the concrete walls.

"Manny, Def, what have you got?"

"Rubble, dust, and smoke. Can't see shit."

"Manny, you cover. Def, help Romeo in back."

"Roger," Ritchie replied.

Crocker pried the side door open and, using a plastic garbage can lid to shield himself from the flames, entered. Immediately felt the heat.

The first-floor store appeared to sell cleaning supplies—mops, brooms, floor polishers, wax. A brilliant orange-blue against the opposite wall was spreading, consuming god knows what. More flames to his immediate left.

He hung a sharp right and was crossing to the stairway in the corner when something exploded and knocked him off his feet.

Fuck.

As he got his boots under him, thick black smoke twisted around his head, crawled down his throat. Smelled like burning rubber. Worse.

Hearing footsteps, he got into a crouch and readied his weapon.

A shadow fell across the second-floor landing, then disappeared. Crocker was about to squeeze the trigger when he spotted a pair of skinny bare legs emerging from the gray smoke and saw that they belonged to a boy in underpants carrying a red plastic truck.

Seeing the American soldier, the little boy froze halfway down and looked back at two women in dark brown burkas. Faces obscured in shadows and cloth. Was one of them the boy's mother? The taller of the two cradled something wrapped in a blanket.

Crocker, assuming it was a baby, held a finger to his lips and waved them down. Whispered: "Come on. Come on."

All three descended quickly and passed Crocker without uttering a word.

Then the whoosh of a rocket and an explosion out back.

Crocker, into his microphone: "What the fuck was that?"

"RPG fired from the back window. A panic shot. Landed near the tracks."

He turned back to catch a glimpse of the taller woman in the doorway. Caught the corner of her left eye in the shadows. Onyx black, defiant. Crocker didn't have time to consider what it meant. AK-47 ready, he hurried up the concrete steps two at a time.

The second floor was completely dark. Desk and chairs overturned. A blackboard swaying from one hook. Papers scattered everywhere.

Sweat rolled down his legs into his boots. Footsteps moved frantically overhead.

They know they're trapped.

He had a choice. Retreat outside and wait for the smoke and flames to force the terrorists out, or push forward.

But how long would it be before Pakistani security forces showed up? Fifteen minutes? Twenty at the most? This op was considered so sensitive that the Pakistanis hadn't been informed ahead of time. Which meant that he and his men had to vanish before they arrived.

As Crocker considered, the third-floor door opened

and a man quickly descended three steps holding an AK-47 like his. Heavyset, hairy legs. A big stomach that protruded from the bottom of a white T-shirt.

Crocker didn't stick around to glimpse his face. Instead, he crouched behind the stairs and waited. Remembering to breathe deeply; heart bouncing in his chest.

When he saw two sets of bare legs near the bottom, he sprung out and, squeezing off a long salvo, cut down both men just below their knees.

Screams of agony. Both of them firing wildly as their femurs gave way and they stumbled down the last five steps. One with a long beard landed on his face. Orange-red blood sprayed out and splattered the wall.

As per team SOP, Crocker finished them both off with bullets directed at their heads.

Akil radioed to say he was ready to toss a couple of fragmentation grenades through the back window. Two explosions lifted Crocker off his feet, like riding a bucking bronco.

What remained was mainly mop-up after that. Crocker called Mancini and Ritchie.

"Get in here fast! Help me search the place and ID the victims."

"Did we get AZ?"

"I think so."

Six Arabic-looking men lay dead. Five had heavy beards.

One had tried to jump out the back window. Another two appeared to have taken their own lives. The last lay in a pool of blood by the third-floor window, bleeding from the neck.

Crocker instructed Mancini to photograph the men's

faces. He and the other three grabbed what looked important—a couple of laptops, identification papers, wallets, a cell phone, some ledgers—and out they all went.

Back in the SUV. Cranking their way over the Napier Mole Bridge just as the Pak Capital City Police were starting to close it down.

From the driver's seat Akil said, "That was close."

"Which one of them was Zaman?"

Crocker: "My money says it was one of those ugly dudes at the bottom of the stairs."

Akil: "Who's taking bets?"

Crocker craned his neck to study the digital images on Mancini's camera. They all agreed that with the black beards, it was hard to tell.

But Crocker had a nagging feeling.

In the backseat, Davis was slicing open Ritchie's pants to expose his wounded leg.

"What happened?"

"Ripped a nasty gash on a piece of metal."

"You up-to-date on your tetanus?"

"Does a bear shit in the woods?"

Nothing life-threatening. But it had to be attended to soon.

Crocker said to Akil, "Pull over for a second so I can get back there and clean it."

He and Davis traded positions, then Crocker extracted gauze and Bacitracin from his emergency medical kit.

They were already halfway to the safe house in Karsaz, near the golf course. There they would find a surgeon waiting. Warm showers, beer, sandwiches, fresh clothes.

Crocker, from the backseat, said, "Brothers... well done."

CHAPTER FOUR

Success builds character, failure reveals it.

—Dave Checketts

THE MUSCLES in Crocker's arms and legs shook as he sat on the back patio nursing a cold Corona. Nothing unusual about that. It always took his body several hours to wind down from the adrenaline rush of an op.

His friends joked that the SEAL team leader's favorite leisure-time activity was kicking back in his rec room with a glass of red wine or a beer and watching reruns of *Everybody Loves Raymond* on TV. *I'd kind of like to do that now,* he thought. Never mind the ribbing he'd have to take from his men.

Besides, something nagged at him. Through the sliding glass door he saw a well-scrubbed officer from the U.S. embassy sorting through stuff they had recovered from the terrorist safe house.

In front of him, the morning sun had burned through much of the haze. Past a row of eucalyptus trees he saw well-dressed golfers walking together down a yellow-green fairway. Like watching a dream. Or a video feed from some faraway place.

What struck him was the deliberation with which the golfers went about lining up and measuring their shots. Kneeling, frowning, studying their scorecards, consulting with their caddies.

Crocker pegged the men as business executives. Successful enough to belong to the exclusive club. Probably with fat bank accounts, diversified stock portfolios, vacation homes.

As they walked together, he wondered what they were talking about. Interest rates? The size of their stock portfolios? The trading price of oil?

Whatever it was probably wouldn't interest him. Crocker preferred to keep his needs to a minimum and direct his energy toward bigger challenges.

Wiping the perspiration off the neck of the Corona, he imagined his father limping up to the kitchen table of their house in Methuen, Massachusetts.

His dad had admired men who played "in the big arena," made personal sacrifices for their country or beliefs, and didn't give in to fear. He'd consumed biographies of George Washington, Thurgood Marshall, Ulysses S. Grant, Andrew Jackson, Simón Bolívar, Francis Marion, Teddy Roosevelt, Alexander the Great, and men like them.

Tom Crocker understood that his destiny had been cast at that little oak table as he listened to his father talk about leaders, his gray eyes shining, his scratchy voice rising in his throat.

Now the patio door slid open and Mancini stuck his thick head out. "We need you, boss."

Crocker cracked his neck and straightened his back. Ran his hand over the scar over his left eye that he'd gotten falling off a motorcycle as a kid. "What's up?"

"Inventory."

Inside, leaning on the dining room table, Officer Williams was checking off a list of the recovered items that he had written on a yellow legal pad. Crocker watched as he slipped on white cotton gloves, carefully wrapped each item in plastic, and packed it in a metal box. He saw the two battered-looking laptops, several notebooks covered in Arabic writing, a half dozen videos, including one that looked like an Arabic version of *Pulp Fiction,* one of Crocker's favorite movies.

"I wonder what the analysts at the CIA will make of that," he said, referring to the video.

Williams didn't answer.

Crocker was reaching out to turn over a charred book that still lay on the table when Williams stopped him with a gloved hand. "We'd rather you didn't touch anything."

We? Who are we?

"Sure thing. But I doubt you're going to find any usable fingerprints on something that's been burned to shit."

Williams stopped. "Is this everything?"

Crocker found his backpack among a pile of gear in the corner. From inside he removed a handful of papers that he'd grabbed off a desk on the second floor of AZ's safe house. He paused to study one of them—the remains of an invoice with the address burned off. He made out an unusual name.

"The name Syrena mean anything to you?"

Williams: "No, sir."

Mancini perked up: "Serena, like the tennis player?"

"No, Syrena with a *y*."

Past his shoulder, in the corner of the sunken living room decorated in a cool pale green, Davis and Akil sat huddled in front of a big-screen TV that was broadcasting a story on BBC World News. Their story. An excited British voice over the *whop-whop-whop* of helicopter blades: "Appears to be a terrorist-type bombing, though details are sketchy. Through the smoke we're seeing a seriously damaged three-story building near the port. Preliminary reports from the Ministry of Interior say that a large explosive device was hidden in a van. Has all the earmarks of the Taliban extremists . . . ."

Taliban extremists. Isn't that rich?

Down the hall, past the steamy bathroom he'd showered in, Crocker stopped at the beige door at the end and knocked.

"Come in," came a no-nonsense woman's voice.

He turned the knob and saw the nurse leaning over the nightstand, placing a stopper in a vial. The thin white fabric stretched to the contour of her nicely shaped behind.

God, what I'd like to do to that.

He stopped. Pushed what he knew was a dangerous urge aside, and focused on Ritchie sitting up on the bed with his right leg stretched out.

The East Indian doctor attending him glanced up at Crocker with a mischievous look in his eyes. He seemed to relish the idea of mixing with shadowy men like them. Probably couldn't wait to get home to tell his wife.

Crocker said: "Doc, did you tell Ritchie that the next time he shaves his legs he needs to stand still?"

The doctor cracked up. "I told. Oh . . . I told him that. Yes."

Ritchie shot him the finger.

"You guys with Delta?" the nurse asked.

"You trying to insult us?" Ritchie asked back.

"Why?"

"D boys look like soldiers," Ritchie explained. "Clean cut. Sticks up their asses. Do everything by the book. SEALs are cooler, more relaxed, until we swing into action. Then watch out."

Her eyes shifted from Ritchie's shaggy hair to the biceps bulging out of Crocker's shirt. Rested on the left one, with the tattoo of a skull smoking a cigarette.

"So you're SEALs."

"That's right."

Ten years and one failed marriage earlier, he would have taken the bait. Invited her out for a couple of beers. He imagined she was the kind of woman who posted overseas in search of adventure. Tom Crocker had it running through his blood. But he was too happily married now to invite complications. Had learned to keep his life clean and compartmentalized. Love, marriage, family, sex in one box. Work, danger, mental and physical challenges in another.

The big SEAL team leader turned to Ritchie with a look that cut right through him.

"We're going up north without you, Rich," Crocker said. "Give your leg a chance to heal. We'll be back in a couple of weeks."

"Hell, I can still outclimb you guys."

"Not on one leg, you can't."

"You want to bet?"

"I'll bring back a yeti if we find one."

"Or one of those cute German climbers."

"Stay out of trouble."

"I'll do the best I can." Then, glancing at the doctor's light-haired assistant, "But no guarantees."

"If he gives you any shit, Doc, you've got my permission to cut his balls off."

The shoulders under the doctor's white coat shook hard. He covered his mouth with a little pink palm and laughed. "I'll remember that," he said. "Oh, my. I don't think it will be necessary. But I'll remember it for sure."

That's when Akil burst through the door looking worried. "Boss, you'd better come see this."

Crocker stopped him in the hall and whispered, "What?"

"They recovered a little girl's body from the apartment. She was crushed to death."

Each of the four men wrestled with the news during the two-hour Pakistan International Airlines flight to Islamabad. It was easy to say, as Crocker had, that the girl was an unfortunate and probably unavoidable casualty of war, and one they had tried very hard to prevent.

But that didn't stop each man from feeling regret. Mancini and Crocker both had wives and children. Davis's wife was almost eight months pregnant with their first.

Crocker had a daughter. Plus, he was the one who had made the decision to deploy the VBIED that partially destroyed the building and probably killed the girl.

How old was she?

It didn't matter. Nor did it help that there were a dozen or so Pakistani and Arabic-looking girls on the flight. Seeing them, he couldn't help trying to imagine her.

What did she look like? What was her name? Was she related to Zaman? Who was her mother? Would she have made a good wife and mother?

Stop it! This is useless. Stop!

Tom Crocker sat up in his seat and reminded himself that he was fighting a war to preserve the freedom of people to choose the kind of life they wanted to live. It was a simple equation.

Yes, there were degrees of freedom and innumerable other factors and influences. But he held tight to a basic proposition. Namely, that Islamic terrorists like Zaman wanted to impose a highly restrictive and repressive set of religious laws on people all over the world, and they were hell-bent on making it come true. He, as an agent of the United States, was fighting to preserve and extend personal freedom at home and abroad.

Crocker said a silent prayer for the girl and vowed to be even more careful in the future.

Entering the baggage claim area, the SEAL team leader spotted a tall man in a light-colored suit and recognized him immediately.

What's he want?

It was Lou Donaldson from the CIA station—their main contact in Pakistan.

Shit...

Crocker had worked with Donaldson numerous times before, and didn't like his superior manner and the way he talked down to people, like a disappointed father or a scolding schoolteacher.

The CIA officer sidled up to him at the first baggage turnstile.

"We need to talk," he said.

"No Hello? Or How have you been?"

"Follow me."

Crocker left Davis, Mancini, and Akil to deal with the gear and followed the man out of the terminal to a light-colored SUV with blacked-out windows idling beside the curb.

Despite the fact that the sun was fading and the sky had turned a vivid shade of salmon, the air was still surprisingly hot. Gods with halitosis, or something like that.

Crocker had perspired through his shirt by the time he climbed into the air-conditioned backseat. Two thick-chested men waited inside. One behind the wheel. One in back, Jim Anders, Donaldson's chief aide and yes-man, whom Crocker had also met before. Lou slid into the passenger seat and slammed the door.

He said, "We've got a major fuckup on our hands, thanks to you."

Crocker chose to remain silent, biting on his anger.

Donaldson craned his long neck past the headrest.

"You hear about the girl?"

"Yes, I did." Trying to hold it back.

"Six years old. Regrettable. But there's more." Donaldson looked quickly at the other two, to add their displeasure to his.

"Zaman. You didn't get him!"

"What do you mean?"

Donaldson wasn't finished. "The guys you killed mean nothing. We've checked their backgrounds. Minor players. Bodyguards. But the guy we sent you in to get... according to our intel, he was there, and you let him walk."

"You know that as a fact?"

"Yes, goddammit. AZ was in the fucking apartment!"

Crocker, his blood pressure rising, immediately flashed back to the two women in brown burkas he had let pass.

"What do you have to say for yourself?"

Rage boiled in his stomach. "How can you be absolutely sure he was there?"

"You screwed up, Crocker. You failed!"

"We carried out the mission professionally, thoughtfully, to the best of our abilities. Of course, everything happened very fast. As you know, every mission involves certain—" His words sounded hollow even to himself.

Donaldson cut him off. "The Pakistanis are fucking irate! They're pretty damn sure that we were involved."

"Do they have evidence? Because we were careful not to leave anything behind."

"Not yet."

"Then that's not my problem."

Donaldson turned to his cohorts—Anders and the driver. "Did you hear that? Not his problem. Fuck."

Crocker struggled to stay calm. He said, "Look, I did see two women in burkas as I was engaged in a firefight on the first floor. One was holding what I assumed to be a baby. The other was leading a four-year-old boy by the hand. I let them pass and assume they escaped the building unharmed."

"Piss-poor decision, Crocker! Jesus Christ! I bet one of those women was AZ." The tall CIA officer punched the back of his seat.

"In the heat of battle I wasn't able to stop and question them."

"It didn't occur to you that one of them could have been Zaman?"

"Like I said, this happened in the heat of battle."

"So?"

"I couldn't see their faces clearly, but neither of them appeared to have a beard."

"Maybe he shaved the fucking thing off!"

"Your intel described him as bearded."

"This is a goddamn disaster!"

"He's on the run. We'll get him. I'll make sure of that."

"No, Crocker. You missed your chance."

The SEAL team leader was determined to extract something positive. "What about the laptops we captured?"

"What about them?"

"You find anything on the laptops that might be useful in tracking Zaman down?"

"Nothing so far."

"Nothing?"

Jim Anders spoke up for the first time. "Seems he liked to download images of half-naked blondes in cages."

"Blondes?"

"Yeah, blondes."

"Does the name Syrena mean anything to you?" Crocker asked.

"Why?"

"I saw it on something that was burned in half that looked like an official invoice."

"How was it spelled?"

"S-y-r-e-n-a."

Donaldson looked at Jim Anders, who said, "Syrena, spelled s-y-r-e-n-a, was the name of a Polish sedan that went out of production in 1983."

"It might be important," Crocker said.

"Thanks, Crocker," Donaldson countered snidely. "We'll keep our eyes out for old Polish cars."

"What about Zaman? Any idea where he is now?"

"Wherever he is, he's probably planning more attacks against Americans."

"I want another shot at him," Crocker said, looking Donaldson in the eye.

"Go climb your mountain. Expect to make contact with a foreign national, six foot one, longish blond hair, early forties. His name is Mikael Klausen."

"What's he want?"

"He has something he wants to discuss with you. We'll talk when you get back."

CHAPTER FIVE

Ever tried. Ever failed. No matter. Try again. Fail again. Fail better.

—Samuel Beckett

LEAVES ME *feeling like a fool,* Crocker thought, referring to the pencil-pushing, risk-averse Agency asshole Donaldson. *Calls the mission a fuckup…*

Unfair.

Anger and anxiety had been eating at him throughout the one-hour flight from Islamabad to Skardu. When he returned to ST-6 headquarters in Virginia, he'd have to prepare a postoperations report. In it, he'd have to explain what went wrong with the mission and how Zaman had escaped.

Following that, he'd be subjected to a briefing called a hot wash, during which every detail of the mission would be picked over and second-guessed by dozens of officers from the CIA, Joint Special Operations Command, and ST-6.

Now he wanted to get up and kick something or do some physical training, but there was nowhere to go in the DC-9 fuselage crammed with passengers, suitcases, plastic bags filled with clothes. A serious—some might say fanatical—athlete, Crocker hadn't missed a day of PT in twenty years.

With no outlet, his indignation metamorphosed into rigorous self-examination. Soon he was questioning the decisions he'd made, his leadership, his intelligence.

Then, he got pissed off for criticizing himself.

What the hell am I doing?

Crocker's father—the most straightforward, hardworking man he'd ever known—had taught his son to be ruthlessly honest.

But what he was doing was something else—a weird form of beating other people to the punch, or keeping himself in line. Maybe it was guilt left over from some of the wild things he'd done as a kid.

Anger begat anxiety, which turned into self-questioning, and then became no-holds-barred self-criticism.

He knew the vicious circle, because he'd traveled it many times. The outcome was always the same. Dizzying mental exhaustion. Emptiness at the pit of his stomach. A feeling of being unworthy and incomplete.

Some wise man had said: You can accomplish amazing feats of bravery and travel to the farthest reaches of the earth, but you can't escape yourself. Or something like that.

The truth in those words chafed at Crocker, who twisted in the upholstered seat. Akil, buckled in beside him, could literally feel the heat radiating from the team leader's body.

"What's going on with you, boss? You look like you're about to explode," Akil remarked, tossing aside the copy of *People* with Sandra Bullock on the cover. Leave it to him to find the one magazine on the plane filled with photos of beautiful women.

Crocker grasped the armrest as the jet banked sharply. "I'll get over it, Akil. I'm just a little... annoyed."

"Why? Because we didn't get Zaman?"

"Something like that."

The plane started to descend through dense white clouds.

"Sniveling coward hides under a burka, pretending to be a woman," Akil remarked. "Which means sooner or later we get to make him our bitch."

Sometimes Akil's devil-may-care attitude cut right through the bull.

Crocker grinned. "It's that asshole Donaldson from the Agency."

Akil frowned. "Where was he when we were in the shit?"

"In a meeting, probably, sipping a cappuccino."

"Or jerking someone off. Next time, tell him to go fuck himself."

Bursts of wind tossed the DC-9 from side to side. Crocker imagined circling back to Islamabad, finding Donaldson, and beating the living shit out of him.

But what would that accomplish, except getting him brought up on charges?

He turned to face the clouds churning outside his window and muttered: "Pencil-pushers like him make a career of second-guessing other people's work. What is their purpose beyond that?"

"Boss, he's not important. Forget him. Just another Washington parasite. The city's swarming with them."

"They get in our way. Live off the blood and sweat of

others. Bureaucrats and fucking power junkies," Crocker continued to vent.

"They whine a lot, but the next time they're ready to nail some terrorists, who are they going to call?"

"Us, I hope."

"We're like the Ghostbusters. Only we eradicate fanatics with automatic weapons and WMDs."

Sharp gray mountains poked through the cumulus clouds. Nanga Parbat, the world's ninth-highest peak, better known as Killer Mountain, glistened brilliantly in the distance. The view of the mountains momentarily pulled Crocker's mind away from Donaldson. One of the things he loved about climbing was the opportunity it afforded to free his mind of the garbage that ate at him.

The work schedule usually provided the SEAL operators with a two-month OCONUS (outside the continental United States) deployment period, followed by two months of Special Skills training, followed by two months of standby. Crocker had convinced his ST-6 commanding officer to allow him to take his crew to the mountains as part of their two-month Special Skills rotation. Having them enter Pakistan as climbers not only provided a convenient cover for the AZ mission, the climb itself would afford Crocker's men some much-needed downtime. They'd been going hard the last five-plus months—deploying on one op after another, with no Special Skills training or standby.

The jet hit another air pocket and fell five hundred feet.

Akil: "You think the pilot knows what he's doing?"

Some kid's DVD player was blasting "Baby" by Justin Bieber, proof that his music had reached every corner of the earth.

Suddenly they saw tin roofs gleam through the swirling mist, which magically dissipated to reveal a valley of deep, luxurious green.

Seatbacks up. Buckles secured. The landing gear groaned as it locked into place.

As they neared an asphalt runway, Akil checked the altimeter on his watch. "Eight thousand one hundred and eighty-nine feet."

Earlier in his career, Crocker had been part of a joint SEAL-Agency mission to La Paz, Bolivia, located at 13,000 feet. Most of the team spent the first two days sick and suffering from massive headaches because they landed without a chance to acclimatize.

He planned for his current team to climb approximately 10,000 feet beyond that, without supplemental oxygen. But they would be taking the ascent in stages.

The plane twisted violently right, seconds before it touched down.

"Hold on!"

Crocker, Akil, and Davis and Mancini, a row behind them, bounced in their seats and were tossed from side to side. A dark-skinned Tibetan-looking woman seated across the aisle leaned forward and threw up on her red flats.

Crocker passed her a headband that he kept in his backpack to clean herself with. She didn't want to take it.

"Go ahead. You need it more than I do," he said in English.

She nodded and replied: "*Shukran.*" (Thank you.)

"*Aafwaan.*" (You're welcome.)

Outside the little concrete terminal, Crocker breathed the thin air tinged with the smell of burning charcoal, then caught his reflection in the building's plate-glass window.

The modern world wasn't an easy place for a warrior with a conscience to find his way.

A girl had been killed and Zaman had escaped.

As the assault leader of ST-6/Blue, Tom Crocker carried a large responsibility on his shoulders—not just for his team, but for the millions of Americans it was their job to protect. Lou Donaldson was right. Zaman probably was planning more attacks against Americans.

Crocker badly wanted another shot at him. But he literally had to climb a mountain first.

Crocker had faced many extreme physical challenges in his decades as a SEAL: jungle ops in the Amazon, Colombia, El Salvador, Nicaragua, Peru, Honduras, Bolivia, and Panama; air assaults in Grenada and Afghanistan; grueling mountain runs in Ethiopia and Korea; desert gunfights in the Middle East; and undercover ops in Iran, Yemen, Saudi Arabia.

Terrorists generally didn't have much to lose. Many of them had experienced day-to-day combat, the loneliness of imprisonment, the agony of torture, and the pangs of starvation. That's why he always pushed his men to strengthen and further develop their combat mind-set. They needed to believe they could take on the most perilous, difficult enemy, and prevail.

As he waited with the others for their gear to be unloaded from the belly of the jet, Crocker's mind doubled back.

How did one fully serve one's country, which he believed in most cases projected good in the world, when duty to country sometimes involved inflicting violence and death on the innocent?

Physical danger he could handle, but the pull of conscience and the need to answer to civil society—the sheep—was more difficult.

That's why the little girl's death continued to gnaw at him.

Some warriors found relief in gambling, womanizing, or drinking. Others put their feet up and, beer in hand, numbed their brains with TV. He preferred to be outdoors, climbing, running, skiing, hiking, biking, kayaking, always physically challenging himself.

For one thing, he had huge reserves of energy. Secondly, as a kid growing up in New England, he'd spent weekends and vacations in the wilderness camping with his brother, sisters, and parents. That's where he'd learned to appreciate and respect the power, beauty, and majesty of nature.

Nature made no judgments, and represented truth. Growth and destruction. Death and rebirth.

The pride he felt in being a small part of it had pushed him to develop his body. A skinny teenager, Crocker had spent many sweaty all-nighters in his father's garage, lifting weights to Black Sabbath, Led Zeppelin, the Stones. He became a fanatic. Some nights he'd work out until an hour or two before his mother got him and his siblings up and ready for school.

He sat remembering those days. The simplicity of knowing what was expected of him; the loving warmth of his family.

"Legs" by ZZ Top just happened to be playing on the cassette player of the multicolored Nissan cab. An old Ford Taurus followed them, carrying Akil and the rest of their gear.

He panicked for a moment, thinking they'd lost

Ritchie, then recalled that he was back in Islamabad with the attractive nurse, waiting for his leg to heal.

The gray-haired driver negotiated potholes as the sweet smell of barbecued lamb wafted through the cracked and taped side window.

"Jesus, that smells good," Mancini remarked.

"Sure does," Crocker echoed.

Davis, his stomach still halfway up his throat from the landing, looked at the two men and shook his head. "You guys got to be kidding."

The joke was that Mancini had a stomach like a cement mixer. He could eat anything.

Mancini: "Boss, you think we can stop and try some of that lamb kebab?"

"We'll eat at the hotel."

"Doubt if the grub there will taste half as good as that. The stuff they sell on the streets is always better."

"So are your chances of getting food poisoning."

Brownish yellow dust covered everything, including the dozens of stalls that sold items that ran the gamut from trekking supplies to souvenirs. The dirt shoulder that passed for a sidewalk was crowded with a mixture of Shins, Pashtuns, Hunzakuts, and Uyghurs. Looked more like Tibet than Pakistan.

Before dinner, Crocker set out on an eight-mile run in the foothills. As his muscles worked and his lungs filled with the fresh mountain air beyond the town limits, he felt better. The starry sky and sliver of moon reminded him of his boyhood home in New England. The shadows of giant peaks looming ahead promised new adventure. The Pink Floyd song "High Hopes" echoed in his head, especially the lyric "consumed by slow decay."

* * *

The next morning, fed and rested, the four Americans set out in two rented Land Rovers for the seven-hour drive to Askole. Zaman and the dead six-year-old girl had faded in the memories of the others, but for some reason Crocker's mind hadn't completely let them go.

Amends had to be made. Scores remained to be settled.

His determination to get AZ didn't dissipate, even in the face of rugged mountainous terrain and thin air.

To call what they traversed a road was something of an exaggeration. But he'd been on worse—recently in Afghanistan, and several months ago in Bolivia, where he and his team had been sent to take out the leaders of a ring of narco-terrorists.

The members of SEAL Team Six wound their way up small hills into lushly vegetated, irrigated farming villages. Between these green oases they passed over stretches of stark desert, through river basins and canyons of sharp granite.

Crocker thought of past missions he'd been on and the casualties they'd produced—Cubans in Grenada, PDF in Panama, Saddam's soldiers in Iraq, Salvadoran rebels, Afghan Taliban and mujahedeen, Colombian, Bolivian, and Honduran drug-war casualties. There was a fellow adventure racer who had died of heatstroke in Utah, fellow bikers he'd seen destroyed in motorcycle accidents, frozen climbers in Alaska and in the Himalayas.

He wondered about the toll they'd taken on his soul.

Not that he'd ever had a problem killing people when he thought it was necessary. At seventeen, he'd taken his first life—that of a sadistic gangbanger fresh out of prison who'd beaten up a female friend of his, a sweet lost soul with blue eyes named Patty Norris.

When a red-hot young Crocker confronted the punk, who outweighed him by at least 125 pounds, the ex-con drew a snub-nosed .38, smiled, and asked: "What the fuck do you want, kid?"

Crocker didn't panic. Surprised the bastard with three sharp punches to the face.

As the gangbanger bent down to retrieve the pistol that he'd dropped, Crocker smashed the side of his head with a large rock. The big ex-con hit the ground, twitched a little, but never got up.

In all the many times Crocker had thought about that encounter since, he'd never felt remorse. One less evil scumbag to plague the innocent. To his mind, he'd made the world a safer place.

They had to stop where a river had washed out part of the road. The four SEALs stripped to their T-shirts and tossed boulders into the narrow, busy channel. Within an hour, they were back on their way, smiling, munching on lamb sandwiches, cracking jokes.

Akil went first. "How do you keep a blonde busy all day?"

"Beats me."

"Put her in a round room and tell her to sit in the corner."

Davis: "Why are tornadoes and marriage alike? They both start with a lot of blowing and sucking, but in the end you always lose your house."

"Your turn, boss."

"What do you call a blind deer?"

"What?"

"No eye deer."

Groans, then Davis: "Jesus, boss, that sucks."

Mancini blew them all out of the water. "What's the difference between acne and a Catholic priest? Acne usually comes on a boy's face after he turns twelve."

"Shit, Mancini," Davis said. "Where did that come from?"

Crocker: "I thought you were a Catholic."

"I am."

By nightfall, they rolled into Askole, the last village en route to the Baltoro Glacier and K2. Despite the late hour, Balti porters gathered around the vehicles to offer to schlep the men's gear for the next ten days. For this backbreaking work, ranging in temperatures from ninety-five degrees to the teens, they were asking $7.50 a day.

Having chosen a dozen porters and one cook, the four Americans set out at six the next morning. Since there were no teahouses along the trek, all food had to be hauled in, which accounted for the fact that each man had to carry at least fifty pounds of expedition supplies and equipment. The porters tied their personal gear in tight bundles on top of their loads.

Most used handmade wooden pack frames; a few had more elaborate welded-steel ones. None bothered with padding or waist belts.

The more fortunate of the porters wore laced leather shoes. Most made do with cheap Chinese molded-plastic footwear, no match for the double-insulated climbing boots worn by Crocker, Akil, Davis, and Mancini.

In addition to their climbing gear, the Americans brought along cold-weather clothing, sleeping bags, compression sacks, self-inflating ground pads for sleeping, cooking gear—cup, spoon, bowl—SPF 40 sunscreen, lip balm, water bottles, pee bottles, knives, toiletries, toilet paper, hand sanitizer, hand and toe warmers, first-aid kits, medications, cameras, and note-taking materials.

The first few miles were gentle, past rich green fields, trees—the valley on one side, villages peeking through the trees on the other. But as soon as they neared the Braldu River, the trail veered sharply upward.

With the sun beating down it was boiling hot, but when afternoon clouds moved in, the temperature quickly dropped into the forties. Dark clouds sped across the sky.

This is the easy part, Crocker thought.

After a long day of trekking, the Americans stopped to set up their tents. While they hammered spikes into the hard ground, the porters called out evening prayers to Allah. The sounds collided and echoed into the valley.

As Crocker watched, the porters, bickering and laughing, created a communal shelter behind three-foot-high rock walls, which they covered with a plastic sheet. For warmth they huddled together, wrapped in thin blankets and woolen shawls while the cook prepared a dinner of *daal* (a bland stew made from dried beans), *chawal* (rice with kidney beans), and *achar* (spiced Indian pickles), which all the men shared. Then they slept.

Two days of trekking later, the team reached the Baltoro Glacier, which slowed them down considerably. Most of the slow-moving ice river they traversed was covered with rocks, sand, and dirt, giving it a grayish aspect. The parts exposed to the sun were slick and especially treacherous.

Crocker led the way, looking to avoid ice ridges and crevasses. To his left, sharp granite peaks covered with snow and ice stabbed the sky.

He wished Holly was with him to see this. She was a government operative like him, also a black belt in karate and an accomplished runner and cyclist. Fit and beautiful, too. Their friends and family called them Mr. and Mrs. Smith.

He wondered what she was doing, and how she was getting along with Jenny. As much as he loved them both, he preferred the excitement of training with the team and missions to the comforts of home.

His first wife could never understand that. But Holly did. Crocker knew that he was lucky to have found her—a woman who appreciated what he did and didn't try to change him. He gave her total credit for making their marriage work.

He pushed ahead, picking his way through an endless maze of giant boulders, all the while thinking he had to track down Abu Rasul Zaman. Shoot the bastard in the head.

One of the Balti porters told him the glacier moved so fast that the route was different every two or three weeks. Sounded a bit like his own life.

Eventually they reached a path that wound a thousand feet up from the glacier to the next campsite, perched high on a hill. It was a slippery, near vertical climb.

"How much farther?" Akil shouted.

Turning to look over his shoulder, Crocker saw Mancini lose his grip on the ice, flip in the air, and slide ten feet before he could perform a self-arrest by sticking his ice axe in the frozen snow and stopping his momentum.

Shit!

He was down, squirming, trying to pull the axe out from underneath his body.

Crocker shouted: "Is he okay?"

Davis, by Mancini's side, shouted back: "The blade went into his thigh. He smashed his knee and ribs."

"Let me see."

A light rain started to fall as they arrived at the permanent camp. Multicolored tents covered a broad grassy slope three hundred yards above the glacier, which formed an enormous granite backdrop, like a giant rippled curtain. As the porters sang and banged out an intricate rhythm on blue plastic drums, Crocker bandaged the ugly slash to Mancini's right thigh. Then he fitted him with an elastic knee brace and handed him a couple of Motrins.

He felt for damage to his ribs, kneecap, and ligaments. "You might have bruised and possibly fractured a couple of ribs. The knee looks bruised, not cracked. If that's the extent of your injuries, you're lucky."

"That's the same knee I smashed playing football," Mancini said.

"You're probably gonna have to stay off of it awhile."

"Fuck me."

"How'd it happen?"

"I was feeling a little light-headed," Mancini said. "I started imagining the smell of my wife's lasagna. Then I thought I heard her talking to me."

The long hours in the thin air were known to play tricks on people's brains.

"Breathe deeply, stay hydrated, and don't lose focus," Crocker warned his men.

When word reached the Americans that members of a Norwegian team had invited them to drinks and dinner in a nearby tent, Mancini and his battered body chose to stay behind.

Crocker, wrapped in his parka, stepped past a group of porters who were roasting a goat on a spit and bent over to fit through the opening in the Norwegians' North Face tent. Davis and Akil entered behind him.

Fluorescent camping lanterns lit the tight, warm space. Half a dozen fit, scruffy men sat around a portable table, drinking, eating, smoking cigars. The air was thick with smells.

All eyes ogled the plates of mashed *aloo*—potatoes and chili peppers fried with onions and spices—*daal,* and *chawal*.

A tall man with a full face covered with reddish brown stubble saluted them with a tin cup of brandy.

"Are you the Americans?"

"Yes, we are."

"Here's to cowboys, apple pie, and cheerleaders," he said.

A man wearing a black ski cap turned to face them. "Would any of you happen to know Chief Warrant Officer Tom Crocker of the U.S. Navy?"

Crocker did a double take. "Why?"

"I heard from my embassy that he was climbing in the area and would like to speak to him."

"Crocker. That's me. Who are you?"

"Mikael Klausen," the Norwegian said, extending his hand and clearing a place beside him. "I work in my country's foreign office."

"Nice to meet you, Mikael."

He probably was the foreign national Donaldson had told him about. But Crocker wanted to make sure.

"Who told you I was here?" he asked.

"A man from your embassy named Mr. Lou Donaldson."

"How do you know Donaldson?"

"I was introduced to him through Ambassador Connelly. Your ambassador and my ambassador to Pakistan play poker together."

"And you trekked all the way up to look for me?"

"I have a proposition for you from my king."

CHAPTER SIX

There's no school like old school, and I'm the fucking headmaster.

—RocknRolla

WIND SMACKED the side of the oval tent, sounding like a machine gun, as Mikael refilled Crocker's mug with Teerenpeli single malt whisky poured from a tin flask. Then the Norwegian slipped the flask into his sleeping bag next to his iPod, water bottles, and other items he wanted to keep from freezing.

The Teerenpeli went down smoothly. Rich and old, its distilled essence of earth warmed Crocker's body.

Several other Norwegian climbers slept in sleeping bags behind them, snoring and occasionally passing gas—which became more of a problem the higher one climbed, according to Boyle's law $(pV = K)$. Mancini had explained earlier that for a fixed amount of a gas kept at a fixed temperature, pressure and volume are inversely proportional. In other words, once you lower the atmospheric pressure the gas will escape.

One of the sleeping Norwegians called out the name Berit. Whoever she was.

The rest of Crocker's team had returned to their tent, where their team leader hoped they were resting for the climb ahead.

He and the Norwegian spent hours comparing backgrounds and sharing stories about their children, tastes in food, music, and women, the economic states of their respective countries. All prelude.

"Last one for me," Crocker announced.

They agreed on lots of things—including love, loyalty, and the need to protect their citizenry from the savagery of certain people.

Mikael frowned and cleared his throat. "For the better part of a year I've been on a fact-finding mission regarding a problem that plagues our country."

"What problem is that?"

"Normal crimes of passion, drugs, prostitution, these aren't things that I like, but as a realist I understand that they're acceptable to a certain extent," Mikael continued. "They don't involve so many innocent victims."

Crocker thought he knew what the Norwegian meant. He said, "That's another way of saying that people get caught up in nasty shit because they're weak for one reason or another. They do, or maybe they don't, see what's coming as a result."

Mikael lowered his voice to a whisper. "What I'm going to discuss with you now is just between the two of us."

"Understood."

"My leader and dear friend the king of Norway, Harald V, has asked me to take this up as his personal mission. It's something that offends him deeply as the leader of our country, and as a husband, father, and grandfather to five young children."

Mention of the king got the SEAL's attention. He wanted to meet him. His fellow Frogs, training buddies, and even his gnarly biker friends would get a kick out of that.

"You see, Mr. Crocker, in the last four or five years an increasing and alarming number of young men and, especially, young women have been disappearing from my country. Snatched off the streets. They're never heard from again. Their bodies are never found."

"How many are you talking about?"

"Dozens. Last year over fifty."

Crocker remembered that Norway had a population of about five million. He said: "That's a hell of a lot."

"You might ask, What do they have in common? They include boys and girls but are predominantly female, all between the ages of twelve and eighteen. They're in good health, usually from good families, with good educations."

"You make it sound like something out of one of those vampire movies."

"It's worse. We have evidence that they're being smuggled out of the country for two very sinister purposes. The physically attractive ones are sold into sexual slavery. The others are used in something called the 'spare parts program.' "

Crocker felt a throb in the pit of his stomach. He'd heard rumors about the latter, but had never seen hard evidence that it existed.

The corner of Klausen's mouth curled into a snarl. "Our investigators have traced some of these children to

Central and South America, and to Middle Eastern countries, particularly Yemen, Syria, and Saudi Arabia," he explained. "They believe they have been kept on farms and used, after being blood-typed and cross-matched, by wealthy Arabs and sheiks for organ transplants for their children when these are needed."

"Disgusting."

"Barbaric."

"Besides collecting evidence, what have you done to stop the animals who are doing this?"

"We passed along our findings to a special committee of the European Parliament. They followed up and issued a report, which was referred to a special rapporteur of the United Nations. Warnings and information were then sent to member governments."

Diplomatic maneuvers like that weren't likely to accomplish much.

"Has any direct action been taken?" Crocker asked, clenching his fist.

"Of course in matters of this kind, getting countries to act is problematic. The nations accused of haboring such criminals protest vociferously. They claim to have looked into the charges and usually dismiss them as rumors."

"So what you're telling me is, nothing has been done?"

"I can't speak for other countries besides my own, but it takes individuals with special abilities and international experience to track down the kind of people who commit these acts. For political reasons we can't use our own people to eliminate them. That's why I've been hoping to connect with someone like yourself."

"I see."

"What do you think?"

Crocker scratched the stubble on his chin. After the climb he and his team were scheduled to take a week to rest and recuperate, and he would then await further orders from his CO at ST-6 headquarters in Virginia. Hopefully, Zaman would surface by then, and he and his team would get another shot at him. But after what had happened in Karachi, he doubted they'd get that chance.

He said, "I'd like to help, but I can't do anything without authorization."

Mikael's eyes lit up. He explained: "Like I said before, our ambassadors here in Pakistan are poker buddies. Also, the king and I have many important friends in Washington, especially some key decision makers at your Pentagon and White House. I believe I can prevail on them for a few weeks of your time. Unofficially, I can arrange for money to be wired into an account to cover your expenses. The king and I are hoping you might convince other members of your team to cooperate as well."

Crocker figured that the Norwegian understood little about the command structure of SEAL Team Six. He said, "Even if you manage to get authorization from my superiors, what are we likely to accomplish in a short period of time?"

"Wait." Mikael got to his feet, reached into a backpack, and returned to the table with a thin Apple laptop. "We've had a very recent case," he said, eagerly firing it up and punching keys. A case file appeared on the screen, along with the photo of a lovely young woman.

"Malie Tingvoll. I know the family. Good, solid people."

Crocker leaned closer. He thought she looked familiar.

"She recently turned eighteen. Disappeared a week

ago from the small hotel she was working at in Oslo. Nobody has seen or heard from her since."

"She didn't run away with a boyfriend?"

"We don't believe so. No."

Crocker winced as he remembered long, light blond hair like hers, glimpsed in the backyard of a grand house in Mosul, Iraq. His memory took him back to the summer of 2003 and a morning when he and his team had been called in to help eliminate a "high-priority" target.

An army intelligence unit searching for Saddam Hussein had stopped to interrogate the owner of a large, gated house in Mosul when people started shooting at them from the second floor. Air support was called in; rockets were fired. By the time Crocker and his team arrived, the battle was pretty much over.

One of the Delta squadrons swept the house. The shredded bodies of two bearded men were found behind a bloody mattress. Army intelligence operatives believed they were Saddam's sons, Uday and Qusay Hussein.

Crocker and his men had gone downstairs to search the basement. Past a workout room filled with Nautilus-type machines and decorated with leopard-skin-patterned wallpaper, they found a torture chamber, the medieval-looking devices covered with bloodstains. There was splatter on the walls and ceiling, even dried pools on the floor. Some of it was still sticky-wet and pungent.

Inside a desk, they discovered a collection of photos of naked, tortured women. Uday and Qusay posed with some of them, bound and gagged, in the act of being raped or sodomized. Many were young and blond, and had been burned, whipped, and cut.

Sick fucks!

Behind the house they found a large cage of lions busily gnawing the remains of some of these women down to the bone.

Crocker and his men saw rib cages, blanched pelvises, skulls. Some looked fresh. Akil had pointed out a head with long blond hair lying in one corner next to a pool of water. It was the one time in the SEAL team leader's combat experience that he'd come close to losing his lunch.

His stomach churning, he focused on the screen again. The young girl in the picture had long, light blond hair and big breasts, which had made her a target.

"What's her name again?"

"Malie Tingvoll."

"Anything about her background that I should know?"

"She's a nice girl, a good student, no record of drug use. Healthy and normal. Like I said before, I know her family."

At times like these Crocker hated being tied down by regulations. Part of him wanted to turn around right now, grab his men, and fly to Oslo.

He said: "If you and the king can buy me a couple of weeks, I'll try to find her." Or what's left of her, he thought.

"Are you confident you can accomplish that in so little time?"

"The more you can tell me about the people who grabbed her, the better chance I'll have."

"Of course," Mikael answered, placing a hand on Crocker's shoulder. "The king will be pleased."

"Tell him he has to act quickly."

"I'll call him in the morning on my sat-phone and start

making the arrangements," Mikael said. "I'll also alert our security police to assemble a file with their best evidence."

"That's fine," Crocker answered. "But I can't wait here. Tomorrow morning I'm proceeding into the mountains with my men."

"I understand."

Crocker thought it was a long shot. Unless Klausen secured the necessary authorizations immediately, Crocker would be almost impossible to reach. In the time it took him and his men to finish their climb and return to Islamabad, the girl would probably be sold into slavery, or dead, or God knows what.

But he'd learned to never underestimate the ability of politics to trump the rules and procedures, and of kings to influence the future.

As he got up to leave, Crocker said, "Nice to meet you, Mikael. Good luck."

A king needed a crown. Towering above the frozen valley floor was a natural one formed by dozens of mountains that grew in size and dramatic splendor as the team picked its way farther north. Like the Himalayas, the Karakoram Range had been violently thrust upward when the Indian and Eurasian tectonic plates collided. Both ranges were still growing at a rate of 2.4 inches a year. The peaks here seemed to have been sculpted by demonic gods.

They'd trudged two hundred yards over snow and hillocks of icy rocks, and already Mancini was lagging. Crocker led, postholing his way through the deep snow, which enabled the others to walk in the holes he created.

He'd just sunk into drifts up to his knees when Davis slapped his shoulder. "Boss, look."

The team leader pulled his legs out and doubled back to Mancini, who was leaning on Akil.

"It's okay," Akil said. "We'll catch up."

"We gotta stay together," Crocker responded.

Crocker saw that Mancini was having a great deal of trouble putting weight on his right foot. When he did, ripples of pain and shame twisted what the team leader could see of his face. "Your knee still acting up?"

"It's a little stiff. I'll be fine."

"Manny, conditions only get worse up there."

"It'll loosen up."

Sometimes the die-hard SEAL mentality got in the way.

"Too much can-do can do you in."

"I'm okay."

"Show me."

Reluctantly, carefully, Mancini rolled up his pant leg and medium-weight Icebreaker long underwear to reveal a bulge the size of a baseball and a livid purple bruise that ran from his calf to the bottom of his foot.

"Looks like you ripped your calf muscle."

"No way."

"That purple is the blood that's drained from the tear."

"What's that mean?"

"It means you won't be climbing. You're going back to last night's camp. I'll send you with two of the porters. We'll meet you in Islamabad on our way back."

Mancini pulled off his goggles and threw them in the snow. "Islamabad? That won't be for another two weeks!"

"Ten days max. You can hang with Ritchie."

"That crazy fucker threw a live rattlesnake at me once."

"As a joke."

"It wasn't funny. I'll follow up the rear with a couple of the porters. In a couple of days I'll be fine."

"You're going back to Islamabad."

"Fuck me."

A day and a half more of slogging through ice sharks—exposed fins of ice that shoot up as high as two hundred feet—they entered the Concordia, which the Baltis referred to as the "throne of the gods." The sky was clear blue, and the view spectacular, unrivaled by anything Crocker had seen.

Before he left them, Mancini had explained that back in the seventh century the Buddhist pilgrim Hsuan Tsang had called this valley the most splendid place on earth.

Located at approximately 13,100 feet, the Concordia is actually a rippling, pitted, pockmarked river of gray and white ice where the great glaciers Baltoro, Abruzzi, and Godwin-Austen slide together before separating and going their individual ways. It forms a proscenium for a 360-degree panorama of peaks. Over forty of them reach over 21,000 feet, and ten of the world's thirty highest peaks are here, including the revered Broad Peak (26,414 feet), Gasherbrum-I (26,509 feet), Gasherbrum-II (26,360 feet), and K2 (28,251 feet)—the second tallest mountain in the world.

"There she is! That's K2, the Savage Mountain, over there," Crocker said, pointing at the spear-shaped thrust of rock.

"Incredible," Davis said.

"And a total bitch to climb."

"Great."

"Arguably the most difficult in the world. Steeper and more treacherous than most of the routes on Everest. And the weather is significantly colder and more unpredictable."

"Whose idea was it to climb that beast?" Akil said.

"Don't worry, we're not going for a summit."

Crocker, who had climbed a few of these peaks before, filled them in on K2's history. First summited in 1954 by two Italians: Lino Lacedelli and Achille Compagnoni. Since then, something like 310 climbers had reached the top, compared to over 2,700 for Everest. Over eighty others had died.

As with most climbs, the descent was even more dangerous than the ascent.

Crocker told them that only ten women had climbed K2. Three of those had fallen to their deaths on the way down.

"And that's the peak Edyta wants to summit?" Akil asked.

"Yeah, she's kind of extreme."

"I can't wait to meet her."

"Piss her off and she'll kick your ass."

The wind picked up, smacking them in the face as it blasted down between K2 and Broad Peak. It took them close to an hour to cross two hundred yards to the camp, a scattered collection of purple, pink, orange, red, yellow, and blue tents in various sizes and shapes.

The Concordia camp served as a meeting place for adventurers from all over the globe. Flags showed that there were climbers present from Korea, Nepal, Serbia, Pakistan, Norway, France, Ireland, and Germany.

While the porters sang and cleared places for the team's tents, Crocker and Akil went to visit the Germans. Eight of them were packed into a rectangular blue structure, seated at a folding table. The two Americans were invited to share *chapatis* (flatbread), yak cheese (which tasted like unsalted butter), and goat-milk tea while one of the Germans relayed the latest weather report out of Switzerland.

"There's a storm coming in tonight," he said in English, "then a forty-eight-hour break before the next one rolls in."

That's when Edyta entered, wearing a bright yellow parka and black wool hat pulled down to her eyes. Crocker, who didn't see her immediately, got an elbow in his side from Akil. "Look."

Recognizing Crocker, her gray-blue eyes sparkled, and she wrapped him in a hug. "Crocker. You old dog."

"It's good to see you again, Edie."

"I pictured you sitting before a fire, well fed and pleased with yourself, with your children and dogs gathered around you."

"I'm still getting in a climb or two a year. How are things?"

She looked leaner, more wizened, but still attractive in a been-everywhere, nothing-will-shock-me kind of way. High cheekbones, a wide, full mouth, strong jaw and chin. Straight, dirty blond hair that barely reached her shoulders.

She said: "My body's stronger than ever. My mind is still sharp. And I'm still hungry. Very hungry. I'm not ready to slow down yet. Too many mountains and too little time."

"I hear you."

"More mountains to conquer, more hearts to break."

Even in her forties, she still projected the aura of a femme fatale. A leaner, much tougher Kathleen Turner from *Body Heat.* Knowing Edyta, it was probably one of her favorite movies.

She whispered to Crocker, brandy on her breath: "I'm going to eat with the Italians after I help them clear up some garbage. You want to come?"

"You're doing what?"

"These Italian environmentalists, they're cleaning all the camps from Askole on. Empty gas canisters, beer tins, Coke cans, packaged food wrappers, batteries. Drop by my tent later. We can catch up."

Crocker knew what she wanted. Edyta made no bones about the fact that she'd slept with practically every attractive climber she'd met.

"I'd like to, but I'm married."

The glint in her eyes was wicked. "That didn't stop you before."

She was right. But that was during his first marriage, when he'd spent over three hundred days of the year away from home. He had returned after a three-week deployment to find the lawn unmowed and no furniture, lightbulbs, or even toilet paper in the house. Had no idea where his wife and three-year-old daughter had gone.

That hurt real bad. Now he limited his days away from home base to two hundred. Crocker wanted this marriage to last.

"Not this time," he said.

"You'll change your mind."

"I doubt it."

Edyta had a voice that sounded like honey mixed with gravel. "You know, a warm body is a luxury in a place like this. And mine gets hot."

Crocker's teammate stood to his right, vibrating with eagerness to take his place.

"Edyta, I want you to meet a good friend of mine. His name's Akil."

She checked him out from head to toe. "You look strong."

"I've heard a lot about you."

"You like Italian food, Akil? You want to come with me and get dirty picking up some garbage?"

Akil winked in the direction of his boss. "Why not?" he answered.

Edyta grabbed his hand and led him out.

CHAPTER SEVEN

I just don't want to die without a few scars.

—Chuck Palahniuk

SNOW AND ice everywhere they looked, interrupted by sheets of gray granite. A buzzing blue sky. Thin air. His mind reaching into euphoria. Lungs and muscles burning.

They climbed four steps, then stopped to catch their breath. Climbed three more, then stopped again—Crocker, Davis, Akil, Edyta, and two of the Germans linked to one another by an eighty-foot rope.

After they had climbed eight hours, the sun continued to beam intensely and brilliantly as they ascended steep snow slopes weighed down by fifty-pound packs. The porters had stayed behind in the Concordia.

And as they passed between rocky towers, wiggled through ice gullies, and stepped carefully across knife-sharp ridges, Crocker replayed a nightmare from the night before. It had occurred in an unusual yellow light. He and Akil were accompanying some U.S. Army Special

Forces somewhere in the Middle East. They stopped and were resting with their backs against a berm. The ground felt warm. The sun bore down on them, hot and heavy. Crocker, who wanted to keep moving, didn't like the fact that they were exposed on three sides.

He sat admiring the way the sunlight turned the dust-filled sky a mustard color, thinking that he should point out their vulnerability to the SF leader, when a convoy of three white pickups sped toward them and opened fire. He saw little white splashes of light from the trucks.

Bullets splattered around them, kicking up dirt and shards of rock.

The closest cover: their Humvees, parked thirty feet away along the two-lane asphalt road.

Seemed like the best option.

"Let's go!" Crocker shouted, getting into a crouch.

He grabbed Akil by the shoulder and started to run. His feet pushed down into the soles of his boots as they gripped the ground. Adrenaline surged through his veins, making him stronger, braver, smarter.

Hot air brushed past his bare arms and face. Then he was hit. His flight interrupted. One-two-three-four times.

Crocker somersaulted forward and landed on his side. *Bam!*

His heart reached up into his throat until it was strangling him. Somewhere below his navel, just under the body armor, life was draining out of him. He knew he was going to die.

Not now! He had things to do. People to take care of.

He couldn't even remember the name of the country he was in as his blood seeped into the thirsty ground.

What will they tell my wife? My daughter? Like it mattered.

He had awakened in his sleeping bag in a cold sweat, thinking about his family and the risks he took daily.

Now, picking his way through the snow and ice, he thought back to some of the real nightmares he'd been through. Like the time in Panama, humping through the jungle on a Special Forces Reserve–led mission in the San Blas Islands. Birds calling, howler monkeys screeching from the canopy of trees, on their way to capture a General Oliverios, who had worked for the drug-dealing dictator General Noriega.

General Oliverios, who in addition to running drugs and illegal guns, and forcing young girls into prostitution, had recently decapitated one of his maids.

Nice guy.

Leading the mission was an out-of-shape, cigar-chomping SF major named Malone. A loudmouthed asshole.

Crocker pointed out that they needed to establish a loss-of-communications plan. The smart-ass major replied: "In the army we have comms that work," because Crocker was in the navy.

A day later, during the hump over the mountains, the horse carrying all their comms fell off a cliff to his death. Which meant no comms for the remainder of the mission.

At the time, Crocker was hugely pissed off at the incompetent SF major. But now, for some reason, he was thinking about the horse. Remembering the horrible brays and thumping as it fell down, then the cries of pain and helplessness as it took its last breaths.

The result of one act of stupidity and one false step.

* * *

The sun had started sinking past his shoulder, which turned the sky a deeper, stiller blue and the snow-covered bank in front of him various shades of gold.

The others were lagging farther behind in the increasingly thinner air. Crocker sensed that they were ready to set up camp, but he didn't want to stop. There was another campsite just 800 feet higher.

He'd wanted to push himself more, until he felt completely spent.

They had reached 23,300 feet.

"Boss! Boss!" He turned to see Akil pulling on the rope behind him, trying to catch up.

During training, Crocker often told his men: "Blood from any orifice." In other words: Push yourself to your limits, and every now and then go past them. Otherwise, how will you know your full potential?

For years, Crocker would regularly take twenty-mile midnight runs. Then wake up the next morning at 0430 hours and ride his bike another forty miles before going to work.

Sometimes after a long run, when he stepped off the trail to urinate, he'd piss a steady stream of red. The first time he saw blood coming out, he went to see the SEAL doctor, who explained that constant trauma to the urethra had caused the bleeding.

People called him an obsessed maniac.

Truth is, he admired maniacs. Maniacs were prepared to face the shit. Like his SEAL buddy Joe M., who on a mission to Iraq saw a car full of insurgents pull alongside the vehicle he was riding in and start firing AK-47s. Most people would have panicked, but Joe kept his cool. Realized he had to protect his driver if he wanted to get out of there alive.

Sitting in the backseat and wearing body armor, he positioned himself behind the driver's head to act as a shield while screaming at the guy in Arabic to hit the gas.

Over two hundred rounds were fired into that SUV. Two hundred! A good number slammed into Joe's body armor. Three slugs found their way below it and landed in his flesh. The bullets were removed, and Joe survived to continue chasing bad guys overseas.

Like Crocker often told his men: The more sweat and tears you put into training, the less blood you'll shed in time of war.

You never knew what you would be called upon to do.

That night, after they had set up camp on the mountain's massive shoulder, the weather changed and a storm blew in fast. First rain fell, then it turned to snow. Winds tore across K2, bringing a blizzard.

They huddled in their two-person nylon tents, wrapped in their parkas inside their sleeping bags. Every hour on the hour, Crocker, Davis, and Akil went out and shoveled the snow off the tents so they wouldn't get buried. Sleep was pretty much out of the question.

Edyta told Crocker that one of the German climbers was coughing up blood. Crocker suspected high-altitude pulmonary edema (HAPE), which could be fatal. He'd had it twice, once in the Andes and once in the Himalayas. As with all cases of altitude sickness, the best method of treatment was to descend. But there was nothing they could do now except wait out the storm.

As the wind pounded his tent, Crocker rolled over in

his sleeping bag, thinking about his mother, who had died recently at the age of seventy-five.

He'd watched her change from a thin young mother with shiny brown hair to a stooped, gray-haired grandmother. But the sweetness in her blue eyes never changed. He saw them looking up at him, pleading, as he held her frail hand.

"What, Mom?"

She was trying to say something, but couldn't speak because she was so weak from the cancer that had started in her lungs and spread throughout her body.

As Crocker held her, she mouthed the words: "Please don't leave me."

The next time he saw her, two days later, she was a gray corpse on an aluminum table in the local morgue.

All he could do was kiss her on the head, say "I love you." Then he crumpled to the ground and wept like a little boy.

He thought about her now as he sat in the tent next to Davis, who was trying to sleep beside him. His parents had been good, brave, loving people who had worked hard for their children. Tried to pass on everything they'd learned.

Where were they now?

A blast of wind ripped at the side of the nylon tent.

Interesting how nature reduced things to fundamentals. Life and death. Disease and destruction, then the smell of wildflowers and a gentle breeze.

The storm outside was violent now. If nature wanted to take him—to bury him and the others in snow, blow them off the mountain, and freeze them to death—it would.

Whispering a prayer to his mother and father, his

brother, sisters, and their kids, his daughter, his stepson, and his wife, Holly, he closed his eyes.

At noon the next day, the snow was still falling. Crocker estimated that another three feet had accumulated. And the winds had picked up to sixty knots, with gusts up to ninety.

The Germans in the lime green tent felt better, and they were all getting antsy, to either climb or turn back once the storm subsided. Edyta, in particular, wanted to push on. She pointed out that they had only another five thousand feet and approximately sixteen to eighteen hours of climbing before reaching the top. Crocker thought she might be suffering from summit fever.

"Not under these conditions," he responded. This was just a training climb for his men. He'd planned to take them another thousand feet at most.

"Then I'll go by myself!" she shouted.

"That would be suicidal," Crocker told her. He and Davis ventured out to take a look.

A few steps from the tent—wearing glacier glasses, fully baffled parkas, and windproof, water-resistant down pants—they were blinded as the wind kicked up a swirl of snow. Crocker tried looking behind him, but the blast from the west was so frigid and powerful that it started to freeze the little bit of exposed skin on his neck.

Using a trekking pole, he gestured to the blond-haired, blue-eyed SEAL as if to say, *You wait here.*

Davis waved him back. "Don't go!"

Taking a step in the fresh snow, Crocker's right leg sunk up to his thigh and his foot didn't touch bottom. Still, he ventured out a few yards and tried to dig some of their supplies out of the snow.

They had camped approximately six thousand feet above the base camp. To move in any direction was perilous, because the slopes were primed for an avalanche.

And conditions were likely to get a whole lot worse before they got better. Since the snow that had been falling was so cold, the crystals hadn't yet bonded. An avalanche that happened now would be soft, not the heavier, denser slabs that they could expect once the sun and wind compressed the crystals into giant chunks of snow.

Armed with his trekking pole and ice axe, Crocker tried to inch up a traverse to the next ridge to get a better look. But when he stepped on the clear, hard ice, he lost his footing and fell back.

He picked himself up and tried again, with the same result. No go.

Back in the Germans' tent, Edyta reported that base camp had received a message from Switzerland that there would be a small break before more bad weather moved in.

She shouted above the roar of the wind outside: "I'm leaving at dawn. Who's coming with me?"

Crocker thought: A chick with a pick, and stubborn as a mule.

Being a responsible team leader, he explained to Davis and Akil that it was better to play it safe and come back to climb another day than try to prevail against conditions that were out of their control.

Around midnight, the wind died down and the snow stopped.

Crocker left his third game of chess with Andreas—the shorter and healthier of the two Germans—put on his boots, hat, helmet, backpack, and mittens, and stepped out to breathe the fresh air.

The wind whispered and the full moon cast weird shadows on the snow.

Looking almost straight up at the snowcapped summit of K2, he felt like he had arrived in another world. Gods and spirits lived on the mountain.

Climbers had a saying: The climb is possible only if the mountain allows it.

Maybe these spirits don't want to be disturbed.

But the still beauty of the night drew him forward. He stepped carefully, boots crunching into the billowy snow until, when he looked back, the camp was only a dim shadow.

Enjoying the feeling of being alone with the mountain, he moved another fifty yards to his left to get a better view of the peak. Stopping and leaning on his pole, he sighed. The moonlight cast an eerie bluish, otherworldly glow.

I wish I had a camera.

His had apparently frozen the night before, even though he'd kept it wrapped in his parka.

Crocker had just pushed off with his right foot when the ground under him gave way and he started to fall.

What the—

Down. Down, picking up speed. Nothing to hold on to. No way to fucking stop.

It seemed that minutes passed before he landed with a thump, adrenaline coursing through his body, the air pushed out of his lungs until he passed out.

He awoke several minutes later, surrounded by a faint blue light. He thought he had died and been transported to another dimension. Then felt his heart pounding wildly.

Somehow, I'm still alive!

Biting cold under him, and pain emanating from his right thigh, hip, and arm. Crocker realized that he was lying on a tiny ice bridge somewhere in the middle of a curved crevasse. Alone and trapped.

It would have been much worse if the backpack hadn't cushioned his landing.

He reached under his jacket and checked for broken or loose bones. There seemed to be none. Just blood on the palm of his right hand from a superficial wound.

I'm fucking lucky.

He pulled his legs up under him and shouted, *"Help!"*

Then realized that his voice would barely reach the surface.

He was a good thirty to forty yards down. The camp was another two hundred yards away. He squatted, embarrassed that he'd made such a stupid mistake. And hoped that sooner or later, Davis, Akil, Edyta, or one of the Germans would notice that he was missing. If the wind didn't kick up again, they'd be able to follow his footsteps and they'd find him—if he didn't pass out from exposure first.

Even though he was wearing only a light down jacket, it didn't feel terribly cold yet. But that could change quickly.

Chasing away an impulse to panic, he looked for a way out.

The icy bridge he rested on was barely four feet wide, and slick. Carefully holding on to a crease in the wall, he climbed to his feet and, using the light on his helmet, surveyed the crevasse above.

It glittered back like an ice jewel, with dozens of

various-sized stalactites and columns sticking out at different angles.

As amazing as it looked, there appeared to be no chance of climbing out without crampons and an ice axe. The former were back in the tent, and he had lost the latter in the fall.

So he slid the backpack under him and curled up in a ball, calculating that he had five hours at most until the others awoke, hoping he could survive that long in the clothing he was wearing. At least he was protected from the wind.

Thinking: *How ironic that I abandoned my mother when she was dying, and now that I'm in danger it feels like she's with me.* Warm and loving. Nothing had mattered more to her than her husband and children.

Crocker bit his lip and willed himself to think of something else.

He tried to recall the names and faces of all the people he'd grown up with. Kids he'd played baseball with, boys he'd gone fishing with, first grade, second, third. The names of his teachers. Miss Moore. Mrs. Murray. Miss Hastings, who told him he'd never amount to anything.

He remembered them more vividly than he had in years. Incidents, facial features, jokes, shards of stories. Like the time he and his cousin Jake had buried a dead crow in his backyard. Marked the place carefully. When they dug up the grave two days later, the bird was gone.

Crocker felt the cold creeping into his body and fought off the urge to close his eyes and sleep.

Not now!

He remembered running with his biker friends. The

names of girlfriends. The first girl he kissed and the color of the sweater she was wearing: pink with white piping around the neck.

He was furiously going back through names. Making a list of his favorite people. His father, his mother, Holly, his daughter…

His favorite songs: "My Way" sung by Frank Sinatra and Sid Vicious, "Gimme Shelter" and "Sympathy for the Devil" by the Stones, "Sky Pilot" by the Animals, AC/DC's "Highway to Hell."

That's when he thought he heard a voice. "Tom!" It sounded like a woman's.

"Mom? Is that you?"

She had told him once that she believed in spirits and ghosts.

"Mom, I'm down here!"

No response. Maybe the wind was playing tricks on him. Maybe it had been his imagination.

Favorite movies: *Pulp Fiction, The Deer Hunter, Dances with Wolves, Apocalypse Now, Platoon. The Godfather* at the top of the list.

Minutes passed before he heard the voice again, faintly: "Tom. Tom. Where are you?"

"I'm down here! *Down here!*"

A column of cold wind found its way into the crevasse and spun in a circle, chasing itself. A chill rattled up his spine.

Crocker thought: *The worst thing that could happen is that I start to lose my mind.*

Extreme conditions could do that. He knew from experience. He had hallucinated several times during multiday nonstop treks. Like once, in the Iraqi desert after almost a week of sleep deprivation, he thought he saw strange objects flying overhead.

Crocker hugged himself into a tighter ball. His mom felt close.

Feelings of mortality started to creep into his head, along with a numbness that moved through his feet, up into his ankles.

He shivered three times in succession. His teeth started to rattle.

Fuck...

His muscles were frozen, and there was no room to move. Not that he wanted to risk slipping off the narrow ice bridge and falling deeper.

So he focused on the sun. And understood why ancient people had gotten on their knees to worship it each morning. Without the sun, there would be no trees, no birds, no life. Modern man paid homage by going on vacation and lying on the beach. He preferred a soft sand run or a swim. He'd done so all over the world: Panama, Vietnam, Florida, Maine, Virginia, the south of France.

Suddenly Crocker felt the slightest warmth, and smiled to himself. The power of suggestion.

He heard something stir. "Mom?"

Looking up, he saw a light at the top of the crevasse, then heard a familiar voice.

"Crocker! Are you down there?"

There definitely was a light.

"Akil!"

"Boss!"

"What the hell took you so long? I'm fucking freezing."

"I had better things to do."

No doubt. The testosterone-loaded SEAL and the East

European climber had been going at it practically nonstop since they'd met two and a half days ago.

"What are you doing down there, boss?"

"I was looking for a quiet place to take a shit."

As they continued talking, Akil lowered a rope. Crocker didn't take his eyes off it as it snaked down the icy blue wall.

When the yellow line reached him, he grabbed it.

Using a small cord he had in his pocket, he tied two emergency Prusik knots on the line and started to pull himself out.

The ice wall made foot placements almost impossible, but the farther he climbed, the better he got. Yard by yard. His heart pounding.

The pressure on his arms and shoulders was so intense that his muscles started to spasm as he reached the top.

"Another couple of yards!" Akil shouted, offering a gloved hand.

Crocker tightened his grip on the rope, his right foot clinging to a little ridge in the ice. He took a moment to reach down deep, through all his experience and training, to the ball of fire that burned inside him.

With a last burst of energy, he got to the top and held on. Akil's sure hands helped him out.

"Thanks!"

"You must have antifreeze in your blood."

"I won't forget this, buddy."

Then, acknowledging his mother, Crocker looked up to the stars spinning in the neon blue sky and passed out.

CHAPTER EIGHT

Adapt or perish, now as ever, is nature's inexorable imperative.

—H. G. Wells

CROCKER DREAMT he was a boy looking at a birthday cake, waiting for his opportunity to blow out the candles. The electric lights were off. Familiar voices were singing in a range of octaves. Most beautifully, one slightly off-key. He turned to look for the face it belonged to. Saw a cascade of beautiful strawberry blond hair, then awoke.

Who does that hair belong to? Not my sister.

His tent was suffused with a warm reddish light. He lay zipped into a sleeping bag, a woolen hat pulled over his head. When he sat up, his right side barked, from his shoulder to his knee.

Which made him remember the ice crevasse of the night before. The eerie blue light.

No more wandering out at night alone.

Pulling on his boots, he returned to the warm image of the cascade of strawberry blond hair and wondered where he'd seen it before. Didn't it belong to the missing Norwegian girl Mikael Klausen had shown him on his laptop, back at the camp in Urdukas?

No, hers was lighter.

Could be he had her confused with another fresh-faced Scandinavian girl. He'd seen hundreds in his travels to Denmark, Norway, and Sweden. Admired their beauty, especially their delicate, perfect skin and smooth features. Like pale pink roses, he thought. Magnificent at the moment of bloom.

"Beauty is unbearable," Camus wrote, "...offering us for a minute the glimpse of an eternity that we should like to stretch out over the whole of time."

Men wanted to possess things, for the power they thought it gave them. But there were boundaries of right and wrong that had to be maintained.

Beautiful young women disappeared all the time. He'd heard stories. Like the FBI friend of his who had helped rescue an American girl of South Korean descent named Suzie. The sixteen-year-old was snatched right in front of her house in Washington DC by some slick dude in a Jaguar.

After being beaten, gang-raped, and locked in a small room for three weeks, Suzie was forced to be an escort to wealthy businessmen and lobbyists in her hometown. Five hours with her went for $15,000. Often she was sold three times a day to different clients.

After months of serving as a sexual plaything, she was informed that she was being sold to a Japanese businessman in Tokyo for $2.2 million. On the way to the airport, she and her female captor stopped at a diner to get something to eat. Realizing this was her last chance, Suzie wrote, "Help! Call Mom!" and her mother's cell-phone number on a napkin while her captor wasn't looking. Then she dropped it on the floor.

A waitress picked up the napkin and called the number. Suzie was rescued—what was left of her.

The general public didn't understand the scope of the problem. Trafficking in young women didn't just happen in Third World countries. It took place in Japan, France, Spain, Sweden, Norway, Germany, even the United States.

They were kidnapped while shopping at upscale malls, traveling with their parents, walking down the street to school. The kids who managed to escape had to overcome enormous physical and psychological problems. Those who didn't get away were used up, then murdered.

It pissed Crocker off.

He thought of his own teenage daughter shopping, walking home from school, going to the movies—unaware of how vulnerable she was to predators.

Sheep and wolves.

Animals who kidnapped, then abused and sold young women, had to be stopped, thrown in jail to rot, or, better yet, made to die a slow and painful death.

Crocker carried his anger out into the brilliant sun, then into a nearby tent, where he found the Germans packing their gear.

"What's going on?" he asked.

"How are you feeling?" one of the German men asked back, as he reached for a kettle to pour the American a cup of green tea.

"Like I was tossed out of a speeding car and fell off a bridge onto a bed of nails, then run over by a steamroller."

The German laughed. "You're a lucky man."

As he sipped the tea and looked around the tent, Crocker willed himself to focus on the present. "Where's Akil?"

"Where do you think? Up into you-know-who's business."

The taller of the two Germans glanced at his watch. "He and Edyta left about two hours ago to set some ropes."

"They think they're climbing farther?"

"Ja."

"What about Davis?"

"He's outside somewhere, waiting for you."

He handed back the cup. "Thanks."

The taller of the two Germans announced, "The conditions are too perilous to climb farther, so we've decided to return to the Concordia. We're leaving in an hour."

"Oh."

"You're welcome to join us."

"I might take you up on that."

Mention of returning to the Concordia brought back memories of Holly and Jenny. He wondered how they were getting along without him and what new challenges lay ahead.

The two Americans stood shoulder to shoulder, looking up at the slope. What had once been swatches of ice and snow interrupted by rocky cliffs was now a soft, undulating sheet of white. The wind blew over it with a gentle hiss and slapped the sides of the tents behind them.

"Amazing, isn't it?" Davis asked.

"It's so pure and pristine, it's almost unreal," Crocker answered.

Again he thought of Malie, Jenny, and other young girls and boys.

It's our job to protect them...

A whistle in front of them announced a larger gust of wind that twisted the new snow into curlicues of spinning powder as it passed. They started to climb slowly. Postholing, following the trail in the powder created by Edyta and Akil.

The mountain turned quiet. Crocker stopped to check that the loops of the gaiters on his snowpants were connected to the laces of his boots. It was important to keep your feet and ankles dry because frostbite was a constant danger.

"This reminds me of a story," Davis said, the sun glinting off his orange-tinted goggles.

"What's that?"

"There was an Indian chief out west named Two Eagles who was being interviewed by a U.S. government official."

"Yeah."

"And the government official asked him: 'You've been observing the white man for ninety years. You've seen his technological advances, the progress he's made and the damage he's done. What do you make of it?'

"The chief stared at the official a long time. Then said: 'When white men find this land, Indians were running it. No taxes, no debt, plenty buffalo, plenty beaver, clean water, women did all the work, medicine man free. Indian man spend all day hunting and fishing, all night having sex.'

"Then the chief leaned back and smiled. He said: 'Only white man dumb enough to think he could improve a system like that.' "

Crocker laughed. "What made you think of that?"

"The beauty of this, I guess."

"You feeling guilty for being a white man?"

"No. But sometimes I get the feeling that we're not supposed to be here."

"My dad said: Only a fool forgets to live in awe of nature."

"He was right."

Crocker started to climb again.

Sometimes he felt that all the reading Davis did made him a little morose. Crocker wasn't a student of history to the extent that the young SEAL was, but he knew enough to understand that mankind had a tremendous capacity for destruction and a frustrating tendency to repeat the mistakes of the past.

Pausing, he turned to Davis and said, "We should be able to see them from the top of that ridge."

He pointed his trekking pole to a crest in the snow two hundred yards ahead. It tapered gently to the right, then ended abruptly in a phantasmagoria of deep blue sky painted with wisps of white.

"When's your wife expecting?"

"In about three weeks."

"Does she know what it's going to be?"

"No, but I'm hoping for a boy. Little girls are so delicate. They kind of scare me."

"It's exciting, either way," Crocker said.

Since the air was dramatically thinner, they had to stop to catch their breath every fourth or fifth step.

As they continued climbing, Crocker thought about how his concern for his daughter and his efforts to protect her had sometimes gone too far. Like the night last summer when he sat up past two waiting for her to return home. His little angel had promised to be back by ten, and Crocker was getting sicker with worry with every minute that passed. Unable to stay still anymore, he climbed into his car and started driving all over town looking for her.

After an hour of increasing anxiety and frustration, he spotted an old Ford Mustang weaving down a local road. He saw the driver, a teenage boy, leaning across the seat with Jenny beside him.

Crocker turned off his headlights and tailed the Mustang into his neighborhood. When the old Mustang stopped in front of his own house, Crocker made a hard right and came within inches of crashing into the driver's side of the car. Then he jumped out and pulled the boy from his car.

The kid was obviously drunk or on drugs, screaming, "You crazy old man! Get your hands off me before I call the police!"

Crocker held him up by the collar, slapped the hat off his head, and said, "If you say another word, I'll kill you right here!"

The kid shut his mouth.

"You *dare* take my fifteen-year-old daughter out in your car when you're drunk off your ass. Give me one reason I shouldn't beat the living shit out of you."

Jenny, meanwhile, was crying, screaming, "Dad, you're overreacting! He didn't do anything. Leave him alone!"

Crocker shouted, "Get your butt into the house."

He threw the little punk to the asphalt, searched him, and had to fight the impulse to wring his neck. Irresponsible little shit. The kid never asked Crocker's daughter out again.

Now the SEAL team leader stopped to catch his breath. *God, I love my daughter.*

Beside him, Davis readjusted his gaiters.

Crocker remembered holding baby Jenny on his right forearm. She had translucent skin like her mother's, and light hair. A sweet, gentle sparkle in her eyes.

He turned to Davis and said, "Yeah, daughters are wonderful, but they're challenging."

"I bet."

Long streams of white condensation issued from their mouths when they reached the crest. The snow-covered ground in front of them dipped slightly, then rose in a sharp U to the last peak, which shot up at a seventy-degree angle.

Following the footsteps left by Edyta and Akil, he spotted them approximately two hundred feet ahead, with Edyta leading the way, breaking trail in the fresh snow.

"Where's she taking him?" Davis asked.

Crocker pointed at a crease in the mountain. "She's going to start her final ascent there."

"What about Akil?"

"I assume she's got him carrying supplies that she'll leave at the bottom. Unless he's so damned pussy-whipped that he's following her up to the summit."

"Knowing Akil, it's hard to tell."

The final ascent looked almost impossible, especially since the entire peak was covered with several feet of fresh snow. Crocker admired Edyta's courage. But it struck him as extremely foolish to attempt the summit in these conditions.

In the whiteness before him, he saw Edyta turn back and measure how far Akil lagged behind. He felt he could read her thoughts—having to do with men, strength, and her unending appetite for sex. Maybe men related to her easily because she thought like they did.

Spotting Crocker on the ridge, Edyta waved with a yellow mitten that matched her parka.

"Stubborn old bird," he muttered under his breath.

She seemed to be shouting something. Her eyes widened and brilliant sunlight glinted off her teeth. Then suddenly her expression darkened, and she turned back to face the mountain.

Crocker stood, wondering what was going through her head, when he heard a deep rumble and immediately understood.

"Avalanche!" he shouted at Davis.

"Where?"

Crocker pointed ahead.

The ground beneath them started to tremble, then shake, and the entire peak in front of them shifted, as though the hard granite mountain had decided to shrug off its white coat.

"Jesus!" Davis exclaimed.

Quickly the roar grew louder. A massive, incalculable amount of snow slid off the mountain, picking up speed and funneling into the crease that Edyta had been climbing to. She and Akil were standing a mere hundred feet away from it, directly in its path.

"They're gonna get hit!"

As Crocker watched, both climbers turned their backs to the mountain and assumed a seated position, with their heads bent forward and arms over their faces.

A horrible chill came over him as he saw the enormous wave of snow bear down and overwhelm them. His mind worked fast, calculating the route the avalanche was going to take and his and Davis's safety. Its momentum and the configuration of the mountain would push the snow into the U, then off the mountain to their right.

He grabbed Davis by the shoulder. "This way!" he said, pulling him sharply left. Around them rose a huge billow of white. A thunderous crunching, rushing sound. The snow and ice shifted under them.

"Davis, hold on to me!"

There was nothing they could do but try to keep from being swept off their feet—and pray. Somehow, through the enormous whiteness, he saw a red object tumble past.

"It's Akil!"

"Where?"

His mouth and nostrils filled with fine powder, making it hard to breathe. The two big men shook.

As quickly as the massive surge had started, it settled, and the roar echoed farther down the mountain and faded. Then the eerie silence returned, and the mountain stood still. Defiant. Clouds of fine powder rose and disappeared.

Davis grabbed Crocker's shoulder. "Jesus, boss. Do you see them?"

"I'm not sure. Hold on."

"Incredible. Fucking incredible!"

Crocker used the rope in his pack to tie the two of them together. He warned, "Walk carefully. The snow hasn't settled. Step into an air pocket and you'll disappear."

"Okay. But you said you saw him."

"I did for an instant. Hold on."

"Where?"

Crocker calculated the approximate spot where Akil had landed, got down on his knees, and used his ice axe and hands to start digging through the mélange of snow and ice. Davis did the same, approximately two feet away.

"They should have been wearing their avalanche beacons!" Davis shouted.

Nothing in that spot.

Crocker said: "Let's try farther right."

Every second that passed felt like a loss. They dug furiously, burrowing into the snow, then moving forward.

Davis found a bone—a human femur. An awful reminder that another climber had died in that location sometime earlier, maybe from the same cause.

Anger, fear, and determination were clashing with one another.

Dammit, Edyta. An experienced climber like you should have known better.

His mind was performing jumping jacks.

Do we keep looking here, or move closer to the edge? Should we shift farther left or more to the right? What are the chances they survived?

Both men were breathing hard. The muscles in Crocker's arms and shoulders burned. His knees and calves were rigid from the cold.

Somewhere in front of them they heard a scratching sound. Davis pointed, "Boss! Jesus, boss. Two o'clock!"

Ten feet closer to the edge of the mountain, they saw the heel of a boot poking through the snow. Pouncing on the spot, they dug frantically. One leg, to his butt, to another leg, then his torso. They found Akil sitting upside down under five feet of snow.

Crocker figured he'd been there two or three minutes at the most as he dug around Akil's head and found a pulse on his icy cold neck. "He's barely breathing and is probably hypothermic."

Working together, they grabbed him around the legs and torso and carefully slid him free. They had him seated on the ground, and were brushing snow off his beard and head when the big Egyptian American opened his eyes.

"What the fuck..."

"Easy, Akil."

"Where the hell am I?" Blinking, grabbing his right shoulder.

Davis gave him a drink of Jack Daniel's from a small metal flask.

Crocker warned, "Just a sip." He knew that any attempt to warm a victim of even moderate hypothermia too quickly could result in metabolic acidosis, which could cause a stroke or heart failure. "We need to get him off the ground and warm him up slowly."

They sat him on Davis's backpack, then wrapped Akil in a lightweight Tyvek blanket, making sure his head was covered. Within minutes his breathing and color returned to normal.

Akil looked up into the faces of his two colleagues and asked, "What'd you do with Edyta?"

"We haven't found her yet."

"What?" Akil tried to pull himself up. He got as far as his knees and fell back.

"You stay with Davis," Crocker instructed. "I'll look for her."

"Hurry up!"

The team leader worked his way to the edge, zigzagging every three or four feet to dig, but found no sign of her. He thought of circling back, but since he was within six feet of the drop-off he decided to get on his belly, slide forward, and steal a look.

Akil shouted behind him. "Boss. Boss! What the hell are you doing?"

The distance down was even worse than Crocker had thought. A two-hundred-foot drop-off at least. The huge mass of snow had hit the gray granite face at an angle and dispersed. Most of it had ended up hundreds of yards lower, on another slope.

He was thinking *No living thing could survive that* when on his left periphery he noticed a bright yellow spot about 250 feet down. His heart sank.

Removing a small pair of binoculars from his pack, he focused on the yellow mitten with the palm facing upward.

Edyta!

He watched and waited for her hand to move. It didn't.

Together the two men helped Akil over the ridge. He was still groggy and having trouble putting weight on his right ankle. They stopped to rest.

"You saw her? You one hundred percent sure about that?" Akil asked for the third time.

"It was her, yes. I ID'd her by her mitten. Yellow. Her hand wasn't moving."

"How can we be sure she's not alive?"

"I can't be absolutely positive. But there's no way anyone could survive that fall."

"Edyta's tougher than shit."

"I know that."

The SEAL team leader tried to be patient. He understood his colleague's distress. "It's at least two hundred feet onto a solid granite face. Like I said before, I watched and waited, but her hand wasn't moving."

"That's all you saw? Her hand?"

"Her gloved hand, part of her wrist."

Hurt and anger burned in Akil's dark eyes. "I think we should go back and try throwing her a line."

Crocker had considered that option and come to the conclusion that it was impossible and too dangerous to attempt. He said, "The ledge won't hold our weight for one thing. Number two, it's impossible to descend from there. Three, if we throw down a line, we're gonna need something like four hundred feet of it, which we don't have. And finally, if by some miracle she's alive and able to grab it, there's no way we'll be able to pull her up without the whole ridge giving way."

"I'm going to try!"

"No you're not."

Akil tried to push past.

Crocker grabbed the front of his parka. "Look, the only way to reach her is from below. That would mean climbing down way past last night's camp and making an ascent from there. We're talking two days at least."

"Two days? Bullshit."

Crocker understood Akil's desire to reach her. He said, "When we get to camp, we'll radio for a rescue party. It's the best, fastest option by far."

"Maybe we do have enough line if we tie everything together. We can try that at least!"

"How is she going to grab onto it if her hand isn't moving?"

Akil stared hard into his eyes. "You don't give a shit about her, do you?"

"I like her a lot, Akil. Edyta's a brave, amazing woman. A good friend. But I'm telling you, I watched for ten minutes at least, and she wasn't moving. I'm sorry."

"Maybe she's unconscious but alive."

"It still won't work."

"If she were your wife, you'd be climbing down there."

"Edyta knew the risk she was taking."

"So what?"

"She died on the mountain she loved."

"She was with you, Akil," Davis added. "She was happy."

"Maybe she belongs here, Akil," Crocker offered.

Akil looked up at the peak and sighed. "Fuck."

CHAPTER NINE

The basic difference between an ordinary man and a warrior is that a warrior takes everything as a challenge, while an ordinary man takes everything either as a blessing or as a curse.

—Carlos Castaneda

CROCKER RUBBED his tired eyes and looked again. There it sat, still against the white-gray landscape, its top propeller slowly spinning in the wind. A big green insect with "Pakistan Air Force" stenciled on the side.

"Boss. Look!"

Davis's light blue eyes were weary and red. Little icicles hung from his mustache and eyebrows. The reddish blond beard on his face was covered with snow and ice.

"I see it, but is it real?" Crocker asked.

Somehow they'd managed to make it back to the Concordia, even though he, Davis, and Akil were exhausted and both Germans had bonked—depleted their stores of glycogen in the liver—several times during the descent.

"Looks real to me," Davis groaned.

"I hope so."

Crocker had weighed the dangers of stopping and getting hit by another incoming storm, and possibly being stuck for an additional three or four days without food or fuel. Instead, he had pushed himself and his men for almost thirty hours straight.

Akil had hallucinated, off and on, all the way down. They heard him talking to Edyta and laughing at her jokes. Rambling, sometimes incoherently, about favorite movies, interesting places they'd traveled to, pets. Fascinating how the human mind deals with loss.

Crocker had kept himself going by thinking about Holly's cooking, sexual companionship, and the smell of clean sheets. A piece of a poem by Pablo Neruda recycled in his head.

Body of my woman, I will persist in your grace.
My thirst, my unbounded desire, my uncertain road!

After he slept for a week, he wanted to lounge in front of the TV and watch something like *The Sopranos*—his feet up, cold bottle of beer by his side, a bowl of pretzels.

Maybe catch Vanna White in a tight dress turning letters on *Wheel of Fortune* the way she had for years. Always neat, clean; a smile on her face. Years ago he'd seen her nude in *Playboy*. Later, he heard that a chick had claimed she had an affair with her.

Like that mattered.

The danger now was that their bodies would completely shut down.

Fifty more yards.

The landscape seemed to shift and wobble with each

step, and the pack on Crocker's back felt like it was loaded with bricks. His shoulders, back, knees, thighs, and feet screamed.

Ahead of them, climbers stood among the variously colored and shaped tents scattered throughout base camp and applauded as they approached.

Or was it a dream?

A Pakistani man in an olive military parka stepped forward and offered his hand. "Chief Warrant Officer Tom Crocker?"

"I think so."

"Lieutenant Colonel Mushavi. I have orders to take you and your men to Islamabad immediately."

Crocker looked at him and his bristling black mustache like he was insane. "My men and I need some food and rest first."

"Jolly good, sir. I'll be waiting."

Whatever.

A Japanese climber helped him to a green tent. Seated on a thick sleeping bag, Crocker slowly and painfully removed his boots, thinking *I never want to wear climbing boots again.*

Then he looked down at his badly blistered feet and saw that the skin hadn't turned black, which meant he hadn't suffered frostbite.

Thank God.

He said, "I need to call my wife."

But before Crocker even saw a phone he was unconscious, dreaming that he was fighting his way through clouds of blinding, whirling snow.

Edyta, walking by his side, said, "We're on the road less traveled, Crocker."

"More like the road to nowhere, or something we don't understand."

"Yes." She laughed hard, revealing a broken front tooth. The wind seemed to be laughing, too.

When he awoke the next morning it took Crocker a few minutes to realize where he was. Light snow fell even though the sun was shining.

The light hurt his eyes.

"Are you ready to fly, sir?" It was the Pakistani lieutenant colonel, all polished and eager to go, standing in the entrance of the green tent, reminding him of Luke Skywalker. Like he was offering to fly him to another galaxy.

"Where are my men?"

"This way, sir."

Crocker was escorted to a larger, rectangular tent where, still groggy and weak, he joined Davis and Akil at a fold-up table to eat bowls of yogurt with honey and drink hot tea.

Then all three of them were in the air. The Pak lieutenant colonel informed him that Mancini's leg had healed.

"Who?" Crocker shouted over the din of the helicopter engine.

"Your man. Warrant Officer Michael Mancini. Waiting in Islamabad, sir," the mustached officer answered.

"My man?"

Crocker had forgotten about Mancini. It seemed like months ago that they had left him at a camp above the Baltoro Glacier.

"Oh, yeah. What about Ritchie?" he shouted above the engine.

"I'm not familiar with that gentleman, sir."

"Chief Petty Officer Richard Maguire. The fifth member of my team."

"I have no information regarding that individual."

Crocker looked at Akil and Davis seated on the bench along the opposite side of the Mi-17 and thought they both seemed gaunt and years older. Akil wore the expression of a kid who'd lost his dog.

"Cheer up, Akil!" Crocker shouted. He wanted to go over and tell him again that Edyta had lived a full life and understood the risks. But the helicopter was banking right, pushing him hard against the side of the fuselage, so he shut his eyes and slept.

Two hours later, the lieutenant colonel stood over him, smiling. "Sir? Mr. Crocker?"

Sun spilled in the side door and warmed his feet. The thick air wafting in from outside felt luxurious in his lungs.

"We've arrived at PAF Base Chaklala. I have instructions to take you to the U.S. coordinator's office. Your military officials will meet you there."

"Military officials?" Crocker was confused. Did that mean that his CO had flown in from Virginia?

"Military officials. Yes, sir."

A long hot shower and shave later, Crocker was starting to feel like himself. Wearing a borrowed pair of khakis and a blue U.S. Navy polo, he tried to keep pace with the U.S. Air Force major who was leading him down a dark hall. Nothing he saw helped him identify the place.

He was hoping to see Mancini and Ritchie, or one of the two. Instead he entered a conference room where the shades were half drawn and an air conditioner groaned in the window.

Two tall men stood at the opposite side of the rectangular glass table, both clutching water bottles, conferring. Crocker recognized the taller of the two as their CIA liaison Lou Donaldson. The second man wore a navy uniform festooned with epaulets showing three full gold bars and a star, which meant he held the rank of full commander (O-5).

But when the man turned, Crocker didn't recognize him.

"What took you so long?" Donaldson asked, setting his plastic bottle on the table and taking a seat. Rude as always.

"I was climbing a mountain. What do you want?"

"What do we want?" Donaldson asked back, raising a pale eyebrow to the man in navy uniform beside him. "When did you become friendly with the king of Norway?"

"I'm not friendly with the king of Norway," Crocker explained. "I met an associate of his in a camp on the way to the Concordia. He said you gave him my location."

"That's correct," Donaldson said, cutting him off. "Mikael Klausen. The king's special advisor. Who's the girl?"

"What girl?"

"Malie Tingvoll."

Crocker had forgotten her name. He'd been focused on returning to Holly and Jenny and his warm home in Virginia.

"Why is she important?" the commander asked aggressively.

"She's a Norwegian girl who disappeared. That's all I know."

"People disappear every day," Donaldson growled. "Regrettable, but not our business."

"I never said—"

"Look, Crocker—"

Crocker didn't like raising his voice in anger but made an exception this time. "Are you going to let me speak?"

"Go ahead. Explain yourself."

After his irritation had abated slightly, Crocker said, "Mikael Klausen told me that the Norwegians have experienced a number of cases like hers, of young people disappearing without a trace."

"Last I heard, we don't operate a people-finding service."

"I expressed my sympathy, and told him the only way I could help is if I got authorization."

Donaldson slapped the table. "Well I'm afraid the king of Norway is going to have to wait."

"Fine with me."

Donaldson reached into his briefcase and removed a manila file. "Remember the laptops that were recovered from Zaman's safe house? Well, we might have found something."

"What?"

"A lead, Crocker. A reference in a coded e-mail to a known terrorist who calls himself Rafiq."

"Who's he?" Crocker asked, relieved that the raid in Karachi had yielded some actionable intel.

"Headquarters believes that his real name is Rifa'a Suyuti. A Saudi national. Midtwenties. Slight, approximately six foot one. Dark eyes, darkish skin, dark hair."

"What's his relationship to Zaman?"

"Unclear. But the NSA traced the e-mail to a motorcycle club in Marseille. The message seemed to refer to the delivery of certain products. It seems to indicate that this guy Rafiq has been procuring materials for Zaman."

"Bomb-making materials, I bet."

"Maybe. We know that Zaman has been looking for ways to inflict major damage. No doubt the raid in Karachi pissed him off. If you kick a hornet's nest, you can expect to get stung."

"What do you want from me?" Crocker asked.

Donaldson handed him the folder. "Look this over quickly and commit it to memory. Then you're headed for the airport."

"How come?"

"You and the French-and-Arabic-speaker on your team have been authorized to fly to Marseille. There's a reservation for you at the Hotel Select by the port. One of my operatives will meet you there."

Crocker eyeballed the contents of the folder, which featured photos of a tall, good-looking man with shock of thick, wavy hair.

"I've wired ten thousand euros to an account at the Banque de France to cover your expenses. Keep all receipts."

Crocker said, "I assume all this has been cleared with my CO."

The commander answered, "Yes."

As Crocker pushed the folder back to Donaldson, he asked, "What about Zaman?"

Donaldson frowned. "You let him get away, remember?"

"I want to find him."

The commander with the buzz cut sounded as though he was reading directly from an intelligence report. "The

Pakistanis have tracked him into the mountains along the Afghan border."

Crocker asked, "Where'd that come from, the ISI?" Meaning Pakistan's Inter-Services Intelligence.

The commander didn't answer. Instead, he said, "NSA has been picking up a lot of chatter about an attack against a major target in the area. Possibly on a U.S. facility. Some people think the two might be related."

Crocker was trying to figure out what two things he was talking about when Donaldson, sneering, got to his feet. "Don't worry yourself, Crocker. We've got other assets working on Zaman. You need to get moving."

"All right."

"Please, no collateral casualties this time. Try to locate this Rifa'a Suyuti character and report back."

"Yes, sir."

CHAPTER TEN

You can go a long way with a smile. You can go a lot farther with a smile and a gun.

—Al Capone

CROCKER ARRIVED in Marseille early the next morning feeling as though a load of bricks had landed on him. The tight airplane seat combined with the residual effects of the climb had caused lactic acid to build up in his muscles. He knew he needed to move, rehydrate, and rest.

The last one would have to wait.

Crocker deplaned from the Air France Airbus surrounded by businesspeople and tourists. He wanted to go for a run or speak to his wife, but knew he couldn't do either because he was on a short-fused mission and had to move quickly.

Beyond the baggage turnstile he found Akil at a news kiosk leafing through a magazine. He looked fit and rested.

"What took you so long?" he said when he saw Crocker.

"They sat me in the last row. Don't tell me you slept."

"Like a baby."

"Who the fuck is he?" the team leader asked, pointing to the bare-chested man on the cover.

"Samir Nasri."

"Who?"

"One of the top young footballers in the world. Born here in a poor suburb of the city. His parents were Algerian immigrants. Plays with a fast, attacking style. Great footwork. Considered the next Zidane. Currently with the British club Arsenal."

"Never heard of him."

"You need to broaden yourself, boss."

"You need to stop looking at pictures of half-naked men. Let's go."

Crocker was glad to see that Akil had recovered so quickly. It made him even happier to watch him flirting with the lashy-eyed girl at the desk who checked them into the three-star hotel they were staying in near the old port, Hotel Port Select.

The room was clean and tight. Two double beds with patterned white coverlets, a mirror over a set of drawers, a little desk, and a small TV.

It seemed like it was built to accommodate people smaller than the two large SEALs.

Ten minutes after they arrived, as Crocker was studying a street map, the phone rang.

The girl at the front desk said, "Your car has arrived."

"Thanks."

Crocker left Akil in the bathroom and returned to the lobby. A tall, attractive young North African woman stood waiting. Jet black eyes, hair, and eyebrows. High cheekbones. She looked like she was ready to break in half anyone who bothered her.

"Are you the one who brought the car?" Crocker asked.

"Yes, I am," she answered with a British accent. "Follow me."

He trailed her out onto the narrow cobblestone street. Parked along the curb was a little green Renault that looked about the size of a bathtub.

"You couldn't find anything bigger?" Crocker asked.

She handed him a set of keys. "My number is in the glove compartment, if you need me."

His eyes followed the back of her tight black pants until they disappeared around a corner, then he crossed the street and entered an Internet café. Ads in the windows advertised cheap long-distance rates to Algeria, Morocco, and the Comoro Islands.

With the smells of the port wafting in the front door, Crocker logged into his e-mail server. As he waited for his password to clear, he noticed that the patron before him had visited www.aljazeera.com. Other destinations included a variety of porno sites.

His e-mails appeared. Mancini, Ritchie, and Davis were already growing antsy in Islamabad, wondering if they could return home since Crocker didn't seem to need them.

"Wait another couple of days. I might require your services," the team leader wrote back.

Entering the address "Club Rosa–Marseille" and pressing Search, Crocker entered an amateurish website that featured videos of local bands like Carpe Diem, 13 Departement, PSYA4 De La Rime, IAM, Bouga, Fonky Family, and the Mystik Motorcycles, news about upcoming motocross racing events and meetings, and ads from people selling motorcycles.

* * *

Crocker and Akil ate lunch—fresh seafood couscous—at a restaurant across from the docks. Then, with Akil consulting the map and giving directions, Crocker drove the tiny Renault through the cramped Noailles quarter lined with Arabic and Indo-Chinese shops, then north into a spiral of low-income French HLM housing. Sandstone-colored high-rises with Spanish tile roofs swallowed them up. All seemed to have laundry flapping from clotheslines on their balconies.

The monochromatic building scheme was interrupted by colorful signs in Arabic. They passed a number of stores selling fake Nikes and Diesel jeans, and makeshift cafés filled with dark-skinned men with faces lined from the sun. They wore button-down shirts with short sleeves and pressed dress slacks.

The young people, in comparison, were dressed like urban American teenagers. Muscle shirts, baggy tees, baseball caps. Some of the young women were veiled; others wore skimpy tank tops and low-rise jeans.

Crocker remembered hearing that Marseille was the most ethnically diverse city in France. According to the Greek historian Herodotus, Phoenicians had taken refuge in the city (then known as Massilia) when the Persians destroyed Phocaea in the sixth century BC. Then as now the city was a haven for immigrants—back then Greeks, Romans, Genoans, Spaniards, and Venetians, in more recent times German and Polish Jews, then Vietnamese and Cambodians, followed by a huge influx of North Africans, predominantly Algerians, Moroccans, and Tunisians.

He'd also heard that 20 percent of the population lived

below the poverty line and something like 40 percent of young people between eighteen and twenty-five were unemployed. Different cultures grew up with different values. But all values frayed in the absence of hope.

Akil asked Crocker to stop near a group of Arabic-looking boys stripped to their waists who were working on an old Fiat sedan.

"How come? You lost?"

"We're looking for the Club Rosa," Akil said to the boys in French. "Can you tell us where it is?"

A skinny kid wearing a Yankees cap pointed them down a narrow alley. "Down there. Turn right."

The Club Rosa was housed in the garage of one of the sandstone-colored high-rises. Posters of Tupac Shakur, Al Pacino in *Scarface*, and motocross world champion Yves Demaria hung in the window.

Crocker knocked and entered. Two young surly-looking guys smoking cigarettes sat at a table working on a hard drive of an old Dell computer as a replay of a Marseille-Lyon football match played on the TV in the corner. A foosball table stood on the other side of the small, linoleum-floored room. Behind it hummed an old refrigerator. Posters of motorcycles and models in bikinis decorated the stained beige walls.

Crocker intuited the rest. Young men gathered here to blow off steam and discuss their common interests in girls, football, motorcycles. They drank beer and Red Bull, bragged about their exploits, joked around with each other, tested their ambitions.

The younger of the two kids, maybe seventeen, was black, with a shaved head and thick black eyebrows. The older one looked Arabic and wore a goatee.

The darker-skinned kid looked up and said, "If you're with the police and you're asking about the cars that were broken into last night, we don't know anything. We left the club right after dark."

"We're not with the police," Akil replied in Arabic. "My friend here used to be a professional motocross rider."

"What's his name?"

"Crocker."

The boys looked at each other and shook their heads. "Never heard of him."

In his youth Crocker had spent endless hours on the motocross track, broken many bones, and won a decent number of pro-am races. He'd also developed the reputation of a daredevil who never backed down.

"He's retired now but is looking to buy a bike and heard that someone here was selling a used Triumph Legend," Akil said.

"A Triumph Legend?"

"My brother used to ride one," Crocker said, in his badly accented French. "I'd like to check it out, take it for a ride. I'll pay cash."

"How much?"

Akil stepped closer to them. "He's got to see the bike first."

The black boy shrugged at the goateed kid, who shrugged back. Neither of them seemed to know what the big Egyptian American was talking about.

"Who told you about the bike?"

"Rafiq. He said it's a great ride. Three-cylinder 885cc twelve-valve engine. Around 30,000 miles on it. Needs some work."

"Rafiq?"

"Yeah, Rifa'a Suyuti. We call him Rafiq."

"You mean the guy who lives out on the road to Toulon?" the goateed kid asked.

"Yeah. Tall. Wavy hair. Big smile."

"Leave me a number. We'll call you back."

"When?"

"That depends."

Akil scribbled down his cell-phone number and told the boys that his Canadian friend had cash and wanted the bike soon for a trip into Spain.

"We'll call you," the black kid said to their backs.

Outside, Crocker decided to visit the local prefecture of police, where the two men were shuttled from one official to the next, only to learn after an hour that the Marseille office had no record of a Rifa'a Suyuti living in their jurisdiction.

The two Americans were near the port, eating dinner and watching the sky turn shades of mustard and red, when Akil got a call from a man named Yasir Simon, who said he was the owner of the Triumph Legend. He offered to meet them at the club at nine.

That gave them a little more than an hour and a half.

Crocker said, "Tell him we might be a few minutes late." His mind was already pushing ahead, anticipating contingencies and what they might need in terms of protection.

Akil said, "My instincts tell me we should expect trouble."

"I think they're right."

Crocker used Akil's cell phone to call the number that had been left in the glove compartment. "I'm going to need a bike rack for the car," he said in English.

"Where are you located?" the female voice with a British accent asked on the other end.

"I'm in town near the old harbor."

"How many bicycles are you planning to carry?"

"Two."

"We'll have someone meet you on the corner of Rue Lafayette and Rue Marcel Sembat, near the Gare St. Charles, in half an hour."

"Thank you."

Right on time, a dark blue Acura SUV pulled up to the curb.

Crocker walked up to the driver's-side window, where the attractive North African woman sat behind the wheel.

"We meet again," he said.

Her black eyes reflected the yellow light from the streetlamp. "Yes. The equipment you requested is in the boot."

All business.

He transferred two black gym bags to the back of the Renault, which was parked half a block away. Then zipped them open to find two M11 pistols and two MP5 submachine guns with magazines and extra ammo. Also tear-gas canisters, flash bangs, concussion and smoke grenades.

"Nice rack," Akil said from the passenger seat.

"We're good to go."

Crocker navigated the Renault through the loops of narrow hilly streets and arrived at Club Rosa ten minutes past the hour.

Yasir Simon hadn't arrived yet, but a half-dozen other young men were gathered in the club drinking beer and discussing something they'd just heard on Al-Manar TV, the Hezbollah propaganda station. Crocker recognized the Arabic words for "Jews" and "Zionists." Sparks of danger electrified the air.

"Where's the bike?" Crocker asked.

"They said he's coming," Akil whispered back.

Crocker bought two Red Bulls from the kid behind the counter, then heard a terrific roar approaching in the alley. He and Akil went out to look. Three guys on bikes. One a Triumph Legend. Green with some chrome, nice-sounding pipes. Decent leather.

Back in Crocker's youth, a green bike was considered bad luck, especially among Harley riders.

The guy selling it—Yasir Simon—had a silver ring through his nostril and a tattoo of a cobra on his forearm.

As Crocker drank the Red Bull, he went over the bike carefully, checking for oil leaks around the engine gaskets, transmission leaks, tires, paint, chrome. Then he said, "I'd like to take it for a ride."

"How much?" Akil asked.

"Two thousand euros."

Crocker shook his head. "I'll give you thirteen hundred. Cash."

"You're American?"

"Canadian. But I want to ride it first."

"Why not? Follow me."

Crocker sensed something was up when all three of them came along, Yasir behind a tall, sinewy guy on a Kawasaki Ninja and the third hard-looking dude alone on an older BMW. All three looked like they'd been spending a lot of time in the gym.

They led him through dark narrow streets to a two-lane highway that dipped and curled along the coast.

That's when Crocker pulled back the throttle that opened up the big engine. He tore into the mottled light, leaving the other bikes behind him, surprised that the guy on the Ninja didn't try to keep up.

The raw wind from the Mediterranean slapped his face. Scents of lavender and rosemary mixed with diesel fumes and the smell of the sea. He took the turns hard and wove around trucks and cars east toward Toulon, watching the landscape zip past, feeling like he owned the road.

Reaching the turnoff to Cassis, Crocker pulled over and stopped. The other two bikes caught up, and he could tell from the expressions of the three men that they were pissed off.

"Great bike!" he exclaimed in French, feeling like a teenager again.

Yasir, the silver ring glinting in his nostril, looked surprised. "You're a crazy driver. You really serious to buy it?"

"Fuck yeah. Tonight. You sign over the registration, I'll give you the cash."

"Très bien."

As the seller translated the news into Arabic for his two companions, Crocker sized them up further. They were rough—all in their late teens, early twenties. Deeply suspicious of him and Akil. They'd come expecting trouble.

He figured he could take all three of them if he had to, as long as they weren't armed.

Crocker said, "I want to show the bike to Rafiq first. You guys lead the way."

"What?"

"He lives nearby, doesn't he? So let's go see him."

"No!"

Yasir sneered, "Forget about Rafiq. He has nothing to do with this."

"He's the one who told me about the bike."

He didn't budge. "No. No, man. We're going back to the club." Then he walked away and pulled out his cell phone.

Crocker's ploy hadn't worked, so he pointed the bike west and cranked up the throttle. The exhilaration of the ride diminished as he tried to figure out what to do next. The person he wanted was Rafiq. These punks obviously knew who he was. Maybe if he could find a way to separate Yasir from the others and get him away from the club...

As he played out several scenarios in his head, the three bikes reentered Marseille and started winding up the hills past some old fortifications.

Crocker saw the light green Renault he and Akil had come in parked on the street before the alley—the same place they'd left it forty minutes earlier. But Akil wasn't in the car or standing nearby. Nor was he among the dozen young men who stood in the alley outside the Club Rosa.

"Where's my friend?" he asked the first kid he saw—a big guy with barbed wire tattooed across his biceps.

"I don't know what you're talking about."

"A big Egyptian. Six feet two. Wearing a black T-shirt and chinos."

"Haven't seen him."

Bullshit.

Crocker recognized the black kid with the shaved head from their first visit. "Where's Akil?" he asked him.

"Who?"

"The guy I came with. My friend."

"Don't know."

Then Yasir and his two buddies were in his face, demanding that he make good on the deal.

"Thirteen hundred euros. You show me the money first."

"I'm not showing anybody anything until I find my friend."

He sensed danger pressing in on all sides, then, glancing at his feet, saw a trail of blood on the pavement.

Akil!

A massive jolt of adrenaline slammed into his system. Pivoting on his right foot, he started to trace the blood out of the alley.

Two punks in black blocked his path, hatred in their eyes.

"Get out of my fucking way!"

He picked up one of them and was about to throw him against the wall when he felt the point of a knife against his back.

"Arrêtez!" (Stop.)

He did.

"Where's my friend? I wanna see him."

Guys on each side grabbed his arms. "We'll take you to him."

He pushed them off roughly.

Yasir said, "There's no reason to get excited."

"I'm cool. I just want to see my friend."

"Come with me. I'll take you to him."

People were craning their necks out of the apartment windows, watching what was going on below. Itching for a fight; more blood.

Crocker was trapped in the alley and on their turf. He

tried to remain calm even though his blood was pounding.

"I want to see my friend first. Then I'll pay you for the bike."

Someone shoved him from behind. "Shut up, old man! Get in the car!"

He stumbled forward and somehow managed not to fall. More punks seemed to have appeared out of nowhere—like hyenas who smelled blood.

"Get in the car! Fucking liar!"

What car?

They pulled him roughly around the corner, where he saw a BMW with blacked-out windows parked on the side of an adjoining alley.

For a split second he considered running. But two big guys dressed in black emerged from the front seat. The punk on the driver's side waved a silver automatic through the sulfuric light.

"Get in!"

The back door popped open.

With a mass of angry punks behind him and armed thugs in front, Crocker had no choice.

He was bending down to look inside the back of the car when someone pushed him so he fell forward and landed on the seat. The barrel of a Glock was literally two inches from his face.

Inside was another motherfucker armed with a handgun.

Before he could say anything, the door slammed and the car lurched forward, tires squealing. That's when he saw eyes looking up at him from the floor near the third thug's feet.

Akil.

CHAPTER ELEVEN

Confront them with annihilation, and they will then survive; plunge them into a deadly situation, and they will then live. When people fall into danger, they are then able to strive for victory.

—Sun Tzu

THE SECONDS pounded in Crocker's head as the coast road flew past, the sky thick, pitch black. Two guys with Soviet-made Makarov pistols laughed at some private joke up front. Another armed thug leered at him in back. Akil was on the floor to the man's right with his mouth and hands taped.

Crocker's own wrists were duct-taped together in his lap.

This sucks.

Crocker figured they were going to Rafiq's place. There they would be interrogated and shot. Tortured, possibly.

He could almost smell the fear and desperation oozing from Akil. From Edyta's death on K2 to this, in less than a week.

He felt bad. Responsible.

He'd met Akil's parents and sisters. Knew the poor bastard's life history.

Born outside Cairo. Moved to the States with his family at age six. Back in Egypt all of them had lived in two rooms. In suburban Virginia, Akil got his own room with his own bed. Remembered jumping up and down on it like it was a trampoline.

No one in school understood him, since his family spoke Arabic at home. Within a few months, he learned English. Adapted. Made friends.

When it came time to graduate from high school, his parents had plans for him to go to college and work for a cousin who ran a small trucking company near their home. Akil joined the navy instead, went through BUD/S, and became a proud member of SEAL Team Six. When he returned home after earning his trident, his father insisted his son wear his dress uniform and go with him to visit all their friends and family in the community. Akil had become the final validation of the family's decision to immigrate to America.

Now this....

Crocker couldn't let the dream end here. He focused intently.

The car was new. Maybe even brand-new, judging from the scent. Black leather seats, dark wood paneling on the doors.

The men were dressed in black. French-Arabic or Middle Eastern. All in their twenties. Slick operators. Far more sophisticated than the punks he'd tussled with in the alley. They carried themselves like they had money.

He searched for the slightest opportunity. A tiny bit of leverage. Anything to get them out of this before they arrived at Rafiq's place, where more of them would be waiting and things could get ugly.

All he could think of was that maybe one of the doors was unlocked. But he wasn't sure. And with the oily-haired fucker beside him sneering and pointing the Glock at his face—with his finger on the trigger—he wasn't about to try.

They zipped by the turnoff to Cassis, the place where Crocker had pulled over on the Triumph Legend less than an hour earlier.

The moment was screaming at him. *Do something. Do something, goddammit!*

But what?

"Who the fuck are you?" the driver asked.

"My name is Crocker. I'm a Canadian."

"You work for your government?"

"No. I'm a climber."

"What do you mean, a climber?"

"I climb mountains and train people who want to learn to climb."

"Why do you want to see Rafiq?"

"I'm here as a tourist. I'm looking for a bike to tour through Europe. Figure I can really get to see the countries that way."

"You're a bad fucking liar."

The driver nodded in the mirror to the man seated beside Crocker, who reached into the American's pockets and located his wallet. Inside he found a thick wad of euros but no ID.

The two men spoke in Arabic, then the driver looked back at Crocker and said in English, "Now I know you're a liar."

Precious minutes passed. Above the smooth growl of the engine and the electronic dance music pumping over the stereo, Crocker heard a choking sound. Looking down and to his right, he saw two streams of yellowish puke shooting out of Akil's nostrils, a pained exclamation in his eyes.

"You'd better do something. My friend's going to choke!" he shouted in English.

The thug beside him smacked him with the back of his hand. "Shut up!"

Some of the vomit had splattered across the leg of the guy's black jeans. He seemed more concerned about his pants than the fate of Akil.

"Cochon!" Spitting at Crocker's teammate. Like choking on his puke wasn't bad enough.

Almost simultaneously the driver screamed in Arabic, "What's that horrible smell?"

Then things happened fast. The thug in the backseat kicked Akil in the stomach with his boot. And the driver went apoplectic, shouting, "My car! Motherfucker! Get that nigger out of here. Throw him in the trunk!"

He steered the car abruptly right and stopped on the shoulder in a cloud of dust.

It took both men—the thug in the passenger seat and the dude in back—to pull Akil roughly out, the driver all the time screaming instructions in Arabic. "Watch the leather seats! Clean it. Make sure you clean it all up! Get rid of that fucking smell before I kick your asses!"

Crocker noticed that the driver wasn't holding a weapon.

So he propelled himself over the seat, grabbed the Makarov pistol that was lying on the console with his hands still taped together at the wrists, and brought his arms up with all the violence he could muster into the driver's jaw.

One, two, three times, quickly. He felt the driver's head snap back and heard a groan.

Then turned immediately and fired two shots through the open front door into the back of the thug who had occupied the passenger seat.

The punk screamed something Crocker didn't understand and fell to the ground.

Simultaneously the guy who'd been sitting in back directed a salvo of bullets that tore into the rear of the front seat. He was firing wildly through the open rear door of the car.

Crocker countered, slithering out the open passenger-side door onto the ground and shooting upward into the guy's crotch. The thug squealed like a cat on fire, twisted and jumped, holding what was left of his balls, then crumpled along the rear wheel of the car, writhing in pain.

Rough justice.

High on adrenaline, Crocker pulled himself up into a crouch, then checked to see that the driver was still unconscious. The other two were dead.

He quickly crawled over to Akil, who lay on his side, and turned him over, pulling the tape from his mouth and feeling for a pulse along his neck. Using his teeth, Crocker ripped the tape from his own wrists, then quickly cleared Akil's mouth and throat with a finger sweep, pulling out a glob of yellow bile and mucus. His colleague coughed up more, started breathing freely, and slowly came to.

Thank God.

Crocker found a bottle of Evian in a pocket on the passenger's door and quickly washed Akil's mouth and face. The smell was awful.

"What happened?" the Egyptian American asked, his right eye swollen nearly shut. "Where the fuck are we?"

"Heaven. How do you like it?"

"Looks like a fucking nightmare."

"How do you feel?"

"My head is on fire. My face aches like shit."

"You're still complaining. That's good."

Akil looked around him, taking in the bullet holes in the car and the dead bodies on the ground, the groaning driver still in the car with blood dripping from his mouth. "You did all this yourself?"

"You pussied out on me, so I had no choice."

Crocker was on his feet, quickly taking in the situation. So far no other vehicles had stopped. The BMW conveniently blocked the view of the dead bodies from anyone passing on the road. It was parked in a dirt turnaround. Ten feet farther the land dropped down into dark brush. There were no lights nearby, only a long deserted slope to the rocky shore.

It would be easy enough to hide the bodies. But he had to deal with the driver first.

He found the roll of duct tape on the floor of the backseat, covered the driver's mouth, and taped together his ankles and hands. Then he slapped his face until he came to.

"Hey! Asshole! You remember me?"

Panic flashed in the man's dark eyes.

Crocker pointed the Makarov at him and called Akil.

"Tell this piece of shit he's going to take us to Rafiq.

Tell him otherwise, I'll shoot him in the stomach and let him bleed. Tell him it will be a slow and painful death."

Akil did, dramatically, in Arabic.

The driver started nodding right away.

Meanwhile, Crocker dragged the bodies into the brush so they were out of sight. Then he circled around to the driver's side, shoved the driver over so he was straddling the console, and slid behind the wheel. He made sure Akil, in the passenger seat, had a loaded pistol ready.

He stuck one of the other two he had recovered into the waistband of his pants, and stashed the third under the front seat.

"Pull the tape off this asshole's mouth. Tell him if he screams or says one fucking word that doesn't directly answer a question, you'll shoot him in the balls."

"Roger."

Crocker hit the gas. Soon they were eating up the asphalt.

The driver started hyperventilating.

"Shoot the motherfucker!"

"Boss, not so fast. Give him a chance to talk."

The driver pointed ahead and started speaking in Arabic.

"He says the house where Rafiq is staying is down a road before we reach Toulon."

"Where?"

A few miles later, the driver directed them north onto a dirt road that wove around a grove of olive trees in a gully between some hills.

"He says the house is maybe two hundred yards ahead. He begs us not to kill him. He has a wife and baby son."

"Tough shit."

"He wants to cooperate."

"Ask him how many men are with Rafiq."

Akil did, and came back with the reply, "He doesn't know."

"Tell him to start praying."

"Boss, he doesn't know."

"Bullshit."

Crocker eased the car to a stop under some trees. "Tape his mouth shut again, then tape him securely to the passenger seat."

"All right."

Crocker ran ahead to recon the area, looked around the bend, and returned.

"It's a one-story farmhouse with a barn-type structure in back. There's a couple of lights on in the house. A jeep and a Nissan sedan parked out front."

"Sounds like we're outnumbered. What's the plan?"

"Plan, my ass. Just go with the flow. We want Rafiq, alive if possible. And any intel we can find. Let's go!"

Some would have called it a suicide mission, but Crocker didn't care. He was amped up to the max. Though he was used to facing danger, most of the risks he took were calculated ones. When SEALs took on a mission, they usually planned thoroughly and rehearsed. It was rare that they would enter a potentially life-threatening situation on the fly, but it did happen.

Crocker couldn't stop. All the anger and frustration that had built up during the last couple of weeks was about to burst out of him.

They moved quickly and quietly along the edge of the little dirt road. Owls hooted in the distance. Then a dog barked a warning.

Fuck.

As they drew within a hundred yards a second dog started up, barking deeper than the first. Sounded like a hound of some sort. The two dogs were near a porch by the side of the house.

He made out the sloping roof and the side of the structure through some thick bushes.

"You want me to silence them?" Akil whispered.

"Too fucking late for that."

"What do we do now?"

It was the oldest trick in the books, one that Crocker had first seen as a kid watching a John Wayne western. When they got within twenty yards of the house, he picked up a big rock and threw it into the bushes on the right, near the dogs, which went ballistic, barking their heads off.

He threw another, and saw people moving in the house.

Crocker turned to Akil and whispered, "You hide behind those trees over there." He pointed to the right. "When the bastards come out, start shooting. One shot at a time. Draw it out. Occupy them. Give me time to circle 'round the other side of the house. I'm going in."

"Roger that."

Akil took off one way, Crocker went the other.

Over the barking, he heard a door slamming and men's angry voices shouting in Arabic and French. Then he heard the first shot from Akil's nine-millimeter.

His adrenaline spiked further.

Entry was easy. An open window on the left side of the house (the opposite side from where the porch was located). All he had to do was punch in the screen, then yank it out.

In less than a minute he was standing in a bedroom, looking down at a king-sized mattress with rumpled sheets. Saw a stack of porn videos, a VCR, a TV, a soccer ball, an AK-47 propped in the corner.

No computers or other potential sources of intel, but the AK was his now. Loaded and ready, thank you very much.

The place was smaller than it appeared from outside. Two more little bedrooms off a hallway. One bathroom with a running toilet. All dark, unoccupied. Then another narrow hallway that led to a kitchen and a living room.

The living room lights blazed.

The racket from outside the front of the house was loud. Dogs barking furiously, men shouting, weapons discharging.

Pressed against the wall, he hoped Akil could hold them off long enough.

Crocker watched a little man in shorts run into the kitchen with an AK slung over his shoulder and quickly turn off something that was burning on the stove.

He stepped through the doorway and downed the man with two shots to the chest and one to the head.

Mozambique! It was the name of the shooting drill he'd practiced thousands of times. Every time he used it on a human target, he was pleased at how quickly and effectively it worked.

He checked for doors that might lead to a basement or other rooms but found none.

Then he crossed to the stove, picked up the pan of liver, bacon, and whatever else had been frying in it and dumped everything on the living room carpet. He emptied the rest of the plastic liter jug of cooking oil over that and the wooden floor, and using a towel lit from the stove, set the whole mess on fire.

The carpet and floor ignited quickly. As Crocker crouched in the hallway and waited, flames spread from the rug to the curtains to the walls.

Pay attention, guys. Your house is on fire!

It didn't take long. A minute or two at most.

As the SEAL team leader was starting to roast from the heat, three men entered and ran to the kitchen, where one of them grabbed a small fire extinguisher from the wall while the other two starting filling pots with water.

He rose from his crouch and didn't stop firing until all three men stopped twitching on the floor.

So much for the plan to take Rafiq alive.

Since he still heard shooting from the direction of the porch, he doubled back, climbed out the window he'd come in, and snuck around the rear of the house past the Kawasaki Ninja he'd first seen only hours before. Seemed like a lifetime ago now.

Above him the roof started cracking and giving way. He peered around the corner. A man in boxer shorts was firing an AK in the direction of Akil. Another was reloading his weapon and backing away from the house.

He took them both down with three-round bursts from their own AK-47, then waited as their screams echoed through the little valley. Their agonies were overtaken by the sound of the house cracking and burning. The dogs grew quiet. The downed men were silent. The two vehicles still waited in the driveway.

He checked behind him. Nothing. No one. Then turned to the barnlike structure he'd seen off to the right and behind the house. A small lake stood behind it.

The barn was actually a large garage with a room on top. No lights illuminated either floor.

He was about to call Akil when he heard something moving, and turned and saw a tall, dark figure run from the garage toward the lake.

Crocker stuck the Makarov in the waistband of his pants and, holding the AK ready, took off past the garage, down a gravelly path that led to the lake.

The tall figure stopped at the water and looked back at Crocker. He was holding something across his bare chest, a pistol clutched in his free hand.

"Rafiq!" the American shouted. It was a hunch.

"Go to hell," the man snarled back in English.

"Rafiq, it's over. Drop your weapon. Hit the ground!"

"Never!"

The tall man lifted whatever he was holding over his head, tossed it into the lake, then started to run into the bushes like a rat.

Crocker thought he might have a chance to take him alive but wasn't about to let him get away.

"Rafiq, stop!"

The rat kept running. It took three shots from Crocker to take him down—one to the back of the thigh, two into his butt. One of the bullets had severed a major artery. He was bleeding profusely when the American reached him.

"Rafiq, where's Zaman?"

"I'm a businessman. I don't know anyone named Zaman."

"Tell me what you know about Zaman."

"You'll be dead soon," the Arab man groaned. "My friends will kill you."

"They already tried. Tell me where he is."

"You...don't...understand..."

Those were his last words.

Crocker left him there and hurried to the garage. He was looking for intel—computers, flash drives, notebooks, letters, anything that could potentially help the Agency locate AZ.

The bottom floor was filled with junk—an old boat, garden equipment, cardboard boxes. He was ripping through the cartons—which contained cans of motor oil and plastic bottles filled with water—when he heard something moving above.

Along the far side of the garage, he climbed a rickety wooden stairway to the second floor. The door was unlocked. The moment he opened it, he was hit with the stench, a thick combination of disinfectant and human excrement.

Several strange pieces of equipment stood in the central room—a weird-looking bench with straps and a harness of some sort. Plastic buckets on the floor. Paper towels on a bench. An old metal desk in one corner. Bottles of pills on top of it. A syringe.

What the hell is this?

He saw six little wooden cells like cages along the far wall. Then heard a whimper, like a dog's.

Strange place to keep dogs.

Looking through the metal bars of the first two cages, he saw they were empty. Dirty mattresses lay on the floor. In the third, he made out something pale. It was a bare human leg, thin and shapely like a young girl's.

"Hello. Can you hear me?" he whispered through the bars. The person didn't move, though he could make out breathing.

Moving to the next, he saw a naked girl covered with what looked like dirt, feces, urine, and bruises. Judging from her eyes, she'd been drugged.

Jesus Christ!

The cages contained four women in total, scared and half alive. More like animals than human beings.

"I'm an American. I've come to save you," Crocker said in a whisper.

All he got back were whimpers.

"Do any of you speak English?"

They didn't answer.

He tried again. "The keys. Do any of you know where the keys are? Tell me where the keys are, and I'll let you out."

As smoke from the house drifted in the open door, they hid their heads and moaned—except for one bold girl, tall and thin, with matted hair, who stared at Crocker defiantly, then pulled herself up and spat through the bars.

At least one of them had some fight left in her.

Crocker wiped off the spittle that had landed on the front of his shirt. "I'm an American," he said again. "I've come to save you."

"Don't touch me! I'll kill you!" she screeched back in heavily accented English.

"I'm not going to touch you. I want to get you out of here."

"You're a liar. A fucking liar! I know what you want!"

"I'm not lying to you. Listen to me. Listen..."

Her delicate long nose sniffed the air. "Is something burning?"

"The house. I set it on fire."

Her expression changed to curiosity. "Where are you from?"

"USA."

"You're American."

"Yes, I am."

She nodded and scratched the skin under her pale right breast. "I have a cousin who is studying veterinary medicine at George Mason University."

"That's not far from me," he whispered back.

She grimaced, pointed past his shoulder, and said, "The keys, I think, are there, in the desk. Try the top drawer."

"Thanks."

He heard a creak on the stairs and froze. Holding a finger up to his mouth, he hid against the wall near the door.

The footsteps got closer.

The girl he had been talking to recoiled to the back of her cage and hid.

He readied the AK and waited, his heart pounding hard.

"Boss," someone whispered. "Boss, are you up here?"

It was Akil.

CHAPTER TWELVE

And whosoever shed man's blood, by man shall his blood be shed.

—Il Duce, *The Boondock Saints*

CROCKER WANTED to get away from the farm before the French authorities arrived. But there were things he had to take care of first.

Continue the search for intel, and question the four female captives.

He and Akil had literally given two of them—the ballsy one from Romania who said her name was Dorina, and a rail-thin brunette who hailed from a small town in the Ukraine—the shirts off their backs. The sweaty, soiled, bloodstained polos hung over the girls' skeletal torsos to the tops of their thighs. The other two sat in the corner, wrapped in a dirty blanket, their eyes staring blankly at the cracked linoleum floor. One hailed from Georgia. The fourth, who had a mole above the corner of her mouth, couldn't remember her name.

They'd been beautiful once. Young and happy, with

boyfriends, friends, and dreams. Now they were a mess. Drugged, raped, and god knew what else.

As much as Crocker's heart went out to them, there was little he could do besides tell them their ordeal was over.

The only one who seemed to understand was Dorina, who gulped water from a Styrofoam cup. Anger and terror churned in her gray-blue eyes. Her bottom lip was swollen, the size and color of a plum.

"You really killed them?" she asked bluntly.

"Yes."

"Dead? You're sure of that?"

"Yes."

"All of them?"

"Five or six," he answered. "We captured another. He's taped to the front seat of the car."

"Shoot him in the face. First in the mouth; then wait a few minutes and shoot him between the eyes."

She translated for the girl from Ukraine, who listened, nodded, then started to sob.

Dorina said, "She wants to see their bodies. To spit on them herself."

"Tell her they've been burned to a crisp. There's nothing to see."

The Ukrainian girl grabbed Crocker's hand like a child. "Thank you. Thank you," she repeated in broken English. "Thank you so much from my heart."

"You're welcome."

She clung to him trembling, and wouldn't let go. "You American? You take us to America now?" she pleaded through her tears.

Crocker tried to remain reasonable and calm. "The French authorities will arrive soon and take care of all of you. They'll send you back to your families. Don't be afraid."

"French?" she asked. "Why not Americans?"

"Because we're in France," Crocker answered.

"But I trust the Americans more."

"The French will take care of you. I'll make sure of that."

As they spoke, Dorina crossed to the desk and started tearing through the drawers.

"What are you looking for?" Akil asked as he kept watch at the door.

"They took everything, those bastards. Our papers, clothing, jewelry, money!"

Dorina removed several DVDs from the top drawer. The rest were empty, except for a wooden ruler and a pair of pliers. She heaved the pliers against the wall and screamed. "Go to hell! *Go to hell!*"

"We've already been to hell," the girl from the Ukraine remarked. "What could be worse?"

Dorina: "She's right."

Crocker wrapped his arms around the tall Romanian girl and sat her on the edge of the desk. He said, "You're alive, Dorina. That's the most important. Passports, jewelry, everything else can be replaced."

Her mouth trembled with rage. "I need to search the house."

"There's nothing left. It burned to the ground."

"They took my rings. One that belonged to my Polish grandmother."

They'd taken their vanity, too. Dorina scratched at a sore between her breasts. He saw the Ukrainian girl past her shoulder squat over a blue bucket and piss.

"Have you seen other girls come and go from here?" he asked.

Staring ahead, she got to her feet and started to leave, even though she was barefoot and half naked.

Crocker stopped her. "Dorina, listen. This is important. Have you seen other girls here who then left?"

"There were others," she answered in heavily accented English. "Yes."

"How many?"

She paused like she was remembering, then held up ten fingers.

"Ten."

"Around ten, yes."

"Was one of them named Malie?"

She wiped her mouth with the back of her hand. "Maybe. I don't remember all their names."

"She would have come from Norway. Oslo. Eighteen years old."

"Same as me." Dorina looked at least ten years older than that. Crocker tried not to appear shocked.

"She was blond. She would have arrived about two weeks ago."

The skeletally thin Ukrainian girl spoke up. "Malie, yes."

"You saw her? Malie from Oslo, Norway?"

"Yes. She was here when I arrived."

"Malie Tingvoll. You're sure of that?"

She pointed a bony finger to the first cage along the opposite wall. "The first day I arrived, I watched them take pictures of her, first in a pretty white dress, then stripped her naked with her legs spread open."

He glanced at the cage, which contained another

stained mattress; there were scratches on the wall. "When was that?"

"When I arrived? Eighteen days and approximately seven hours ago." Even though she'd been drugged and abused, she'd been keeping track of time in her head.

"Do you know what happened to Malie?" Crocker asked.

"She left two days ago with a man named Cyrus."

The name meant nothing to Crocker.

"Who is Cyrus? Can you describe him?"

"Arabic-looking but dresses European. Around thirty years old. He acted like the nicest one. But he was sick, too. Ask her," the Ukrainian said, pointing to the girl with the mole, who was wrapped in a blanket and still staring at the floor.

Crocker knelt beside her and asked gently, "What's your name?"

She didn't shift her gaze and didn't answer.

Dorina answered for her. "Justine."

"Justine looks so young."

"She's fourteen. Cyrus raped her, then bathed her. Raped her, then bathed her. Over and over and over."

"I'm sorry."

The girl finally looked up and asked, "Why?"

"Because I feel for you and what you've been forced to endure."

She said something in a language Crocker didn't understand. Dorina translated. "She asks, Why did he degrade me, then bathe me so gently?"

"I don't know."

Dorina said, "We were forced to watch everything."

Crocker looked at Akil, who shook his head in disgust,

then asked, "Do you have any idea where Cyrus took Malie?"

"They treated us like animals. Worse than animals."

"I'm sorry. But that's over now."

"What did we do to them?"

"Nothing, Dorina."

"Nothing." She twisted up her mouth like she was trying to comprehend the injustice of what had happened.

"Dorina, please. I need you to focus."

"What do you want?"

"Did Cyrus say where he was taking her? Taking Malie?"

She shrugged. "I think somewhere east."

They were interrupted by the sound of sirens approaching. *EE-OO...EE-OO...* Akil hurried outside to look.

The thin Ukrainian girl mumbled something in Russian and pointed to her breasts.

"What'd she say?"

"She said that Cyrus bragged to her," Dorina answered. "He told her that he'd sold the Norwegian girl for a million dollars, to a sheik, because she had a big chest."

"A sheik?"

The Ukrainian girl nodded.

"Did this sheik have a name?"

Not that either one of them remembered hearing.

Akil gestured from the doorway and said, "They're here, boss. Two fire trucks. Half a dozen men."

Crocker tried to sound gentle and reassuring as he addressed the young women. "The French authorities are here. They'll look after you. They'll send you back to your families. Don't be afraid."

Dorina smiled ironically, as if to say: What could be worse than what we've been through?

The Ukrainian girl muttered one last "Thank you very much."

He stuffed the DVDs in his pocket and took off in the direction of the lake with Akil at his heels whispering, "Boss, you're going in the wrong direction. Boss, what are you doing?"

"I'll explain later."

Arriving at the approximate spot where he'd seen Rafiq, Crocker removed his shoes, placed the DVDs, AK, and Makarov on the ground, and jumped in.

"Boss..."

The water was cool and thick with algae, no more than six feet deep. It was impossible to see anything, so he felt along the bottom. Mostly silt and rocks. He swam in a circle until his lungs started to burn, then came up for air, which was pungent with the smell of burnt wood.

Flashing blue lights swept the lake and surrounding hills.

Akil looked anxious. "Boss, they're coming!" he exclaimed in a whisper. "They're close."

"I need a minute."

"Why? What are you looking for?"

Crocker took a big breath and went down again, this time pushing out farther from the shore. He swam as fast as he could with one arm, found something that felt like metal, and came up.

"Boss!"

It had once been the top of a small chest. He tossed it aside.

"Last time."

Kicking hard, he swept the bottom with both hands this time, over smooth rocks covered with slime. Then he reached something hard and slick. Grabbed it under his arm and pushed to the surface.

It was an Apple laptop. White and a little banged up.

"Let's go!"

Akil helped him out and pointed to a spot on his shoulder. "What's that?"

A sliver of wood or metal had created a long gash, he couldn't remember when. Blood mixed with the water from the lake smeared across his chest.

"It's nothing," Crocker said, removing the sliver and finding his shoes, the DVDs, the weapons.

He ran barefoot, making a long arc around the house, through the woods.

All the time he was thinking: The French firefighters won't call the police until they find the bodies.

Not that he felt in any real danger. But he didn't want to be detained and have to answer questions. The local CIA station and U.S. diplomats would go ballistic. Bureaucrats were always highly sensitive to anything that upset the local authorities—like American operatives doing violence on their turf.

They reached the road about fifty meters in front of the car, with scratches on their chests and arms.

Crocker ran to the BMW and checked the Arab driver still taped to the passenger seat. He'd pissed his pants.

"Where's your fucking manners?" Crocker asked as he started the engine. He spun the car around.

"He doesn't have any," Akil growled from the rear seat, backhanding the driver across the side of his head. The driver groaned.

Later, Crocker would have to decide whether to shoot him in the head and dump him somewhere or hand him over to the French police.

Now he pushed down on the gas as Akil reached around the prisoner and checked the glove compartment.

Akil reported that the car had been purchased two months ago from a dealer in Nice. The driver's name was Marcel Saloud, with an address in Cap d'Antibes.

"Easy come, easy go, right, Marcel?" Crocker said to the driver, who squirmed in the leather bucket seat. The heavy tape gave him little room to move.

At the junction with the D-455, the road was empty except for emergency vehicles coming from both directions. Crocker pointed the car west and picked up speed.

"They found the bodies," Akil said from the back, with the wind in his face.

"Donaldson is gonna be pissed."

Crocker's heart burned with outrage as he thought about the four girls. But when his attention shifted to the dead men, his anger morphed into satisfaction.

He was thrilled that they'd killed them. Almost ecstatic.

Entering the outskirts of Marseille, he pulled over into an empty parking lot and checked the trunk. He was looking for something to throw over his bare chest—a T-shirt, windbreaker, anything—but found instead a box of large plastic garbage bags, a pick, and two shovels.

"You know what those were for, don't you?" he asked, looking at Akil.

"Looks like you saved my life."

Crocker caught sight of the Arab driver through the back window.

Akil asked, "What do you want to do with him?"

"Let's pull the tape off his mouth and find out what he knows about the sheik," he instructed.

Crocker kept an eye on the passing traffic as Akil questioned the driver in French. The Arab swore up and down that he didn't know anything about the activities at the farm. He'd simply been doing Rafiq a favor, and offered to drive some of his friends.

When Akil responded, Crocker recognized the French word for liar, *menteur.*

Crocker said, "Tell him that if he tells us what he knows about Cyrus and the sheik, we'll let him live."

The driver started blubbering and talking a mile a minute. Crocker slapped the side of his head. "Shut the fuck up!"

The driver composed himself, then turned to Akil and said in French, "I know nothing about the girls. I didn't know what these men were doing. I swear."

"What did he say?"

"He claims he doesn't know anything."

Crocker leaned into the car and punched the driver in the face, breaking his nose.

"Fuck you."

Then they retaped his mouth, wrists, and ankles, and threw him in the trunk.

Returning to their hotel past midnight, Crocker dialed the number he'd committed to memory. The woman with the British accent answered on the third ring. "Yes."

"We had some problems with the vehicle."

"Meet me at the same location. Fifteen minutes."

"Thanks."

He summoned Akil from the bathroom, where he was taking a shower, and the two men returned to the corner of Rue Lafayette and Rue Marcel Sembat. The same attractive North African woman sat behind the wheel of the Acura SUV, as composed as before.

"How can I help you?" she asked.

"We've got someone for you. He tried to kidnap us when we went to the Club Rosa."

"What's his name?"

"His car is registered to a Marcel Saloud, who resides in Cap d'Antibes."

Akil handed her the car registration papers. She scanned them with fierce, dark eyes.

"What's his relationship to Rifa'a Suyuti, aka Rafiq?"

"He admits to nothing, but they were working together."

"Where is he now?"

"In the trunk of his car."

She thought for ten seconds, then asked, "And Rafiq?"

"Dead."

She raised a dark eyebrow. "You killed him?"

"It couldn't be helped. Akil and I got in a firefight with some suspicious individuals in a farmhouse off the road to Toulon."

"That was you?"

"That was us."

"French television is reporting six bodies recovered from a house burned to the ground. They also recovered four young women who claim they were being held prisoner."

"That's the place."

"Charming."

"Not really. We need to get out of the country as soon as possible."

"That can be arranged. Where's the Renault?"

Crocker had forgotten about the car. "As far as I know, it's still parked near the club in Noailles."

"All right. Put the individual you captured in the back of my vehicle. Cover him with a blanket."

"There's one last thing."

She looked at Crocker's outfit. "I don't do laundry."

"We need someone who can help us recover data from a laptop that's been underwater."

She checked her watch. "It's two in the morning."

"This is important. It has to be done now."

"Fine. Throw the guy in the boot and get in."

"What about his car?"

"I'll deal with that later."

She picked up a cell phone from the seat next to her and dialed while the two SEALs returned to the BMW to get the driver.

Crocker liked her style.

She drove them to a modern apartment building located on a bluff overlooking the port and waited in the SUV. Crocker and Akil hurried through the white lobby decorated with mirrors and fake flowers.

Up on the sixth floor a pale man with glasses and thinning, disheveled reddish blond hair answered the door. Wearing sweatpants and a dirty white tee, he introduced himself as Albert Hayes.

"You guys want coffee?" he asked, listing to his right. "It's in the kitchen."

Hayes took the laptop from Crocker and hurried inside.

The apartment was dark, disorderly. Magazines, newspapers, half-empty containers of food strewn over sofas, tables, counters. A framed poster from *Chinatown* on the wall.

Crocker poured himself a cup of black coffee and walked back into a narrow bedroom where Albert Hayes sat at a long desk covered with computers. The shades were drawn, the bed unmade.

"What'd you do to it?" Hayes asked, waiting for the laptop to boot.

"Someone threw it into a lake."

He shook his head and hooked up the laptop to another computer, started punching keys. "They generally don't like water. What are you looking for?" Hayes asked.

"Information."

"What kind?"

There was movement on the laptop screen. Code scrolling slowly.

Hayes looked disappointed. "Well, I can tell you one thing: the hard drive is fucked."

"Then thanks for the coffee."

"Not so fast."

Hayes worked the keyboard, disconnected cables, reconnected them again. Then slipped a disk in the drive and waited.

Something happened. A message came up on the screen. The tall man leaned forward and slapped more keys.

"I found some e-mails," Hayes reported. "Recent, it looks like. Check 'em out."

Crocker and Akil leaned in over his shoulder. Some were in French, others in Arabic. Akil started translating.

Most of them didn't make sense. "The furniture has

been moved to Naples." "JS has a new carpet. Returning home." "Give the girl three candy bars after lunch."

"It's in some kind of rudimentary code," Hayes offered.

"Looks like."

"Not my department."

Crocker instructed Hayes to stop at one, subject "Carpets," which read: "We have stored the carpets here. The one you ordered for the sheik will be delivered to the port in K-P on the 25th. I hope he appreciates its exceptional quality."

Crocker asked Akil to read it again.

"Could be something."

"The sheik."

"Yeah, the sheik."

"What's K-P?

"Karachi, Pakistan?"

Crocker remembered that Dorina had said that Cyrus was taking the girl east.

Hayes found references to S. Rastani in two other recent e-mails.

"Any mention of a leader, someone named Zaman?" Akil asked.

"No," Hayes answered. "Even though the e-mails come from different addresses, I believe they're from the same source."

"Why?"

"They're all directives. They sound like they're coming from someone who is moving pieces on a big chessboard."

Crocker turned to Hayes and said, "I need to use your phone."

He pointed to a console on the nightstand. "Use that one. It's secure."

Crocker handed Hayes the DVDs he'd been carrying. "Check these out."

He reached Mancini at the hotel in Islamabad as he was finishing breakfast. "How's your knee?" he asked.

"A hell of a lot better. Thanks."

"Good. I need you to jump on two things. First, call Donaldson in Islamabad and tell him to contact Mikael Klausen. They both need to meet us in Karachi as soon as possible."

"Wait a minute. Where are you?"

"I'm still in Marseille, but I'm on my way to Karachi as soon as I get authorization. So are you."

"Me?"

"All three of you."

"When?"

"As soon as we get a nod from Donaldson, drop what you're doing, fly to Karachi, and go directly to the port."

"That'll take several hours."

"You'll be looking for a Norwegian girl named Malie Tingvoll: eighteen, blond, beautiful. She'll be with a Middle Eastern–looking guy named Cyrus. He'll either be hustling her onto a ship or handing her off to representatives of a sheik possibly named Rastani."

"All right. Let me write this down."

"The important thing is to get there fast."

"Understood."

"Akil and I are leaving as soon as we get an okay."

"You want me to wait for you?"

"Don't leave the port until we get there."

"I understand."

"Maybe Donaldson has someone in Karachi who can help. Tell him we've got to recover the Norwegian girl and stop this sheik character and this guy named Cyrus from leaving the country."

"You got a description?"

"Cyrus is in his late twenties, early thirties. Middle Eastern looking. Medium height. Big smile."

"The sheik?"

"No idea."

"Roger."

Crocker hung up and turned to Akil, who pointed at a large computer monitor on the desk and said, "Boss, look."

It was Justine—the young girl with the mole over her mouth—the one they'd last seen in the barn, wrapped in a blanket, staring at the floor.

On the screen she wore a pink dress and had her blond hair pulled back. She looked beautiful and innocent, walking through a garden in bare feet. As she bent to pick a yellow flower, the camera zoomed in on her face, which was glowing from within and unmarked.

Next she stood inside the farmhouse, in what Crocker thought was the living room, looking away from the camera. Someone out of the frame said something that couldn't be heard, and she turned and crossed her arms over her chest.

The girl looked frightened. She hesitated. A man stepped into the picture and with his back to the camera slapped her across the face.

"Fuck."

Casting her eyes to the floor, she started to slowly remove her dress until she stood naked, trembling, hands at her sides, tears splattering her upturned breasts.

Crocker wanted to punch something.

"What the hell is this?" Hayes asked.

A man out of view of the camera shouted something, and the girl turned abruptly and bent over until her hands touched the floor. The camera zoomed in on her ass as she reached back and spread her cheeks.

"Turn it off!" Crocker shouted, holding out his palm to Hayes, who ejected the DVD and handed it over.

If Crocker had even a smidgeon of regret for blowing the men away, it disappeared now.

"They used the DVDs to sell the girls," Akil muttered, breaking the silence.

"We've got to stop Cyrus. Let's go."

CHAPTER THIRTEEN

You're not a star until they can spell your name in Karachi.

—Humphrey Bogart

AN HOUR later Tom Crocker was still in Marseille, stuffing clothes into his bag and waiting for authorization to fly to Karachi. Minutes earlier he had spoken to Mikael Klausen in Oslo, who told him that Cyrus was the name of the man who was last seen with Malie Tingvoll at the café there.

His mind was working feverishly. There seemed to be a million things he needed to do.

Why was Donaldson taking so long?

He started pacing the little room and stopped. The texture of the yellowish morning haze through the dirty hotel window reminded him of summer days on the beach in Nantucket. Suddenly he felt a strong desire to be with Holly, to tell her how much he missed her.

He thought how good it would feel to hold her hand and walk barefoot across the wet sand. Blueberry pancakes with fresh maple syrup. Broiled lobster with red wine for dinner. The smell of her hair. Making love.

As he started counting the days he'd been away from home, the phone rang. It was the North African CIA officer.

She said, "Meet me downstairs in ten minutes. I'm driving you to the airport. The flights for you and your companion are confirmed."

That meant Donaldson had given his approval. But Crocker wanted to double-check.

"Our destination is Karachi, correct?"

"Yes."

"Thank you. You're very efficient."

"You're welcome, Mr. Crocker," the North African said. "But I'm afraid I just heard some unfortunate news."

"What's that?"

"French authorities have discovered the bodies of several young women buried near the lake at the house in Toulon."

Crocker was struck more by the sadness in her usually emotionless voice than the significance of what she was saying.

"Bodies?"

"Yes, other girls were buried near the lake."

He hadn't considered that possibility.

"I regret to report that one of them was a blonde," she continued. "Approximately eighteen. Same approximate height as the Norwegian girl you're looking for."

Crocker felt like he'd been kicked in the stomach. "Oh."

For an instant he imagined Malie's parents, whom he'd never met, clutching each other and sobbing.

Through the mottled light of the narrow room, he saw

Akil exit the bathroom and point toward the door. Crocker nodded as if to say "Yes, we're going."

The woman on the phone continued, "I've just finished contacting the Norwegian police security service. They'll be e-mailing her photos, fingerprints, and dental records presently to expedite the identification."

Crocker felt his pulse quickening. "How many girls did they find?"

"Three so far. But they expect to unearth more."

The implications of what he'd just heard spooled out in his mind.

"Fanatics and psychopaths," she remarked. "Different shades of evil."

His mind was occupied with another line of reasoning. If the body that had been recovered was that of Malie Tingvoll, why was Cyrus on his way to Karachi?

Crocker explained the dilemma to Akil as they waited outside for the SUV.

Akil scratched his freshly shaved jaw and suggested that they wait in Marseille until Norwegian PST was able to confirm the identity of the body. "In the meantime," he said, "let's return to Albert Hayes's place and see what else we can find on the computer."

"I hate wasting time."

"Why's that wasting time, if the guy we're looking for isn't even there?"

Crocker's gut still pulled him to Karachi. He couldn't explain why.

Akil said, "You've always got to push ahead, don't you, chief?"

"It's not about me doing what I want. It's about stopping these fucking savages."

Crocker didn't like pushing people. But it was his job to lead.

Akil wasn't letting go. "How long is it going to take to get the results from Oslo? An hour at most?"

"We're going to Karachi. End of story."

"Boss, you're not thinking straight."

"Maybe not. But we're going anyway."

As they put their bags in the SUV, Akil shot him a look of pride mixed with hurt and a bit of defiance. Crocker took note. Part of being a successful SEAL assault team leader meant tracking the psychology of your men, especially on long and serpentine ops like this. Instead of breaking down physically, operators were more likely to experience nervous or mental exhaustion. The constant pressure of working undercover, the changing scenery, the emotional ups and downs—all took a toll.

Crocker stopped Akil as he started to climb into the vehicle.

"I can count on you, can't I?"

Akil looked him in the eye. "Yes, you can, boss."

"You still mad at me about Edyta?"

"I don't want to talk about her anymore."

Crocker said, "I know something about losing people you care for. The pain won't go away, but you'll get used to it."

"Fuck you."

The North African woman dropped them off at the international terminal, where they checked in and ran to their flight—Emirates to Doha, Qatar, then Doha to Karachi.

The Airbus was crammed with businessmen and wives. Mostly Arabs—some in robes, others in business suits. A sprinkling of South Asians. Women in chadors working at laptops. One of them glanced at Crocker from across the aisle, then quickly looked away, her big eyes glistening with curiosity.

Even a fleeting look like that could be dangerous in the potent mix of cultural influences and interests. Money battled with religion, obedience clashed with personal ambition—creating an undercurrent of danger and anxiety.

Nine and a half hours later, when they changed planes in Doha, Crocker read a text message from Mancini. "Preliminary tests DO NOT link Malie. More results pending. Headed to KP."

He leaned over and showed it to Akil, who had just come back from the men's room. "Take a look at this."

Beads of water still clung to his chin. "You're right this time. Good for you."

In the air again, the SEAL assault team leader closed his eyes and dreamt that he was being chased by a pack of wolves through dark, unnamed streets. Sweating through his pale blue polo shirt, he opened his eyes and, blinking, realized he was somewhere over the Indian Sea in an aluminum cylinder with two hundred or so people he didn't know. The air tasted sour.

He was keenly aware of the space between himself and his fellow passengers. Each of them lived in the bubble of their own experiences, beliefs, circumstances, wants, and needs.

Akil, with his big head leaning on the headrest and his eyes closed, stood out. He was the only one of many Middle Eastern men on the flight dressed casually, in jeans and a black T-shirt. And he was fit. Crocker had noticed other travelers looking at Akil askance.

"No man is an island," a poet had written. Still, people acted as if they were islands and defended them like wild dogs. To extend oneself and try to cross over from one island to the next was to invite hostility and conflict. Which explained why the Western ideal of personal freedom challenged those who clung to the strict boundaries of dogma. In the state of Virginia, which Crocker called home, you could believe anything you wanted to, dress according to your personal tastes, say whatever you felt like saying, worship the deity of your choice.

He considered personal freedom to be a key ingredient to human progress. And it was a desire that he believed all human beings harbored somewhere in their hearts. To those who wanted to impose a uniform set of beliefs, Western-style freedom—with its invitation to individualism and experimentation—was a loaded gun. A threat.

Crocker liked to compare his team to the Greek three hundred—the free Spartans who chose to fight to the death to resist hundreds of thousands of invading Persians in 480 BC. It was a story that had inspired Crocker his entire adult life. A small, free people had willingly outfought huge numbers of imperial subjects at Thermopylae who advanced under the lash. The Western idea of freedom was proved stronger than the Eastern notion of despotism and monarchy.

Things hadn't changed that much. Maybe weapons and methods were more sophisticated today, but the war still raged.

Like the day before, at the farm.

Crocker counted his bodies, then added them to the tally. Another two or three in Panama, a half dozen in Iraq, one in Paraguay, six or seven, maybe eight, outside

Kandahar in eastern Afghanistan, another two on the Guatemalan border. All men who made the world more dangerous, who threatened the right of free people to live the way they wanted.

The twenty or so lives he'd taken had never caused him to lose a minute of sleep. But, looking out the Airbus window, Crocker wondered if maybe he'd paid a karmic price. Because sometimes he sensed a dark place in his soul.

Maybe one day I'll face a reckoning and will be punished, he said to himself.

He couldn't worry about that now. He'd chosen to be one of America's elite warriors. And as such, he'd proudly and steadfastly fend off and defeat the wolves.

Karachi airport was a confusing, smelly, noisy mess of anxious bodies trying to get from one place to the next. The two Americans hired an expediter—in this case a short Pakistani man named Ahmed—who helped them navigate immigration and customs.

On the way out they passed two strutting Pak security guards with bristling, shining mustaches. Behind them followed lower-ranked guards pulling along a young man with long blond hair and his wrists chained together who was shouting curses in German. A smuggler or drug courier, probably. Crocker imagined that he'd be screaming even louder when the Pakistanis got him behind doors.

The scene outside was equally chaotic. Even though it was late at night, almost 11 p.m. local time, the conjoining streets presented an incredible tangle of cars, people, bicycles, and honking horns. Crocker was reminded that

Karachi was a city of over eighteen million, and the primary banking, trade, and business center of Pakistan. A large proportion of its inhabitants were refugees—Muhajirs and Punjabis from India, Biharis and Bengalis from Bangladesh, Pashtuns from Afghanistan, and Rohingya from Burma.

"This way, boss!"

Akil pointed to a blue Mercedes taxi. Inside, he instructed the Sikh driver to deliver them to the port as quickly as possible. They took off at breakneck speed, retracing the path they'd taken the night they went after Abu Rasul Zaman—the Shahrah-e-Faisal Boulevard to Napier Mole Bridge. Judging from the number and prominence of billboards advertising Bollywood movies, that form of popular entertainment had managed to bridge the venomous rivalry between India and Pakistan.

Interesting, Crocker thought as they entered the port area, this time with a chance to look around a little more. He hadn't expected to be mesmerized but was, by a deep purplish gray sky festooned with lights from ships, booms, loading elevators, and Panamax cranes of all sizes. The effect was otherworldly. Significant in a way he couldn't grasp.

During the day this was one of the busiest harbors in the world—a long natural channel protected by a thin finger of land with elaborate wharves east and west. At this hour, half past eleven, the port was eerily calm. Gently lapping water with Sufi music playing somewhere in the background. The fire from some sort of refinery burned in the distance, projecting a golden glow along the horizon, which made the water appear even lighter than the sky.

He'd heard that neighboring Afghanistan was the country with the highest percentage of fecal matter in the air. Judging from the quality of what he was breathing, Pakistan couldn't be far behind.

After an exchange of cell-phone calls, Crocker learned that Davis, Ritchie, and Mancini had arrived ahead of them and were haggling with officials at the Karachi Port Trust.

They ran. Five minutes later, out of breath, he and Akil entered a regal colonial-style building that reminded the SEAL leader a little of the U.S. Capitol. They were directed to an office on the second floor where they found Davis nose to nose with a Pakistani official.

"What's going on?"

The two men were approximately the same height, but otherwise were very different.

Davis was broad-shouldered and blond, with blue eyes; the Pakistani, dark-skinned and frail, with a brush of black-silver hair and turned-up mustache. He introduced himself as Ayud Nasiri, the assistant port safety manager.

"He's stonewalling us, boss."

Ayud Nasiri to Davis: "You're a very rude man."

Crocker summoned all his diplomatic charm. "We're American officials," he explained, "on a mission for the king of Norway."

Nasiri responded in a high-pitched voice. "I keep telling your man here that I'm not allowed to release any passenger lists without the approval of the port facility security officer, and that individual won't be available until later in the morning. It's nothing personal, of course."

"But, you see, Mr. Nasiri, this is an emergency. A girl's life is in imminent danger."

"It seems that everything is an emergency these days, my good sir."

A good-natured fellow with a ready smile, Nasiri was also stubborn. He clearly did things by the book and wasn't about to make an exception, even after Crocker called Mikael Klausen in Oslo, who managed to get the Norwegian deputy foreign minister to talk to him.

"The PFSO will arrive in several hours," the assistant port safety manager said with a sly grin. "He's usually prompt, at nine o'clock. I'm sure you'll find him to be a very good fellow."

It was a polite go-fuck-yourself.

"Now what?" Davis asked.

That's when Mancini and Ritchie returned from the port's passenger terminal, looking fit and rested. They told Crocker they'd shown everyone they could find a photo of Malie Tingvoll.

"Any luck?"

"Negative, boss."

Crocker and Akil were irritable and tired, having traveled all day to get to Karachi. Crocker's lower back ached from the long flight. He'd broken it in two places during a HAHO jump (high altitude–high opening) a year before.

The crackers and tea in glasses Nasiri ordered an aide to serve didn't help.

Mancini, who liked to focus on details, drew a quick sketch of the port—seventeen vessel berths on the east wharf, thirteen on the west. Each wharf held a large container terminal. The west pier also accommodated three oil berths, two ship repair jetties, a shipyard, and an engineering facility. In addition there was a large harbor adjacent to the western wharf that contained thousands of smaller fishing vessels.

"What do we do now?" Ritchie asked, his longish, straight black hair setting off his Cherokee cheekbones.

"We wait."

They sat on a rough wooden bench and watched the clock on the opposite wall tick slowly past one-fifty-five to two.

Crocker asked Akil to go inside and ask Nasiri if they could see a list of vessels that had recently left the port. He referred him to the traffic manager's office on the first floor. The lone official on duty there, a tall, thin man with large hooded eyes and thick lips, announced that the office was closed to visitors until 8 a.m. When Akil tried to reason with him, he waved him away and tried to close the door. Akil managed to wedge his foot inside and claimed he was from the U.S. consulate. When that didn't work, he offered the night traffic manager forty dollars for the names of all vessels that had left the port in the past several days.

Five minutes later, a one-page printout was passed through the crack.

"You understand, of course, you cannot tell anyone that you got this from me."

"I won't."

On the sheet about a dozen names were printed in type so faint it was hard to read. Akil ran up the stairs and handed it to Crocker, who had been considering checking into a nearby hotel.

"What's this?"

"It's the list of vessels that left the port over the past six days, including yesterday, the twenty-fifth."

The team leader's eyes burned. The names meant nothing to him as he read them out loud: "*Lucky Arrow, Northern Valour, Ginga Panther, Eastern Highway, Bunga Raya Tujuh, Rolldock Sun, Syrena, Aristea M*—"

"Wait a minute," Ritchie said. "What's the next-to-last one you mentioned?"

"The *Rolldock Sun*?"

"No, the one after that."

"Syrena?"

"Yes, *Syrena*. Didn't we see that name on an invoice we found at the house?"

"What house?"

"AZ's safe house, the one we raided a couple of clicks from here."

Crocker looked at the printout again and read the name—*Syrena*. "You're right," he said, trying to fight through the dull fog of exhaustion and recall what else he knew about the *Syrena*.

"It might mean something, boss."

"An interesting coincidence, at least."

Crocker straightened his back and turned to Akil, who was biting his nails. "Take the finger out of your mouth and go see the night traffic manager again. Ask him to tell you where the *Syrena* is headed. What time, exactly, did it leave? When is it scheduled to dock again, and where?"

Akil said, "It's gonna require cash."

Crocker reached into his wallet and handed him three twenties. "Bargain with the bastard. If that doesn't work, beat it out of him."

"Yes, sir."

His mind picked up speed. Carpets, S. Rastani, the port in KP, the *Syrena*... the shards of info were starting to fit together. Now they had something that linked Zaman to the kidnapping operation and Cyrus.

"We're gonna need a helicopter and equipment," he said to Ritchie. "Get Donaldson on the phone."

"Aye-aye."

"Davis, call Klausen in Norway."

"What time's it there?"

"Doesn't matter. This is important. Tell him we've gotta stop that ship!"

CHAPTER FOURTEEN

Never, never, never, . . . never give in.

—Winston Churchill

HE COULDN'T tell if it was the thick midmorning heat, his fitful, truncated sleep, or the fact that he was bracing himself for another meeting with CIA officer Lou Donaldson. Likely it was combination of the three that fouled Tom Crocker's mood and set his mind whirring and turning in on itself like a rabid dog. Fueling his anger was intense frustration—the kind he felt squeezing his bones.

The sky beyond the wisps of white clouds and gray-orange patina of pollution was vast and infinite blue. He hated waiting.

Something important was happening while Crocker and his men napped, played video games on the hotel computer, and talked to their families. Maybe it involved an attack Zaman was planning, since the name of the ship *Syrena* had been found on an invoice in his hideaway. Maybe it held a clue to the location of Malie Tingvoll.

Why were they cooling their heels in the Karachi hotel room? Why?

In practical terms, he knew the answer. One, their evidence was slight—a coded e-mail about a "delivery" that could be the kidnapped Norwegian girl had led them to the port of Karachi, through which a ship mentioned in papers found in Zaman's hideout had passed.

Two, they needed money and equipment to move forward and intercept the ship. That required authorization from the CIA as well as his CO back in Virginia. Now, because of the girl's nationality, the Norwegian government was involved, too.

Lou Donaldson was on his way from Islamabad. Mikael Klausen had changed planes in Oman and was scheduled to arrive within the hour.

But couldn't something be done sooner? Like... now!

All that was really required was a couple of phone calls to the right people, and Crocker and his team could be on their way.

He blamed the culture of Washington and the millions of bureaucrats and officials who were like a layer of fat covering the muscle of the rich men and politicians who made decisions and set policy.

The bureaucratic mind-set put a premium on climbing the ladder, which meant serving superiors and avoiding risk. Agency officers were particularly risk averse. They cloaked their cowardice and self-interest with words like "policy," "options," "strategic goals," and so on.

Imagining the billions of words that had been spoken and churned out in papers when real contingencies required action—all the arguments that had been carefully reasoned to support one theoretical outcome or another—

made Crocker want to put his fist through the window.

He kept seeing the withered, bruised bodies of the girls they had found above the garage at the farm near Toulon. In his current state of torment their faces morphed into those of other women he'd known, including Jenny and Holly back home. All of them had come from families that were part of communities, departments, and countries served by armies of officials whose job was to protect them. But somehow the girls had managed to "slip through the cracks."

Were they so hard to find, in fucking Toulon, France?

The real truth was that most citizens, even in modern Western countries like Norway, felt powerless. And the men and women whose job it was to protect them were too often incompetent and lazy. They just didn't give a shit about people who in their narrow view weren't important.

"Any word from the embassy?" Crocker shouted from the balcony into the hotel room where Davis was reading a book about Willie Mays.

"Donaldson has landed. He's on his way."

"It's about time."

A muezzin in a minaret across the street began to recite the call to noon prayer.

> Allahu Akbar. Allahu Akbar.
> Allahu Akbar. Allahu Akbar.
> Ash-hadu an la ilaha ill-Allah.
> Ash-hadu an la ilaha ill-Allah.

Loudspeakers amplified his voice so it echoed off the nearby buildings.

Crocker thought that everyone in the U.S. government, from the president on down, should be required to come to Pakistan and experience the country firsthand. The intense devotional pleading. The desperation and crushing poverty, with millions of slum dwellers pressed cheek to jowl. The cruelty and greed of those with any power. The enormous disparity between the rich and poor—and people thought it was bad in the States? The hovels that passed for hospitals, schools, and prisons. The millions of illiterate, ignorant people essentially living in the fifteenth century, who were perfect fodder for religious fanatics and demagogues.

Admitting that he was neither a prognosticator nor an intellectual, Crocker sensed that something important was happening in this far corner of the globe. Pakistan—with 180 million people. Its enemy India, with over a billion poised across the border. Both countries armed with nuclear weapons. As was China, with another 1.3 billion people, which loomed over both.

They were standing at the nexus of something. A moment in history. A cultural and political battlefield.

Crocker and his men weren't just boots on the ground. They were part of the most highly trained and versatile military unit in history. But as talented as they were, they depended on political leaders to deploy them wisely.

Crocker was thinking about all the missed opportunities to crush al-Qaeda dating back to the late '90s, when Davis emerged through the curtains, his blue eyes squinting into the hazy glare.

"Donaldson's here," he announced.

"Thanks." Crocker took a deep breath and stepped inside, where the air-conditioned air cleaved to his skin.

Donaldson's long face and body moved in deep shadow. Two shorter men in gray suits hung by his sides. He'd seen the shorter and stouter of the two before, at the meeting in Islamabad weeks earlier—Jim Anders.

"This is turning out to be one long, crazy fishing expedition," Donaldson started off in his deep Carolina drawl. He wore a tan cotton suit with a white shirt open at the collar. "Where the hell are we now?"

The SEAL team leader recounted what he had learned so far, starting with his trip to the Club Rosa in Marseille. When he got to the raid at the farm, Donaldson leaned forward on the cream-colored leather sofa.

"I thought I told you I didn't want any more casualties," he said, clasping his hands in front of him.

"You said 'collateral casualties.' I wouldn't put the men at the farm in that category."

A big smile creased the CIA officer's weathered face. "I wouldn't either, Crocker. Nicely done."

Maybe he wasn't so bad after all.

"Thanks."

Donaldson turned to the thick-necked, gray-suited man to his right and asked, "What do you think, Anders?"

Anders pulled at the front of his Brooks Brothers shirt. "Feels thin."

Crocker: "I assume you're talking about the trail of evidence."

"Yes," Donaldson answered. "Feels thin."

The suit on his left agreed.

"Which part?" Crocker asked, trying to keep his composure. "The evidence linking Zaman to the *Syrena,* or the trail of Malie Tingvoll?"

"Both, Crocker. Both."

"I don't disagree. But what does it cost us to go after the *Syrena*?"

"Potentially a great deal."

Anders popped open a briefcase and handed his boss a sheet of paper. The senior officer propped a pair of gold-framed reading glasses on his long nose. "First of all, what do you know about this ship?"

"Nothing, really. The port facility security officer told us it was some kind of freighter. Medium capacity."

Donaldson glanced at the printout. "Turns out that it's registered in Yemen."

Crocker knew that was bad.

"The Yemenis don't like us much," Donaldson continued. "We touch a ship of theirs and they're going to scream bloody murder."

The guy on Donaldson's left agreed. "They'll use it as an opportunity to create an incident. Get the White House involved, the UN. We don't want that."

Donaldson clasped his hands together. "So we can expect zero cooperation from the Yemenis."

"Understood."

"Number two, the *Syrena*'s next scheduled port of call is Salalah, in Oman," the CIA officer continued. "Arrives there tomorrow morning."

Crocker sat forward on the edge of his chair. "Which means that if we're going to board it in Salalah, we have to move quickly."

Donaldson took a long swig of the Coca-Cola Davis had brought from the minibar under the desk on the opposite wall, then wiped his mouth with the back of his hand.

"The Omanis are reasonable people," he explained, "who happen to be our friends. But they're also extremely proud. Which means whatever kind of operation is launched on their soil they're going to want to do themselves."

Crocker spent a moment considering how to negotiate the obstacles that had just been put in his way.

"Can we ask the Omanis to monitor the ship when it docks, to see who gets off?" he asked.

Donaldson looked at Anders, who frowned.

"I don't know how seriously they'll take our request, but we can try."

"How about a couple of us go there ourselves to watch what comes off the ship?" Crocker inquired.

"I expected you to ask that."

"Nothing official. We act like tourists. Witnesses. If we see anything, we alert the Omanis."

"Unwise."

"Completely undercover."

"And what happens if no one debarks in Salalah?"

"We proceed to the next port of call and do the same thing," Crocker answered.

"That seems unnecessary."

"Why?"

"We've got local assets who can do that."

"You know as well as I do that we can't rely on people who aren't ours."

"I said no."

"Some of them sympathize with the fundamentalists. They don't have as much at stake."

"Dammit, Crocker. You think this is the only operation we're running here? Let it fucking go!"

Crocker bit his bottom lip and started to tremble with an anger he had to use all his self-control to contain.

Shifting his gaze from the glass table between them to Donaldson's knotted-up face, he said, "All of us on the team feel badly that Zaman got away. We don't want to give up on him or this girl from Norway. We all have families. It was sickening to see what they did to those kidnapped girls. There must be something we can do." Crocker immediately scolded himself for pleading. For sounding weak.

Donaldson looked at Davis and Mancini, who were leaning on the wall behind their leader, and smiled. "It's my job to look at the bigger picture. To look at the totality of all the things we have going on. You might think this is important, but I'm telling you that in the grand scheme of things, it isn't. You and your men have done enough."

"We don't feel that way," Crocker snapped.

"I appreciate your commitment and understand your frustration," Donaldson said as Anders shut his briefcase. "We have experts back at Langley working on the laptop you fished out of the pond. They're not convinced that the e-mails Rafiq received even originated with Zaman."

"I disagree." Crocker sensed what was coming next.

"We brought your team in for a specific mission, which unfortunately went wrong. It's time to send you and your men home."

No!

Donaldson rose; his bookends followed. "I'm sure you gentlemen miss your families. I'm sure they miss you, too," he said with all the sincerity of a Hallmark greeting card.

Crocker resisted the impulse to reach out and grab Donaldson by the throat. Struggling to keep his cool, he watched the tall man in the tan suit turn and saunter out, with the two suits following. One of them cracked a joke he couldn't hear. Their laughter was muffled by the closing door.

Crocker's heart pounded so hard he thought it was going to jump out of his chest. His fists and teeth were clenched. All the hatred of authority he'd accumulated since he was in grade school rushed to the surface.

He looked up to see the defeat on Davis's face. It was like a dagger pushed into his throat.

The three men were quietly packing their gear when Akil arrived from the port, looking pleased with himself. Sweat had formed two large *U*s under the arms of his pale blue shirt.

"What have you got?" Crocker asked.

In his big hand Akil clutched a quarter-inch sheaf of papers he said contained the lists of crew members and passengers who had passed through the Karachi port in the past eight days.

The four men abandoned their packing and tore through the lists, but found no Malie Tingvoll or Abu Rasul Zaman. Not that they had expected to see either name.

The dozen people listed as the crew of the *Syrena* were all men, mostly of what seemed to be Somali and Lebanese descent.

Davis did notice something—the ship was described as a tanker, not a cargo ship.

"What kind of tanker?" Crocker asked.

"I wasn't able to find that out," Akil answered.

"Hmm..."

"You want me to go back?"

Crocker stood looking down at the top of the table he

had punched and cracked earlier, wondering how much it was going to cost to replace, when Ritchie walked in pulling a suitcase on wheels. Behind him followed a very tired-looking Mikael Klausen, wearing a beige raincoat, a sky blue shirt that matched his eyes, jeans, and brown loafers, his straight blond hair sticking up.

In his cloud of frustration and regret, Crocker had forgotten about him.

Now the Norwegian stood before him, asking what they'd learned so far. It surprised Crocker how hard he found it to answer.

Klausen knitted his pale brow and listened carefully. His hand rubbed his jaw like he was hoping a genie would pop out.

"And your government turned down your request to proceed to Salalah? Is that correct?"

"Yes. Their main interest is Zaman, and they believe that the evidence linking the ship to him isn't strong enough to justify the problems it could cause with the Omanis. Our contact, Mr. Donaldson, said he would pursue the matter with the government of Oman. I don't know how strongly he'll do that."

Klausen folded his short arms across his chest. "Give me an hour or so to make some calls. I'm checked into a room down the hall."

Minutes after Klausen left, Crocker was in the bedroom talking to his wife. He was interrupted by a knock at the door. It was Davis, reporting that Lou Donaldson wanted him to attend a meeting at the U.S. consulate in half an hour.

"Why?"

Davis handed the phone over. According to Anders,

who was still on the line, the meeting concerned Abu Rasul Zaman.

"I'll have a car waiting for you downstairs in ten minutes," Anders said.

Crocker told Holly he'd call back, then reminded Anders that he was staying in the Sheraton, which was only a few hundred yards from the consulate.

"It's almost impossible to enter the diplomatic enclave if you're not in an official vehicle," Anders explained. "Security here is very tight."

"I'll manage."

"Dammit, Crocker."

"See you in ten."

Nine minutes later, a perplexed Tom Crocker was ushered into a video conference room and shown to a large leather chair in front of a crescent-shaped table that faced a wall displaying a series of TV monitors. At the opposite end of the walnut crescent sat Lou Donaldson talking to Jim Anders, who was beside him. Another gray suit stood behind them, leaning on the back of Anders's chair.

A big woman with a pile of brown hair occupied the middle seat and spooned yogurt into her mouth when she wasn't speaking into a cell phone. Next to her was a quiet, almost invisible Asian man in a shirt and tie, sparse black mustache, and black-framed glasses.

Donaldson frowned at Crocker and growled to the assembled, "All right, he's here. Let's get started."

Anders picked up a phone from the console in front of him, and soon the lights dimmed and the monitors lit up. Serious-looking men and women appeared on five of the ten screens. They introduced themselves as the director and deputy director of the Al-Qaeda Working Group from CIA headquarters; the deputy director of the Counter-terrorism Center (CTC), also at Langley; the CIA station chiefs in Kabul and Oman.

They were all business.

Crocker learned right away that the officials at Langley were taking the *Syrena* more seriously than he'd thought. The station chief in Oman reported that the Omanis were prepared to board and search the vessel as soon as it docked at Salalah.

Donaldson seemed pleased.

The woman to Crocker's right asked about the latest intel on Zaman. She pointed out that Crocker was the last American to see him in person.

The two representatives of the Al-Qaeda Working Group did most of the talking. They cited reports that tracked Zaman's recent movements into north Waziri-stan, then into Khost, in eastern Afghanistan, where he was believed to have attended a meeting of local tribal leaders.

"There's no question that he's the operational leader now," a bearded male analyst said from Langley. "We hear through our assets that he's planning something big. You know, to make a statement that al-Qaeda is back."

"He needs to," the woman next to Crocker said. "Lately, Lashkar-e-Taiba has stolen their thunder." She was referring to the Pakistani terrorist organization that had carried out the bloody attack on Mumbai, India, in November 2008, which resulted in the death of 175 peo-ple, including dozens of Westerners. Crocker had passed through Mumbai only a week before the attacks and had eaten dinner at the Leopold Café, where the terrorists later sprayed the crowd with automatic-weapon fire, killing ten tourists.

The CTC woman on the monitor drew Crocker's attention back to the conference with her shrill, loud voice. "If we got that intel regarding Zaman and his current location from the ISI, I wouldn't give it a whole lot of credence," she said through the speaker.

He agreed. He knew that a large portion of the Pakistan intelligence outfit known as the ISI (Inter-Services Intelligence) secretly supported the Taliban and al-Qaeda, and had for years. The Pakistani government steadfastly refused to acknowledge the ISI's duplicity. And many U.S. officials didn't want to believe it.

But the Pakistanis were playing a double game—officially expressing their opposition to al-Qaeda and other Islamic terrorist organizations, but secretly colluding with them through the ISI. The reasons for this were complex, and reflected the treacherous nature of Pakistani politics and the country's obsession with India.

But that's not what they were there to discuss. The CIA analysts turned their attention to an official al-Qaeda proclamation that had come out of Peshawar the week before.

A man with a salt-and-pepper beard who was identified as the head of CIA's Al-Qaeda Working Group explained that the statement was mainly a reiteration of al-Qaeda's longtime goals: one, to involve the United States and its proxies in a war of attrition in the Middle East; two, to drive the Jews out of Jerusalem and Palestine and return these areas to the Palestinians; and three, to overthrow the Saudi monarchy and establish a caliphate to rule the Arabian Peninsula. What stood out, he said, was a paragraph at the end that vowed "to soon unite the trinity of objectives in one important event."

None of the CIA analysts seemed to know what that meant.

The Asian man with the mustache read from a chart of NSA statistics and algorithms that measured the frequency with which "attacks against the West" had been mentioned on jihadist websites and monitored phone calls. They had spiked in recent weeks. "The confluence of Muslim holidays and the recently stepped-up Israeli-Palestinian peace talks could explain what we're seeing," he cautioned.

The head of CTC disagreed. He felt that some sort of attack was imminent. So did the woman to Crocker's right.

As they debated, the SEAL team leader looked down at his watch. The meeting had already lasted an hour and fifteen minutes. From his perspective, it hadn't accomplished anything. Mikael Klausen and his men were waiting. He had nothing more to add to the discussion.

In his mind's eye he saw the girls' pale, bruised faces. The faraway looks in their eyes.

The anger he felt brought clarity and purpose.

He rose and walked quickly to the elevator, ignoring the footsteps that hurried after him.

"We're not finished, Crocker," Anders called, out of breath.

"I am."

"Where the hell are you going?"

"There are things I need to accomplish."

"What things? What are you referring to?"

He stepped into the elevator and watched the doors close and shut out Anders's troubled face.

Outside the consulate, Crocker moved purposefully.

Action, not talk.

Passing the waiting limo, he walked briskly through the iron gate, through ranks of heavily armed soldiers guarding the perimeter of concrete barriers stacked high with sandbags, and continued down Abdullah Haroon Road.

Although the sultry air caused his shirt to stick to his skin and sweat to run down his pant legs, he felt better. Almost exhilarated.

Crocker was at his best when in motion. When the fear or danger grew so intense that he acted without thinking. When he did what he knew he had to do.

CHAPTER FIFTEEN

The only easy day was yesterday.

—U.S. Navy SEAL motto

HE RODE in the Sheraton Karachi elevator with a youngish couple from Vancouver who'd just been shopping on Tariq Road. Both tall and full of pride, wearing designer jeans, carrying multiple shopping bags. She had blond windswept hair, a tight little mouth, a dimpled chin. Assuming that the SEAL team leader was an American, the young couple started complaining about the room service at the hotel.

He half listened, still wrestling with his emotional response to the meeting. But the outrage behind their words drew his attention.

"It's a crime, with what we're paying," the man said, thrusting out his square chin. "My wife ordered eggs Benedict for breakfast and they brought us something that looked like it had been scooped out of the sewer."

"Completely disgusting. It smelled bad, too."

"I'm sorry to hear that."

She tossed her head back and swiveled her narrow hips as she stepped off. "We're never coming back!"

Why? Because of the eggs? What about the fact that Pakistan is harboring terrorists who want to destroy our way of life?

He wanted to put her over his knee and spank her; tell both of them to wake up. But what good would that do?

His annoyance was quickly drowned in the flood of concerns roaring through his head.

What happens now? What do I say to the men?

The room he returned to smelled of burnt coffee and mildew. Klausen stood by the bed, speaking Norwegian on the hotel phone. Confusion, anger, frustration.

"He's working on something," Davis whispered from one of the chairs by the window. He and Mancini were watching a soccer match on TV with the sound turned off.

Crocker couldn't hear clearly over the guttural sounds coming from Klausen's mouth.

"What did you say?"

"Klausen is trying to get us to Oman."

He wanted to change into shorts and go for a long run, but instead waited on the Norwegian, who slammed down the phone.

"Corruption," Klausen snorted. "With all the other things we have to deal with, they add this! Always! Human complications."

"Who?"

Klausen crossed the pale green carpet to Crocker and took him by the arm. "What do you say we go back to the mountains? It's so good there. It's healthy. We climb as far as we feel like. The air is pure. There's nobody in our way. Here... we have to deal with one son of a bitch after another. You deal with one greedy person, you pay a second. A third one pops up behind him with his goddamn hand out!"

Crocker watched Klausen's cheeks turn a rich crimson color.

"Davis said you were working on something," the American said, hoping to turn the conversation in a positive direction.

"Yes." The special advisor to the king of Norway inhaled deeply and shifted gears.

Mancini punched off the TV. He and Davis turned in their chairs and listened.

"I've arranged for a Gulfstream to fly you to Salalah."

"When?"

"As soon as possible. You'll land at the military airport. A man from the Norwegian embassy will meet you there. Since you don't have visas, you'll avoid immigration. It's all arranged."

"Wait a minute," Crocker interjected. "Donaldson has agreed to this?"

"That's correct. You have three hours to board the ship and search it," Klausen continued. "Then you have to get back on the Gulfstream and return to Karachi."

It wasn't a lot of time, but it was something.

"What do you think?" Klausen asked, running a hand through his hair.

"That's great news."

"At least it gets you there, yes? If you find anything, this man from my embassy, his name is Halvor Reiersen. He's an ex-soldier who is in charge of security."

"Halvor?"

"Hal for short. He'll meet you at the airport. If, God

willing, you find Malie, Halvor will contact the proper Omani authorities. He's a close friend of an influential Omani general. They will make any arrests, or seize the ship, if necessary."

Crocker and his team had loads of experience with Visit, Board, Search, and Seizure (VBSS) operations. In fact, Crocker had taught the course to various platoons of SEAL Teams One, Two, and Six, and to combat troops stationed in Central America at Special Boat Unit 26.

During Operation Just Cause in Panama, he and his team had boarded and searched hundreds of vessels on the Panama Canal, capturing hundreds of General Noriega's PDF combatants, weapons, demolition supplies, and valuable intelligence. Everything from large oil transports to carved canoes. He'd also run VBSSs on the open seas, in which he and his men would parachute in and, using cigarette boats, overtake ships. As the assault team's lead climber, Crocker was responsible for being the first SEAL to ascend a telescoping pole with a ladder attached to get onto the deck of the target ship.

Klausen said, "Of course, you're to communicate immediately with Mr. Donaldson if you uncover any information that might be of value to him."

"Of course. What about weapons?" Crocker asked, thinking ahead.

"What kind of weapons do you need?"

"Submachine guns preferably, but automatic handguns at least. Chances are we'll encounter resistance if we board the ship."

Mikael Klausen, who hadn't thought of that, considered the problem now. "This could be difficult."

"Weapons are necessary. We entered the country without them. I can't risk sending my men onto the ship unarmed."

"How many of you are there?"

"Five, including me."

"I'll talk to Reiersen and see what we can arrange."

"All right."

"Anything else?"

Crocker said, "Get us to Salalah, and we'll take care of the rest."

The Gulfstream V loaded with five SEALs landed shortly past one in the morning on a straight asphalt strip along the alluvial plain before the rough Jebel Akhdar mountains. A big half-moon hung slightly off-center in the blue-black sky.

"That's where Job is buried," Mancini said, pointing to the rough outline of peaks in the distance.

"Who the hell is Job?"

"You don't know Job? The prophet from the Bible. The blessed, righteous man who was tempted by Satan."

"Oh, him."

"Remember the story of how God tested Job's faith by taking away his children, wealth, and health?"

"I didn't pay attention in Sunday school," Crocker said. In fact, he'd hardly given any school a thought until he joined the navy at age eighteen. Before then he'd been a bat-out-of-hell shitkicker more interested in riding motorcycles and raising hell with his friends than in any form of study. The navy and SEALs had given him a purpose and goals.

"Where do you find this stuff?" Ritchie asked Mancini.

"I'm curious about things. I read and retain."

"Read and retain—I like that," Akil remarked.

They taxied past jets from Air India Express and Jazeera Airways, and stopped before the military terminal. A thick-shouldered man in camouflage pants and a white T-shirt waited outside.

"I'm Hal Reiersen," he said in a thick Norwegian accent, extending a hand with stars tattooed on the knuckles.

Several French-made helicopters, two British SEPECAT Jaguar jet fighters, and a C-130 Hercules transport all painted with Royal Air Force of Oman insignia stood behind him.

"My name is Tom Crocker. This is the rest of my team."

The night air was warm and fragrant with the lemony smell of frankincense, which grew in the nearby mountains.

"Let's proceed to the port."

"Good idea."

They piled into a black van. Crocker sat up front next to Reiersen, who was built like a weightlifter and had an undistinguished round face and short, very light blond hair.

"The port is a few minutes from here. There are only two major hotels."

"We're not planning to spend the night."

"Oh."

There was no one on the highway that hugged the rocky coast stretching west, past a small fishing harbor. Then came a long strip of moonlit beach on their right.

"The Bedouins used to control this area," Mancini explained from the back row of seats. "It was the beginning of the legendary frankincense trail."

"Thanks, professor."

A few miles past the city of Salalah, they entered the port area, which was bigger and more modern than Crocker had expected, with a half-dozen modern cranes and wharves stacked high with containers.

The gate was locked, so Reiersen had to get out to find the person in charge. He returned ten minutes later accompanied by a short man in tan overalls and a round Bedouin-style hat.

"This is Samir, the night manager of the port."

"As-Salamu Alaykum." Bowing like a character out of a movie.

"*As-Salamu Alaykum*. Peace be with you, too."

"The night . . . it is beautiful."

"Yes, it is."

Moonlight glistened off the whites of Samir's eyes.

Reiersen cleared his throat. "He told me the *Syrena* never docked here."

"What!" Crocker did a double take. *Did we land in the right fucking place?*

The night manager spoke a little English in short sibilant bursts. "The *Syrena,* no. Never dock here, sir. Not this day."

"But it was supposed to dock yesterday at noon, correct?"

"Cor-rect."

"What happened?"

Samir threw up his arms. "No here. You can see." He waved at the pier where a half-dozen ships lolled in the water.

"You're sure about this?"

"Yes."

"It's a tanker, isn't it?" Crocker asked.

"A not very big one."

Mancini, who had climbed halfway up the fence, shouted over his shoulder, "I don't see any tankers here, boss."

"This is messed up."

"What you mean?" Samir asked.

"Bad, Samir. Not good."

The night manager twisted his mouth into a curious half-smile. "Why? You have friend on the ship? You are expecting something?"

Crocker slapped the side of the van. "Where the fuck did it go, then?"

The Norwegian and the five Americans waited the better part of an hour at the gate, trying out various theories, while the night manager went inside to see if he could ascertain the *Syrena*'s current location.

As the minutes ticked by, defeat wormed its way into Crocker's head, started slowly eating away at his confidence. *I screwed up. What have I done?*

This would be the second or third really bad decision he'd made in the past month. The first was letting Zaman slip away. His CIA handlers would probably report their displeasure to SOCOM in Tampa, Florida, and Naval SpecWar in Coronado, California.

Complaints would be filed. Disciplinary action taken.

Holly was annoyed at him, too. *She'll be even madder if she finds out that I've been court-martialed.*

He imagined various responses to that possibility—hiring a good lawyer, writing a detailed report that explained all his actions, retiring and finding other employment, even leaving the States to work with Klausen in Norway. But none of them seemed to dampen his growing sense of dread.

"Where the hell is Samir?" Crocker asked out loud.

At half past two the moon was high in the sky, and they were running out of time. Reiersen, who was the only one with the credentials to get past the sleepy guards, went inside to check, grumbling to himself in Norwegian.

Fifteen minutes more of standing around and yakking about college football, and Ritchie shouted, "Here they come!"

Three men strode toward them—Reiersen, Samir, and a guy in a white robe. Samir waved something over his head.

"What he's got?"

He had news. The *Syrena* had in fact bypassed Salalah, where it was scheduled to stop, and docked at Port Sultan Qaboos, some 540 miles up the coast instead.

"Where's Sultan Qaboos, exactly?" Crocker asked.

"Right outside the capital of Muscat."

"And the ship's still there?"

"According to the latest communications, yes," Reiersen answered. "But Qaboos doesn't know for how much longer."

Now what do we do?

Crocker, who had led his men way out on a limb, wanted to get to Muscat asap. But there were myriad complications. Like the fact that he and his team didn't have the visas that were required to enter Oman. Secondly, the pilot of the Gulfstream V had been hired only to fly them from Karachi to Salalah and back. Third, Akil was running a fever.

Reiersen offered a solution. "We can all travel in the plane I flew in on."

It was something.

So an hour later the six men crammed into the single-engine plane, which puttered up the Gulf of Oman coast. Dawn was breaking when they touched down in Muscat. A majestic glow from the east turned the faces of the minarets and white buildings of the capital gold.

Reiersen had radioed ahead for help: SEAL candy, aka 800-milligram Motrin for Akil. Weapons. A satellite phone.

They were met by two SUVs and a Norwegian who called himself Jakob and had spent two years at USC as a member of the track and field team. He looked like a Trojan. Square jaw, wide shoulders, a close-clipped mustache and beard.

They sped to the port as fast as the vehicles could take them—only to find that the *Syrena* wasn't at Sultan Qaboos, either.

"You got to be kidding!" Like some kind of cosmic joke.

According to the port manager—a Muslim from Bangladesh named Mohammed—it had left at 11 p.m. Approximately eight hours ago. His records showed that the tanker had docked at two in the afternoon, received two hundred gallons of diesel fuel, and left for the Persian Gulf.

"What's its current destination?"

"Bushehr, Iran."

"Iran?"

"Yes."

That posed a whole host of other complications. First

and foremost, the Iranian government—a declared enemy of the United States—would never give Crocker and his team permission to enter.

"Did anyone disembark in Qaboos?" Crocker asked.

"What do you mean, sir?" Mohammed asked back, smoothing his black handlebar mustache.

"Did your people see anybody leave the ship while it was docked here?"

Mohammed had a few missing teeth. His longish hair was greased back. He projected goodwill and sincerity. "I don't have that information."

"Can you find out?"

Fifteen minutes later he returned with the answer. "One of the fuel men saw some people get off. He thinks there were four of them, but isn't certain."

"Four men?"

"Three Arabic-looking men and at least one woman."

Crocker's eyes lit up. "Was she blond?"

"He couldn't tell. She was wearing a chador."

"Can you find out their names?"

"We don't have that information," Mohammed said. "You will have to check with immigration."

That was a risky proposition, since Crocker and his men had entered Oman illegally. Jakob volunteered and ran off.

"Does this fuel man have any idea where those four individuals who got off the ship went?" Crocker asked the port manager, praying that he had an answer.

"No. I'm sorry. He said they were met by two men in a black Mercedes. A large one. One man never got out. He saw the four passengers get into the Mercedes limo and drive off very fast."

"Thanks."

Very fast. Like they were running away from something, which apparently they were. Because Jakob came back to report that the port immigration official said that no passengers had disembarked from the *Syrena*.

"Impossible," Crocker remarked.

"He was probably paid to look the other way. That happens here."

No shit.

Crocker's stomach growled as he sorted through this new set of challenges.

Their minds sharpened by chai tea and grilled sardine sandwiches purchased from a canteen nearby, the five Americans and two Norwegians put their heads together. Time was critical. They decided they needed to fan out in order to be most efficient.

Hal would call his Omani friend General al-Maskari and see what he could pry out of immigration. Mancini would use the satellite phone to communicate with Mikael Klausen, Lou Donaldson, and others to try to ascertain the current location of the *Syrena*. Reiersen and Ritchie would eyeball outgoing flights at Muscat International Airport. Crocker and Davis would go with Jakob to check the registers at the major hotels.

Crocker's thinking went like this: A transfer seemed to have taken place. In other words, Cyrus delivered Malie to "Sheik Rastani." Assuming that his supposition was correct, Crocker doubted that a sheik would risk doing something so potentially embarrassing on his own turf. Likely he'd flown to Muscat from a neighboring Arab country—Yemen, Saudi Arabia, Kuwait.

If Rastani could afford to spend a million dollars on

a girl, he'd probably be staying at a local luxury hotel, where he could examine the goods—i.e., Malie—before a deal was concluded and money exchanged.

The city, which was just coming to life, boasted a handful of five-star hotels—the Al Bustan Palace, Shangri-La's Barr Al Jissah, the Chedi Muscat, the Grand Hyatt, and the InterContinental. They were located downtown, in the upscale government and residential district along the beach.

Jakob drove the SUV past the recently constructed and very majestic Sultan Qaboos Grand Mosque, which, he said, "Cost a couple billion dollars. Contains the world's second-largest woven carpet, which weighs twenty-one tons."

"That's a lot of bald sheep," Crocker remarked.

"Where's the world's largest carpet?" Davis asked.

"Tehran," Akil answered weakly. He was running a fever and drifting in and out of sleep.

The InterContinental wasn't nearly as impressive as the mosque, but it was still elegant and large, even by Western standards. Crocker and Jakob entered the tall white lobby and strode to the front desk. The big American said he was there for a breakfast business meeting with Sheik Rastani, who might have checked in as Mr. Rastani.

The polite young clerk reported that there was no one by the name of Rastani registered at the hotel.

Crocker told him that Mr. Rastani would have checked in sometime the previous afternoon or evening with an associate or two and his daughter.

"No, sir. I'm sorry."

They followed the same routine at the Chedi and Grand Hyatt and were met with the same response.

The Al Bustan Palace was the most luxurious by far, an impressive Indian sandstone hexagon surrounded by a lagoon and lush gardens against a backdrop of rugged charcoal gray mountains. It faced the deep blue Gulf of Oman.

The lobby, lined with white marble, reminded Crocker of the inside of a mosque.

"My name is Mr. Wallace," he said to the clerk in the immaculate white robe and red-and-black Omani cap. "My associate and I are here for a lunch meeting with Sheik Rastani."

The man consulted a computer hidden in the counter and asked in English, "Mr. Wallace, do you have an appointment? Because I don't see your name here."

"The sheik is expecting me."

"I'm sorry, sir. I'll have to check. Please have a seat."

Does that mean he's here? Crocker asked himself excitedly, as he led Jakob over to a fountain where they couldn't be overheard.

"Go outside and tell Davis and Akil to watch the garage. They might try to run."

"What about you?" the former Trojan shotputter asked.

"I can handle myself."

Crocker studied the Islamic pattern of the floor tiles, trying to appear inconspicuous and stay calm.

Hearing footsteps approach, he looked up into a face that caused him to stop midbreath. Big, with a large forehead and bulging eyes, a nasty sneer on his thick lips. Both eyes drooped, and one was set lower than the other. A long, deep scar ran from the lower eye to the side of his mouth. He was a thick, muscular man with very short black hair, dressed all in black.

"Mr. Wallace?" he asked in rough American English.

"Yes. Is Cyrus here?"

Malice poured from his eyes. "Follow me."

Crocker did, to an elevator, thinking that the man moved like a wrestler. It was a private lift around the corner from the public ones, which the big man opened with a key.

"How long have you worked for Cyrus?" the American asked.

The big, swarthy man said nothing. Stared ahead.

They stopped at the sixth floor. Two other large Middle Eastern men in white shirts stood waiting in the teak-paneled hallway.

Not a good sign.

One wore tailored gray pants, the other, jeans. They positioned themselves on either side of Crocker and grabbed him by the arms.

"I can walk by myself, thanks."

When the American tried to pull away, the one in the tailored pants with the pockmarked face pointed a Makarov pistol at his head.

They guided unarmed Crocker eight paces down a hallway, then pushed him into a private bathroom, crowded in, and locked the door.

This is trouble.

Four big bodies filled the tight space. Resplendent gold-colored glass tiles covered the walls. The dual-sink counter, fixtures, and floor were all black. Elaborately etched glass doors hid the toilet, urinal, and shower.

Strange place to hold a meeting.

Trying to push back the fear that was pressing in on all sides.

The wrestler put the full weight of his body behind his forearm, which he smashed into Crocker's chest. The American fell back and hit the tile wall.

Fuck…

He saw stars spinning; fought to catch his breath.

The pockmarked guy pushed the muzzle of the weapon into his face.

"Who are you?"

"A Canadian business—"

Smacked him hard in the face.

"What do you want?"

"Cyrus…" Crocker tried to answer, gasping for breath.

"How do you know Cyrus?"

The third guy in jeans was rifling through his pockets. Crocker was glad he'd left his wallet and ID in the SUV.

"Answer! How do you know Cyrus?" the pockmarked dude asked again, grabbing the collar of Crocker's polo and twisting it until he started to choke.

"I met him at a farm…outside Toulon."

Crocker managed to remain calm, in part because his brain was releasing a higher level of a neurotransmitter called neuropeptide Y than was normal with most people. The neuropeptide Y worked as a natural tranquilizer to control his anxiety. He'd also developed his mental toughness over years of vigorous training and experience.

The guy going through his pockets was slick and handsome in a predatory way. The kind of man, Crocker thought, who could easily charm a naïve eighteen-year-old girl.

"Cyrus?" he asked him.

The wrestler reared back and clocked him in the mouth.

Christ!

He tasted blood.

"How do you know Cyrus?"

He tried to pull free, only to get kicked in the nuts. All the air went of him, and he struggled to stay on his feet.

Crocker wanted to say something clever, but his mind wasn't working. He heard the man he thought was Cyrus mumble in Arabic, and tried his best to translate. It went something like this: "Take him away from here. Into the mountains. Shoot him in the head. Dump his body somewhere where the vultures will get to him." Then he started to leave.

"It's over, Cyrus. You're fucked," Crocker said to his back.

The fists came at him rapidly from two directions. He tried to defend himself and fight back, but there was very little room to move.

The wrestler grabbed the front of Crocker's shirt, spun him, and threw him through the shower door, which shattered loudly.

The SEAL chief warrant officer lay half-conscious on the tile floor, hurting, his mind wobbling.

He understood now that it was insane to go in the way he had—no backup, no commo, completely solo.

Sharp pains issued from the back of his head. Blood dripped from his mouth. Figured he had a couple of broken or chipped teeth, maybe a broken rib. Later, he'd have Davis or Mancini tie his chest with binding wrap to immobilize his rib cage.

If I get out of here alive.

Through blurry eyes he saw the pockmarked thug lean down to pull him up, the gunmetal pistol clutched in his fist. The savage leer on his ravaged face told Crocker how much he was going to enjoy torturing an American and watching him die.

"Get up!"

The SEAL team leader flashed back to the video Akil had shown him on the first flight into Karachi.

No fucking way! he said to himself, aware of a thick triangle of glass near his right hand.

"Get up, dead man!"

Grabbing the glass so that it sliced into the edges of his palm, Crocker pushed off the floor and thrust it into the man's neck with all the force he could muster—ripping through cartilage, skin, and bone. The man's half-screams reverberated against the tile walls as he fell back against the sink and, twisting, fired wildly into the ceiling, walls, and floor.

Smoke and cordite hung in the air.

Before Crocker could scramble to his feet, the wrestler was on him, spitting curses and reaching for his throat. Crocker could feel the man's sweat and smell the madness on his breath. His thick hands were strong, with nails that sunk into Crocker's neck.

Doubting that he had the strength or leverage to pry them loose, the American reared his head back and smashed it into the wrestler's nose. Then again, and two more times, until its bridge gave way and he felt the man's warm blood on his face.

But when the American tried to get his feet under him, he slipped on the broken glass, blood, and sweat, and went down hard on his ass.

The wrestler roared and kicked Crocker in the stomach. Then the big man threw himself on him, and the two grappled on the shower floor. Body against body. Strength versus strength.

The physical dynamic of wrestling had never been Crocker's strong suit. But here he was side by side with a beast who was using his powerful legs to push against the door opening and pin him against the wall.

Crushing him.

Each man had his arm around the other's neck, but the wrestler had the advantage, because Crocker couldn't move his legs or arms. The pressure against his ribs and chest was growing by the second, making it increasingly hard to breathe.

Trapped and losing ground, Crocker heard something move by the sink.

Peering past the wrestler's thick head and chest, through the shower doorway he saw the pockmarked guy trying to push himself up on his elbow and steady the pistol as blood gushed from his neck. It was a desperate last effort. His hand shook badly. But he still had the determination to curl his finger around the trigger and squeeze.

Shit…

Crocker ducked behind the wrestler as the shots rang out.

Three bullets in succession glanced off the floor and struck the wrestler, who jerked and groaned.

The pistol clattered across the tile floor.

"In sha'Allah," moaned the man by the sink. God willing.

The big wrestler was trembling and loosening his grip

enough that Crocker could pull away and stand in a crouch.

On the floor by the sink, the pockmarked man lay still in a dark pool of his own blood, his mouth caught between a smile and grimace, a look of expectation in his eyes.

Crocker stepped quickly out of the shower and recovered the Makarov pistol. Then turned and pointed it at the wrestler's head.

His big yellowish eyes pleaded up at him. "No."

"Yes!"

Two quick rounds into his skull. Then silence.

Just the loud thumping of Crocker's heart as he reached down and retrieved a hotel keycard and passport from the dead man's pocket.

CHAPTER SIXTEEN

Without knowledge, skill cannot be focused. Without skill, strength cannot be brought to bear. Without strength, knowledge cannot be applied.

—Alexander the Great's chief physician

USING A wet paper towel to wipe the blood from his face and neck, Crocker remembered his circumstances—the hotel, his men waiting near the garage, Sheik Rastani, Cyrus and, hopefully, Malie, in a suite not far away—and knew that more trouble was coming.

He strode down the hallway unaware that he was leaving a trail of bloody footprints.

He felt like Clint Eastwood in *The Good, The Bad and the Ugly,* walking straight into the face of evil. Determined to stop the wolves. But there was no Ennio Morricone music playing in the background. No two-note howl to let the bad guys know he was coming to kick their asses.

Just the pounding of his boots into the carpet.

Nor was there time to call for help.

Crocker assumed that the shots fired in the bathroom

had been heard and that Sheik Rastani, Cyrus, and others were scrambling to stop him and/or escape.

He wasn't going to let that happen, not when he was so close he could smell victory in the air ahead of him.

His heart pounded. His mouth, ribs, and neck hurt. His teeth ached; so did his face and jaw.

The adrenaline shoved all physical pain aside and pushed him forward, around the corner, where he saw the double mahogany doors to Suite 6C.

Bingo!

He knew this was his destination because of the bloody keycard and cardboard sleeve he clutched in his right hand. In his left he held the Makarov the pockmarked thug had dropped on the floor of the bathroom. Still warm.

He put his ear against the door and listened. An announcer's voice in English reporting on a flood in the Philippines. A rescue was under way.

I'm glad.

Then tried the keycard. The lock flashed green and beeped. One deep breath later, he swung the door open and waited.

Come out, you motherfuckers.

The newscast segued into a Madonna song on the radio, her voice soaring and pleading at the same time.

His mind made thousands of lightning-quick calculations—the depth of the space, the darkness of the shadows, the quality of the light, the smell in the air.

It was a big, luxurious open space divided into functional areas. His eyes scanned right to left. A big flat-screen TV on a paneled wall. Tan leather sofas, a vase full of orchids, a view of the ocean, a prayer rug on the floor near the window. A half-eaten plate of scrambled eggs, a cup of tea, steam rising from a metal and glass table, and a hallway at an angle to his far left. Someone had been here seconds before.

Every second marked with a beat of his heart.

The song climbed to a crescendo.

He sensed that there was at least one other door into the suite, and somewhere people were escaping.

Gritting his teeth, he held the pistol in the ready position—like an extension of his arm—and stepped inside. Crossed past the sunken sitting area, swung around the table with the orchids, and entered the hall.

Like entering a bubble that was about to explode.

His back against the wall, he waited as the seconds ticked from a clock in a room to his right. Thought he heard a low voice like a moan. Maybe the wind? Or a big cat?

How likely is that?

Then something moved behind him and he spun, half expecting a panther or a cougar to lunge at him.

Phugt! Phugt! Phugt! Like someone spitting.

Bullets from a silenced pistol whizzed by his chin and tore into the wall. Throwing himself back, he crouched behind the corner. Residue of wallboard pelted his face and stuck in his eyes.

Tearing. Wiping the dust away. Trying to focus.

Aware of footsteps hurrying across the floor in the opposite direction, he stole a quick look only to see the blurry backs of two men running to the door. One wearing a long white shirt and pulling a large black suitcase, the other in a white dishdasha and *ghutra.*

The one pulling the suitcase turned and squeezed off a succession of shots. Crocker aimed and fired back.

A bullet tore into the man's arm, causing him to let go of the suitcase and scramble out the door.

Crocker had a split second to decide whether to pursue them or keep going.

The person he was really looking for was Malie, so he wiped his eyes with the back of his hand and continued down the hallway, inch by inch. Rooms to his left, two doors to his right.

Trying to calculate how much time the men had to get away. Confident that Davis, Akil, and Jakob would do what they could to stop them. Then considering the problems they might encounter.

There was absolutely nothing he could do about that now.

The first opening left led to a kitchen. Lots of cherry wood and stainless steel. A shiny double-doored refrigerator purring. Toblerone chocolate bar, a bottle of Evian water, two Orangina bottles, a roll of paper towels, and a money belt on the counter, but no people inside.

Four steps farther down the hallway, he pushed down on the polished chrome handle and kicked the first door open. The mirrored closet door reflected back his image. Not recognizing himself, he almost fired.

The ferocity in his own eyes surprised him.

Shit, do I really look like that?

He took a deep breath from his diaphragm and counted to four before exhaling, then repeated the process a half-dozen times, the way Holly had taught him. Boxed breathing, she called it. Something she'd learned from yoga class at the gym.

He felt more centered in his body, clearheaded.

The room appeared empty. Opened suitcases. Clothes

scattered across the double bed and floor. A travel guide to Oman open on the nightstand, next to a stack of CDs. A copy of the French edition of *GQ*.

A pair of women's white high-heeled shoes by the drape-covered window. The shoes new. Barely worn, if ever. He stepped over them and opened a door to the right of the nightstand.

Another dark hallway that reeked of gasoline, with a sitting room to the right that overlooked the hotel gardens. To his left, a walk-in closet. Mostly empty, except for a silver-gray man's suit wrapped in clear plastic, a pair of men's sandals.

Sensing something emerging from the sitting room across the hallway, he twisted his body left to reduce the angle of access through the door. His heart skipped a beat as a gun behind him discharged.

Bam! Bam! Bam!

Intense heat splashed against his face, and searing metal grazed the skin above his jaw.

His ears numb, he spun down to the carpeted floor and held himself up on his left forearm. Caught sight of the dark figure out of the corner of his eye.

A torch of some sort illuminated the man's face and torso.

With the pistol in his right fist, Crocker fired repeatedly into the man's shins and knees. First the sound of cracking, splintering bone, then a bottle exploded against the edge of the doorway and flames burst into the closet.

An eruption of gold singed Crocker's eyebrows, eyelashes, and hair.

He jumped back into the closet as the man wailed from the sitting room and fire spread in the hallway between.

A patch of gasoline flames jumped onto the right front of Crocker's shirt. He ripped the polo off and flung it against the wall. Smelled his own burning flesh.

Lying on his back, he raised the pistol in both hands and discharged round after round in the direction of the groans across the hall, spending the ammo completely. Then, pulling the suit from the hanger and ripping off the plastic, Crocker used it as a shield to cover his face and torso as he hurried through the flames into the sitting room.

Breathing hard, he stood over the man who had thrown the Molotov cocktail, watching his face relax with a final sigh, a kind of prayer. Then heard a rattle from his throat.

Another wolf down.

Crocker's whole body throbbing with determination and fear, he felt above his right jawbone where blood oozed from a shallow crease. The skin near his right shoulder was red and tender. The smoke and heat burned his eyes.

He had to dismiss the pain now and recover the pistol from the man on the floor, because the one he'd been using was empty.

A terrible, soul-wrenching grimace leered from the man's gaunt, bearded face. It didn't appear to be Cyrus or anyone else he could identify. Dark pants, a white shirt, a round gold pendant around his neck engraved with the throne verse of Ayat al-Kursi from the Koran.

After prying the Glock 19 from the dead man's fingers, he waited, expecting others. Then squeezed past the flames that were climbing up the wall and entering the closet. Through thick, astringent smoke, five more paces to a door that was locked.

A smoke alarm screeched and overhead sprinklers went off.

His head and shirt were practically drenched when he tried the a door second time.

Same result.

He had to get inside. So, holding the Glock in his left hand, he cocked his right foot back and smashed his boot into the door near the lock. The slick wood splintered and buckled but didn't break. The second time he lifted his foot back, he slipped on the carpet and fell.

Bracing himself against the back wall, he kicked again. This time a piece of the frame shattered and the door came halfway open.

Standing behind the right door frame, he pushed it in with the hand holding the Glock. No response came from inside the bathroom. Just the hiss of falling water and smoke, which seemed to grow thicker by the second.

Seven rapid beats of his heart before he poked his head in. Through the light gray haze, he saw opulent green marble and gold interrupted by a large white object hanging from a hook on the left wall.

Crocker identified it as a wedding dress with a ruffled skirt and a lace top.

He thought he caught a whiff of flower-scented perfume in the acidic smoke.

On the double-sink counter rested a brush, a toothbrush, a tube of Colgate, a pair of scissors. To the far right corner an oversized tub. To his immediate right a glass-enclosed shower. And in front of that another door that he assumed hid the commode.

His eyes burning, Crocker turned the knob and swung it open.

Sitting on the toilet, bent over forward with her face toward the floor, was a pale-skinned woman in a frilly white bra and panties. Thick silver tape had been wrapped around her ankles, wrists, and mouth.

Crocker couldn't tell if she was dead or alive.

"Malie?" he whispered, praying that she was still breathing.

No response.

"Malie, can you hear me?"

He saw the taunt skin near the base of her neck quiver.

"I'm an American. I've come to save you."

He felt pride in saying it.

"Malie, look at me. Please."

She lifted her head. With the light streaming through the window to her right and the fumes surrounding her, she reminded him of a painting of a Flemish Madonna. One eye blue, the other green, both wide with terror. The tears that had run down her cheeks left red streaks. Her wet, light brown hair was gathered on the sides in white ribbons.

"Malie, your ordeal is over."

His heart clenched, imagining all she'd been through.

He tried to smile, but the effort hurt. And sensed that he must look frightening with the gash along his jaw, the claw marks, the blood running down his neck.

As she straightened up, her expression changed from a pleading anguish to a raw kind of anger.

She mumbled through the tape over her mouth. "My name isn't Malie."

"What?" Heavy disappointment. "Your name isn't Malie?"

She shook her head. "No."

Where the fuck is Malie? he asked himself, ignoring for now the consequences of what he'd done so far.

Even though the fire was out, thick white smoke still poured in from the hall, burning his throat and eyes.

When she did look up, he was struck by the expression of hurt and shame frozen on her oddly inert face.

That's when he realized that the body heals, but the psyche inside it is more fragile. Thinking about the hundreds of thousands of children's and young people's psyches that had been shattered because of some kind of abuse or war, he peeled the tape from the girl's ankles and wrists. He took special care with her mouth, then brought her a wet towel to clean her face.

With the tape removed, she looked no more than sixteen.

"You have a name?"

"Brigitte."

"Brigitte, do you know Malie?"

"There was another girl. But they didn't allow us to speak."

"Blond?"

"Yes. Very light hair."

"She came over on the boat with you and was here, in this suite?"

"Yes."

When he helped her up, she trembled on legs that appeared atrophied. Makeup had been applied to cover purple and blue bruises on both thighs.

"Do you know where they took her?"

"No, I'm sorry."

He found a white terry robe on a hook behind the door and wrapped it around her. As delicate as a porcelain doll.

"Keep the towel over your mouth and nose," he said, the smoke clogging his throat.

Her brown hair hung in limp curls and ringlets around her soft pink face. "I don't know where I am."

"Muscat, Oman."

She shuddered. "I'm—I'm not sure I can walk," she said through the towel.

"Lean on me. I'll help."

They made it halfway down the hall. But seeing the smoldering corpse lying in the scorched entrance to the sitting room, her knees buckled. The smell was horrible.

Crocker lifted her in his arms.

"Cover your nose. Close your eyes."

He felt her frail bones under the robe. Her heart beating against his chest like a little bird's.

Through the wider hallway to the living room, out the door of the suite. He followed the bloody footprints he'd left, hoping that Akil and Davis would find Malie so he could return to his family. Spend time with Holly and Jenny. Laugh, play games together, maybe take a vacation.

Rounding the corner, he saw a dozen soldiers in black riot gear and visored helmets pointing automatic weapons at him.

Reminded him of an image he'd seen in a video game.

A shorter soldier on the right of the group, holding a 12-gauge M1014 combat shotgun with a telescoping tubular stock, shouted in British-accented English: "Freeze right there or we'll shoot!"

Stopping, he suddenly felt exhausted. The smoke was creating havoc in his head.

"Now slowly hand the girl to my men."

"Okay." Coughing.

Brigitte, in his arms, whimpered.

Crocker, feeling lightheaded, tried to reassure her. "They're government soldiers," he whispered. "It's okay."

He transferred her to two big men who carried her away. Two other soldiers stepped forward and pointed their weapons at his head.

"Now get down the floor and hold your arms over your head!"

"I'm an official of the U.S. government." Actually, his situation was a bit more complicated. But he couldn't explain that he was a leader of a U.S. Navy SEAL Team Six unit on assignment with the CIA.

"Get on the floor!"

"I need to talk to—"

"GET DOWN, NOW!"

Crocker didn't have the energy to argue. His head was wobbling. As he bent his knees, his legs gave out.

He was already unconscious when he hit the floor.

CHAPTER SEVENTEEN

Pain is temporary. Quitting lasts forever.

—Lance Armstrong

HE WOKE up dreaming that he was floating in clouds looking for something below in the choppy blue water.

What?

The question was immediately lost in the flood of messages that crowded his brain. Pain first, emanating from his arms, legs, face, and ribs. Then, impressions of his current surroundings.

He lay on a metal hospital bed in a pale blue room approximately twenty feet by twenty. Steel bars painted white over the one window that faced another wing of the hospital. Birds chirped playfully outside. A uniformed guard watched him from a folding metal chair by the door.

"Where am I?" he asked.

The guard put his hands behind his head and yawned.

Crocker pushed himself up on his elbows, and as he did, a thick knot of pain traveled from his shoulder up to the base of his skull.

There was no phone on the nightstand. No immediate means of connecting with the outside world.

For the moment he welcomed the peace and quiet. The space to think.

An IV fed a vein in his left forearm. Two monitors attached farther up relayed information to a series of machines on a cart—blood pressure, heartbeat, and so on.

"How long have I been here?" he asked, realizing that he was wearing a light green hospital gown and that his clothes and other personal belongings were nowhere in sight.

"How long have I been lying here?" he asked the soldier again. He looked to be in his thirties. A wide, flat face, clean shaven. Hooded dark eyes. A green-red-and-white Omani flag patch on the shoulder of his uniform.

The soldier tapped his watch, held it to his ear, then stood and opened the door. Crocker watched him turn from the waist and say something in Arabic to someone in the hallway.

That's when he remembered the girl, Brigitte, and the events at the Al Bustan Palace hotel. The terror, gunfire, and flames returned.

Malie? I wonder what happened to Malie?

Dozens of related questions begged for answers. First of all: Where's the rest of my team? Did they find her? Were they able to stop Sheik Rastani, Cyrus, and the others?

He made a careful evaluation of his body, starting with his feet and ankles—all bare and sore, but otherwise functional. Pain pulsed from a bruise below his right knee, which was covered with a bandage. Both hamstrings were tight. His lower back ached, especially on the right. His ribs were tightly wrapped in bandages. And there was a big dressing near his right shoulder where he'd been burned.

Raw claw marks on his neck. His mouth swollen, sore, and dry. Lower lip ripped and stitched. His right incisor had been broken, a triangular-shaped piece missing from the top.

He'd been in worse shape than this. During previous operations, he'd broken his back and other bones, fractured his pelvis, suffered high-altitude pulmonary edema, and nearly drowned.

When he tried to move, sharp warnings rose from almost every part of his body. The guard stood at the door looking anxious, fingering the pistol that hung from a leather holster at his side.

"I have to use the bathroom," Crocker explained slowly, trying to recall the words in Arabic.

Just a frown from the soldier. A threatening look in his eyes.

"The bathroom. *Le pissoir.*"

The Omani shouted something urgently down the hall.

Crocker considered disconnecting himself from the machines and taking his chances, when a nurse in a brilliant white uniform entered. Short, straight brown hair cut in a pageboy. Her features were somewhat Hispanic.

"How do you feel?" she asked in lilting English.

"Sore as hell."

"Sore's not so bad." She introduced herself as Luci, from the Philippines. Told him he'd arrived at the hospital yesterday in the early afternoon. It was now 3 p.m.

"I assume I'm still in Muscat."

"Yes, you are. Lovely city. This morning I watched

dolphins playing in the water from the window of my apartment."

What he would do to change places with those creatures now.

"I need to talk to someone from the U.S. embassy."

"We need to get you to a dentist first."

"No, the embassy. It's urgent. How do I get to a phone?"

"I'll ask."

She helped him out of bed and to a bathroom down the hall. The guard walked beside them, muttering a prayer under his breath, and waited outside the door.

Crocker's face looked worse than he thought it would. His right eye was practically swollen shut, and the blue-and-purple bruise around his mouth extended high up his cheek and down across his jaw. Long red gashes marked his neck.

Returning to his bed exhausted, he fell asleep. Dreamt he was watching his mother iron clothes with a cigarette clenched in her teeth. The expression on her tired, weathered face said Learn to take the good with the bad, son.

I will, Mom. I will.

When he awoke hours later a bright light burned overhead. The sliver of sky through the window had turned deep Prussian blue. He felt like he was floating.

Three dark-skinned men stood at the end of the bed, two in military uniform, the third in a doctor's white lab coat.

"U.S. Navy Chief Warrant Officer Thomas Crocker?" the uniformed man with the thick black mustache asked.

"Who wants to know?"

"Colonel Najar Bahrami of the Internal Security Service."

"Then maybe you can answer some questions."

"When did you arrive in Oman?"

"I need to talk to someone from the U.S. embassy first."

"Your embassy already knows you're here."

"Then please let me use your phone."

"When did you arrive here?"

"I lost track of time. Am I under arrest?"

"Do you realize that you landed in our country without permission?"

"I'm an official of the U.S. government. I came here on a mission for the king of Norway."

"The king of Norway?"

"Yes."

The men whispered back and forth. The doctor put a hand on Crocker's forehead to check his temperature, just like his mother used to do.

When the American awoke the next morning, the guard at the door was gone. Sunlight streamed past the bars in the window and fell across the empty chair.

He felt stronger. More alert.

The same nurse arrived to bathe him and change his bandages, then supply him with a fresh hospital gown. Like an angel.

"I need immediate access to a telephone."

"Your American friends are waiting," she said as another nurse arrived with a bowl of yogurt and a cup of hot tea.

As soon as Crocker finished eating, a sandy-haired man with a long face entered. He didn't look American.

"Mr. Crocker," the man said, beaming as he crossed to the bed and offered his hand. "Claude Mathieu from the French embassy. Thank you for saving Brigitte."

"Brigitte? Yes. How is she?"

The whole messy episode came back.

"You're a hero in my country! The president himself sends his regards."

"Is she okay?" Wondering how much damage the smoke had done to their lungs.

"She's recovering very nicely, I think. She'd like to thank you in person when you're feeling better."

"I'm ready to get out of here now. Maybe you can help."

The Frenchman smiled quickly, then excused himself to attend to some urgent business, promising to return soon.

Almost immediately a half-dozen serious-looking U.S. officials in suits entered. The faces of the five men and one woman were all unfamiliar.

One of them stepped forward and said that the Omani government was extremely annoyed about the incident at the Al Bustan Palace and the fact that they hadn't been briefed about Crocker's mission.

The SEAL team leader hadn't expected this and didn't know what to say. "There was no time. Everything happened so fast."

A tall, red-haired U.S. embassy officer explained that the Omanis had spent years carefully cultivating an image of a tolerant, peaceful haven on the Arabian Peninsula, an ideal place to conduct business. The violence at one of their most prestigious international hotels had shattered that image. It could take years for them to repair it. In the meantime, hundreds of millions of dollars in revenue could be lost.

"Two things you need to understand," Crocker said.

"One, I didn't initiate the violence. And two, it couldn't have been avoided. Besides, I entered the hotel unarmed."

"Maybe not. But the Omanis are still upset."

"They're not completely innocent, either."

"What do you mean?" the lone female asked.

"I mean they allowed human traffickers and two kidnapped girls to enter their country. That girl, Brigitte, and the Norwegian, Malie, obviously weren't carrying passports with valid visas."

"How do you know that?"

Crocker took a deep breath and took them through the incident step by step, beginning with meeting the man in the lobby. Then he answered questions. At the end, one man of the half dozen said, "I admire your courage."

The others looked skeptical and worried.

Crocker, who didn't care about their judgments, was starting to feel tired. "Listen," he said. "There was this girl, a Norwegian named Malie. Do you know if she was found?"

They didn't.

"Where are the other members of my team?"

"I believe they're still in Muscat," the red-haired officer answered.

"If they're here, I need to communicate with them immediately."

"Certain things need to be straightened out first."

"What things?"

They gave no answer.

"I need to get out of this hospital as soon as possible."

"We're working on that."

* * *

An hour later Crocker was thumbing through a back issue of *Time* magazine, reading about the dangers of global warming, when Claude Mathieu returned carrying a vase of white roses.

"To cheer you up," the Frenchman said with a wink.

"Thanks."

"They're from Brigitte's parents," he added, setting them down on the bed table. "They'd like to thank you in person."

The SEAL chief warrant officer usually didn't like thank-yous, but this time he welcomed any excuse to get out of the room. Moving slowly down the hall like a broken old man, he tried to look dignified despite the ugly bruises on his face and neck.

The door at the end was guarded by two serious-looking plainclothesmen with guns. Through the crack in the door Crocker saw large bouquets of flowers and bunches of balloons.

"The story of her rescue has been headline news throughout my country," Mathieu whispered.

A week ago, French authorities had been mad at him and Akil for the raid in Toulon.

The second he entered, a middle-aged couple rose to greet him. Seeing the state of Crocker's face, the pretty woman with a bob of graying brown hair covered her mouth with her hands and gasped, *"Mon Dieu!"*

Mathieu muttered something in French, and the woman, who was about to throw her arms around the American, stopped. Instead, she grabbed both of his hands in hers and kissed them.

Her husband joined her, a well-built man with a square, worn face. He was sobbing, too, muttering something in French that Crocker couldn't understand. He grabbed the American's hands and squeezed them so that the three pairs of hands were linked together.

A bolt of emotion traveled up Crocker's arm into his chest.

They showed him to a chair by the bed. That's when the SEAL focused on Brigitte—small and radiant, surrounded by white pillows. She looked like a sad little doll. When she opened her eyes, he saw that a very faint flame still burned inside them.

Despite the tube in her mouth she formed the words "Thank you."

Crocker bit his lip and nodded. "It makes me very happy to see you with your family."

Brigitte took his big hand in hers, which felt as delicate as flowers.

Crocker remembered all the psychic pain he'd endured to get to this moment—his turbulent youth, his mother's death, his divorce, his training, all the violence he'd witnessed.

Didn't matter if he was dismissed from the SEALs for his actions or given a medal. He had to stay focused, trust his instincts, overcome his fears. All that he'd learned, and everything he was, boiled down to that.

He asked Brigitte's parents if he could ask their daughter a few quick questions before he left.

"Of course," her mother said in French. "Please do whatever you can so that these horrible people are stopped."

"Brigitte," he asked. "You and the other girl, Malie, traveled on the ship together?"

She nodded yes.

"And you disembarked together here in Muscat?"

Yes again.

"And the two of you were together in the hotel suite."

She nodded a third time.

"How many men were there?"

She held up five fingers, then pulled the tube away from her tongue.

"All Middle Eastern," she said. "I think they were speaking Arabic. One man was in charge."

"Cyrus?"

"I don't know his name."

"And Sheik Rastani?"

She winced. "A fat man with thick lips. I found him disgusting."

No clues to the Norwegian girl's location, but she had confirmed that he was on the right trail.

Walking back to his room, hoping that Klausen or someone would arrive with good news, Crocker felt something darker lingering on the edge of his euphoria, demanding his attention.

A scowling Lou Donaldson and Jim Anders stood in his room, waiting.

"We thought you'd escaped the hospital," the CIA officer snarled.

"I was visiting the French girl and her parents."

Crocker sat on the edge of the bed listening to their complaints, trying to figure out what was bothering him. They, too, like the officials from the embassy, seemed more concerned about the irked Omanis than about the fact that a girl's life had been saved and a kidnapping ring quashed.

Apparently, maintaining smooth relationships was

more important than protecting young women from predators.

"Did Davis and the others find the Norwegian girl?" he asked.

"I don't think so, but they did stop the men who tried to escape from the hotel," Anders answered.

That was something. "Are you sure they didn't find her?"

Donaldson, in khakis and a rumpled blue blazer, groaned. "Listen, Crocker. Your men have created another huge headache."

"How come?"

"Because they pistol-whipped a personal friend of the sultan's. A Sheik Rastani, from Kuwait. And when Omani security forces tried to intervene, they fought them, too."

"Good. Where's Sheik Rastani now?"

"No idea, but your guys Davis and Akil are currently being held in an Omani jail, along with a security officer from the Norwegian embassy."

Crocker felt his blood pressure shoot up. "What the fuck are they doing there? I want them released."

"We're waiting for our ambassador to convince the sultan of Oman to turn them over to us."

Crocker jumped to their defense. "Sheik Rastani is the pig who bought those girls and smuggled them out of Pakistan."

"Allegedly."

"Not allegedly. It's a fact!"

"He's also a good friend of the sultan."

"My men and I need to be released immediately, so we can locate the other girl."

"If she's here, the Omanis will find her."

"I don't trust them."

"When did you turn into the fucking Masked Avenger?" Donaldson snarled.

"When did you turn into a goddamn pussy?"

The CIA officer's face turned a bright shade of red. "Watch your mouth, Crocker! I'll have you railroaded out of the service right now!"

The SEAL team leader didn't doubt that the CIA official was capable of doing that. So he softened his approach. "Look. We know the sheik is dirty. We got his name from a computer that was in the possession of the kidnappers. And we have evidence that he purchased the Norwegian girl for a million dollars."

"So what?"

"We need to locate him."

"Sheik Rastani? My money says he's left the country."

"He needs to be arrested."

Jim Anders, who was standing with his arms crossed against his chest, chewing the inside of his mouth, chimed in. "Your men beat up the other two kidnappers so bad they're not going anywhere."

"I hope they die and rot in hell."

"You might get your wish," Donaldson snapped. "One of them sustained a major head injury and is barely alive."

"What's his name?"

"I don't know."

"They get a guy named Cyrus?"

"Yeah. We've ID'd him as Cyrus Aghassi."

"He's the one who snatched Malie in Oslo. I want to talk to him."

The CIA officer cleared his throat. "You're not talking to anyone, Crocker. You're going home."

The thought of ending the mission brought the dark idea that had been looming to the front of his consciousness.

Still seated on the edge of the bed, Crocker said, "Wait a minute. What's the latest on the *Syrena*?"

Donaldson looked at bland-faced Anders, who was scrolling through his BlackBerry, then back at Crocker. "Why?"

"Where is it now?"

"I have no idea. I traveled here to get you to sign an apology to the Omanis and give you your orders to return home."

"It could be important."

Donaldson snapped his finger at Anders, who reached into a manila envelope and produced the typed apology.

Crocker quickly scanned the letter on U.S. embassy stationery and tossed it on the bed. "I'm not signing anything until you get me out of this hospital."

"Hurry up, Crocker, I've got more important things to do than cleaning up your messes."

"You're forgetting something."

"What?"

"The connection between the kidnappers and Zaman."

"Just sign the letter."

"Last I heard, the *Syrena* was headed into the Persian Gulf. Remember, this is a ship that first came to our attention on an invoice we recovered during the raid on AZ's safe house. It just happens to be the same ship that was used by the kidnappers to smuggle Malie and the French girl out of Pakistan."

"So?"

"There were photos of blondes in cages on Zaman's computer."

Donaldson's thin lips curled into a disgusted snarl. "That blow to the head must have scrambled your brains, Crocker."

"I think Zaman was selling those girls as a way to raise money for his other terrorist activities."

"That's a stretch."

"Look. If the ship is part of AZ's operation, so are those two kidnappers in the hospital. They need to be interrogated, we have to find Malie, and, finally, the *Syrena* needs to be boarded and searched."

Donaldson stared hard at Crocker, then turned on his toes and started pacing back and forth across the tile floor.

"Don't you ever fucking quit?" the CIA officer asked.

"You should be thanking me and my men for stopping the kidnappers and recovering the girl."

"Sign the apology so we can get you out of Oman."

"I'm not signing anything."

"Then enjoy your stay, Crocker."

Donaldson gestured to Anders, and the two started to leave.

"I thought you cared about stopping Zaman. I guess I was wrong."

The CIA officer turned.

"If you weren't busted up already, I'd punch you in the fucking mouth."

Crocker tightened the belt of the hospital robe and stood. "Go ahead, Donaldson. Take your best shot!"

Donaldson started toward him, then halted and growled, "You'll regret the way you've conducted yourself."

"Interrogate the kidnappers and find the girl!"

"You're finished here, Crocker. Go home."

CHAPTER EIGHTEEN

A hero is a man who does what he can.

—Romain Rolland

TOM CROCKER found himself somewhere in the desert behind the wheel of a pickup truck. A big saguaro cactus behind him cast a long shadow, which made him think he was in the American Southwest, or maybe northern Mexico, along the border.

The morning sun burned through the windshield and stung his eyes.

Squinting, he turned the ignition key and tried to remember what he was doing here and where he was going. The starter burped and turned, then very quickly ground to a stop.

He tried the ignition again, only to hear the same terrible churning sound and get the same result. The alternator light shone red.

Now what?

He got out warily, boots crunching the sun-baked dirt past the motel sign that he couldn't read through the glare. Five paces back, he popped open the hood, which was already hot. As he swung it up, the thick smell hit him like a brick to the face.

He almost passed out.

Hot damn!

A small animal, a cat maybe, had crawled up into the engine compartment and gotten chewed up in the fan belt. The stench thick and horrendous, a cloying sweetness mixed with burnt flesh and entrails. He felt bile rising from his stomach and grabbed his throat.

Struggling to keep his breakfast down, Crocker awoke. Opened his eyes in the Omani hospital room, which was more familiar and real.

But the nausea was still with him, and the smell surrounded him, stronger than ever—entering his mouth, nose, skin, and eyes. Pulling the sheets aside, he searched for its source in the bed and underneath it, then in the room's shadows, and found nothing.

Strange.

The room was empty. Walls painted with long dark shadows created by the moon. And he was alone.

Still the smell grew thicker, and his stomach was about to spasm.

Unable to stand it anymore, he removed his hand from his mouth and shouted, "Nurse! I need to see you! Quick!"

He slid out of bed and inspected his hospital gown again. Clean.

Where the hell is it coming from?

Growing more intense, traveling up his nose into his brain. If the bars weren't blocking him, he would have jumped out the window.

Christ!

A young Asian nurse in white flung open the door and turned on the light. He stood squinting and doubled over in his light blue hospital gown by the edge of the bed.

"Sir, what's wrong?" she asked, hurrying to his side.

"The smell is making me sick."

"What?"

"The stench! The smell. Get rid of it. I can't stand it. Please."

"What smell?"

"What? You don't smell it?"

She sniffed the air, then shook her head. "No, I don't."

"But—"

Unimaginable. Yet her face, her demeanor, the sound of her voice were all sincere.

That's when Crocker remembered where he'd experienced the awful stink before. Emanating from the smoldering, eviscerated body on the floor of the suite in the Al Bustan Palace hotel.

The Asian nurse saw the troubled look in his eyes.

"Is there some way I can help you?" she asked.

The smell was some type of flashback. An echo of the trauma he'd endured, the violence, the fact that he'd narrowly escaped death.

"I'll call a doctor," she said as she helped him back into bed.

"That won't be necessary." He'd experienced flashbacks before, but they'd always been visual.

"It will just take a minute."

"I was having a bad dream. I'm okay."

Her expression remained compassionate and sweet. "If you want, sir, I can crack open the window."

"That would be helpful. Thanks," he said, slipping back under the covers, feeling like a little boy who had disturbed his parents' sleep.

When he'd had nightmares as a child, his mother had told him to think of pleasant things. So he imagined himself and Holly hiking in the Shenandoah Valley. A beautiful late October day. The trees blazed with fall colors. As he conjured the smell of leaves and grass and burning firewood in the distance, the stench disappeared and he fell asleep.

"Boss?"

"What?"

"Wake up, boss."

The SEAL team leader pushed himself up and rubbed his eyes, aware that he was still in the hospital and thinking he had to be somewhere else.

"Boss."

"What is it?" Grasping for details in the half-conscious fog.

The face looming over him was unidentifiable because of the angle, but he recognized the voice—deep and resonant, with a hint of foreign accent. Akil.

"Akil, what's going on? Did you find the girl?"

The Egyptian American looked thinner and paler than before.

"Not yet, boss. You feeling better?"

Funny, coming from him.

"Fine. Yeah. How about you? And how'd you get in here?" The reality of his circumstances was coming back, along with familiar aches and pains.

"I was running a fever," the Egyptian American explained, "so they transferred me to the hospital, where I met Colonel Bahrami. You remember Colonel Bahrami, don't you?"

"Who?"

A stiff-backed, uniformed man stepped out of the long shadow across the door, and Crocker recognized the intelligent, mustached face from the afternoon before.

"Oh, yes. Hello, Colonel."

"Sorry to interrupt your sleep, sir, but your colleague told me you wouldn't mind," he said in his clipped British accent.

"Did I hear correctly? You still haven't found the Norwegian girl?"

"Not yet, sir."

Akil explained that the colonel had visited his room the night before and the two had started talking about their experiences growing up, their respective intelligence services, and what they perceived to be the primary threats to their countries.

Colonel Bahrami's interest had been piqued when Akil mentioned Abu Rasul Zaman. He said that Omani intelligence was very concerned about al-Qaeda activity in the area, and particularly in Yemen. The colonel had explained that Oman, which continued to make an effort to get along with all countries, had a complicated relationship with its neighbor to the southwest that dated back to the 1970s, when Yemen had supported the pro-communist Dhohar rebels who were trying to overthrow the sultan of Oman. After the rebels were defeated, Sultan Qaboos bin Said Al Said had launched a diplomatic campaign to improve relations between the two neighbors, which had been successful in fostering trade and commerce.

But now Yemen was embroiled in political turmoil. Al-Qaeda in the Arabian Peninsula (AQAP) controlled important territory in the south of the country, near the borders of Oman and Saudi Arabia, and seemed to be growing in strength. Meanwhile, Houthi Shiite rebels in the north were fighting a civil war that threatened to overthrow the government.

"What does this have to do with me and my men?" Crocker asked, shifting to the edge of the bed and flexing his knees.

Colonel Bahrami stood before him in his clean khaki uniform. His white teeth, dark eyes, and black mustache all gleamed, set off by his caramel-colored skin.

"The fact that this ship, the *Syrena,* is registered in Yemen and was used to smuggle these kidnapped girls into my country intrigues me," he said with great seriousness.

"It intrigues me, too," Crocker said.

"Your colleague Akil explained how a document found in Zaman's safe house seems to connect him to this ship. Do you agree?"

"Yes. I do."

"According to our people stationed in Khasab, the *Syrena* has already passed through the Strait of Hormuz and has entered the Persian Gulf," Colonel Bahrami added.

Crocker looked up. "Bound for where?"

"Bushehr, Iran, apparently."

The SEAL leader remembered, and as he did, the noxious smell seemed to rise again from the floor.

"I was under the impression that security at the strait was relatively tight," Crocker remarked, squeezing shut his nostrils.

"All we know is that the ship had the necessary papers and clearances to get through. Where they came from, and whether or not they were fraudulent, is unclear."

"And your people are a hundred percent sure that it has entered the Gulf?"

The Omani colonel grinned sheepishly. "The question I have, sir, the one that continues to trouble me, is this: Why would a Yemeni ship be bound for Iran? These two countries are barely on speaking terms. I think this is highly unusual."

"I agree."

Crocker ran a hand gently over his mouth and right eye. The swelling seemed to have subsided considerably, and most of the soreness was gone.

"I might know a way to find out more about the ship," the American offered. The more he focused on the unfinished aspects of his mission, the more the smell seemed to subside.

"How?"

"I heard that two of the kidnappers were captured. Is that correct?"

"They're under guard on an upper floor of this hospital."

"Would it be possible for us to pay them a visit?"

"That could be complicated."

"They were on the *Syrena*. They might be persuaded to tell us what they know," Crocker reasoned.

Colonel Bahrami considered for a minute, then looked at his watch. "This will require permission from my superiors."

"How long will that take?"

"Several hours at least," the colonel answered.

"In the meantime, help me find the missing girl."

Bahrami looked surprised. "But the Norwegian ambassador has already expressed his concern to our sultan, and our sultan told him he's not convinced that this girl ever arrived in Muscat."

Crocker sat up. "I'm almost certain that she did."

"We're not."

"And I think I can prove it."

"How?"

"I can show you, if you bring me my clothes and get a car to drive us to the Al Bustan Palace hotel."

Crocker's pants, underwear, and shirt, which had been washed and pressed, were still stained with blood. But he didn't care. The three men exited the black Mercedes. It was lunchtime, and several groups of businessmen and tourists sat eating at metal tables overlooking the hotel's lagoon and garden. They craned their necks to watch the big American with the badly bruised face and the pronounced limp pass. These well-heeled travelers hardly registered with the SEAL leader, who was hoping that his hunch was correct.

The head of hotel security—a short, stocky former ISI officer named Waleed—recognized Crocker and confirmed that yes, all entrances to the establishment and elevators were monitored by security cameras.

"I figured they would be," Crocker said.

"We take pride in our security," Waleed offered as he escorted them to a dark room behind the front desk. There, the men leaned forward to study grainy video footage from the passenger elevator that serviced the sixth-floor suite.

"It takes a special key to operate this particular lift," Waleed explained.

"I rode in it," Crocker told him. "I know."

When the time signature on the bottom of the video registered 03:14:05 two mornings earlier, a corpulent man wearing a dishdasha and a black goatee entered with two large men in suits.

"There he is," Crocker said pointing to the man in the dishdasha. "That's Sheik Rastani."

"Perhaps. But that proves nothing," Colonel Bahrami replied.

"Wait."

Approximately five minutes later, another group of passengers entered the same elevator on the ground floor, four men and two women in dark burkas. When the woman on the right side of the screen turned away from the camera, Crocker recognized Brigitte's profile.

"Two girls entered. You see?"

He couldn't make out the second young woman's features, but thought he spotted strands of light hair sticking out of the hood of her burka.

"That's Malie," he said, excitedly. "There she is. There's your proof!"

"That's hardly proof," Colonel Bahrami countered. "How do we know she's not a servant, or some other sort of employee?"

Good question.

"Did anyone see this woman leave the hotel?" Crocker asked.

Mr. Waleed stuck his bottom lip out and shook his head. "We saw the sheik. We saw his men. At least, the ones who survived. But not this girl. No."

Crocker asked the hotel security officer to fast-forward the tape. Images of a mostly empty elevator overlapped one another on the screen.

At around 08:42:23, according to the time signature on the bottom, Crocker saw his own image standing with two other men.

The events that had happened soon thereafter returned to Crocker's consciousness, along with the stench of the smoldering body.

"Slow it down!" he shouted a little too loudly.

Waleed complied.

Crocker felt uncomfortable as he and the other three men watched his black-and-white image exit the elevator. It was like looking at one's own ghost.

Roughly twelve minutes later, Sheik Rastani, wearing a white dishdasha, and several other men hurried into the tight space and started to descend. They seemed highly agitated, which made sense, because they were running away from Crocker, who had entered the suite.

They had left Brigitte in the bathroom, where he found her. But where was the second girl?

Another ten minutes of videotape passed before a group of armed Omani soldiers were seen entering the same elevator and going up to six.

"I didn't see the second girl anywhere," Crocker said.

Colonel Bahrami snapped, "Play it back."

They reviewed the tape six more times, once so slowly that they were watching it one frame at a time, then viewed it again from 3 a.m. two mornings ago all the way to the present.

Two young women in burkas had gone up, but only one of them had come down, and that was Brigitte.

"What the hell happened to Malie?" Akil asked. "She couldn't have just disappeared."

Colonel Bahrami: "Maybe they took the second female down the stairway."

The emergency stairway and all the exits were also monitored by security cameras. But none of them had captured the second woman either leaving the sixth floor or exiting the building.

All the men who had assembled looked perplexed.

"The suite was thoroughly searched?" Crocker asked.

"Yes. Of course."

"And nothing was recovered?"

"Some articles of clothing. A pair of women's shoes. Books, CDs. Mostly belongings of the sheik."

"Anything else?"

"A suit wrapped in plastic. Some foodstuffs. A pair of sandals."

"Where are these items now?" Crocker asked.

"They were locked in a room in the basement on orders from the sultan," Waleed answered.

Crocker was reminded that the sultan and Sheik Rastani were friends, both prominent members of the Ibadhi sect of Islam.

He suggested that they go up and inspect the suite again.

A scowling Colonel Bahrami gave his approval.

While Waleed went to fetch the electronic key that would let them in, Crocker recalled something else—the black pull suitcase he'd seen one of the men abandon as he was running out the door.

"There was also a large black suitcase," the SEAL team leader said. "I passed it on my way out. It was to my left, near the door of the sixth-floor suite."

"What suitcase?"

"A black pull suitcase. About this big," the American said holding out his arms.

When Waleed returned, he admitted that he hadn't personally seen the items that had been removed from the suite and locked downstairs.

The two Americans followed the Omanis to the lift. The experience of ascending in the elevator was strange for Crocker. So was retracing his bloody footprints on the carpet. But it wasn't until they entered the suite and he was hit with the lingering smell that the muscles in Crocker's neck and stomach tightened and he started to feel sick.

Leaning against the wall, the bitter taste of bile reached his mouth.

"Boss, you all right? You want to sit down?" Akil asked, noticing his leader's discomfort.

"I'm good."

Crocker lingered four paces inside, just far enough to scan the foyer/dining/living area and establish that the suitcase wasn't there.

The other three men inspected the interior rooms of the suite and came out empty-handed.

"It's completely clean," Akil reported.

"Let's go see the room in the basement."

This required permission from the minister of interior, who was at his country club eating lunch. They waited in the lobby while Bahrami called.

The suitcase. The suitcase...

Pacing and looking at the clock, hoping that the items in the basement would provide some clue, Crocker sensed there was something else he should be remembering, but his mind was too exhausted and agitated to identify it.

Cups of coffee and tea were consumed and stories exchanged in the hour that passed before a black SUV stopped in the driveway and a tall functionary from the ministry jumped out and handed the colonel a set of keys.

"With the approval of the minister, who says we can look but not disturb anything."

"Gentlemen, this way," Waleed directed.

They descended in a service elevator to the belly of the hotel, the space thick with the smells of garbage and vinegar.

Four sets of footsteps resounded through hallways lit with buzzing fluorescent lights, Crocker praying that somehow Malie was alive.

They turned left at a locked cage stacked to the ceiling with cases of expensive wines and brandies, into a darker corridor, to a door on the right.

"Here it is," Waleed announced.

Bahrami opened the door with a yellow-tabbed key and threw the switch.

Crocker's heart started to leap in his chest.

In the left corner behind the door stood a metal footlocker and the black hard-shelled suitcase, which were chained together and secured with a brass lock. Signs in English, Arabic, and Farsi warned the curious not to touch without signed permission from Oman's interior minister.

Bahrami opened the lock with a red-tabbed key. Crocker leaned over and pulled the chain free. He was so juiced he was having trouble breathing as he felt along the little holes that been punched in the smooth front of the hard plastic suitcase.

"Wait," the colonel barked. He produced another key, a little green-tabbed one this time.

Crocker laid the suitcase on its side and opened the lock. He dreaded what he was about to see so much that he turned his eyes away as he swung it open. The smell of sweat and piss met his nostrils.

The men behind him gasped.

"Dear God—"

"It's the girl!"

"She's dead."

He had to will his eyes to focus on the awkwardly folded little body, knees at her chin, silver tape around her wrists and ankles and across her mouth. The skin on her arms a smooth yellowish gray. More mottled near her shoulders.

"Malie?" he whispered, fearing the worst.

Light blond hair like that of an angel.

It had to be her.

"Malie?"

He reached inside, along the cool skin of her neck, and tried to find a pulse.

The men breathed heavily behind him.

On his knees, his hand shaking, he prayed to his mother, God, and all that he held dear. He thought he felt a flicker of life under her skin.

Is it my imagination?

He waited and felt it again.

And a third time, before he looked up and said firmly, "Call an ambulance and an EMS team. Tell them to hurry!"

CHAPTER NINETEEN

In the darkest night one can see the most stars.

—Persian saying

MIRACLES DO happen, Crocker said to himself. He'd witnessed one. At least he thought he'd heard the hospital's doctor say that Malie's breathing, blood pressure, and heartbeat had stabilized and were returning to normal.

"The doctor said she's going to pull through, right?" he asked Akil, who stood to his right.

"It was touch and go for awhile, but she's improving, yes."

He pinched himself to make sure he wasn't in a dream.

Then he felt strong arms around him and saw Mikael Klausen's beaming face. "Like Lazarus. It's like Lazarus, the way she's come back to life!"

"Yes. Yes." Trying to remember how long Klausen had been there with him.

"The doctor said another hour, maybe less, and her heart would have stopped."

He saw tears in hard men's eyes. Felt the joy in their faces. American, Norwegian, Omani, French. There were over twenty people crowded into the little waiting area. Only three green chairs. The Filipino nurse who had helped him before was passing a bottle of Australian white wine.

The clock behind her head was approaching twelve. Midnight, he thought. It had to be midnight. In the worry and exhaustion he'd lost track of time.

Klausen looked up from one of the green chairs, where he was dialing a satellite phone. "Don't go too far, Crocker," he said, pushing strands of blond hair off his forehead. "The king will want to thank you personally."

The American said, "I've got to do something. I'll be right back."

He felt the sudden urge to call someone, too. Hurrying down the pale green hallway he almost crashed into an African nurse cradling a dozen cans of Coke.

"Excuse me," he said, "but I need to place an international call."

She had kind eyes and parallel tribal scars carved into her cheeks. "The second door on the right. There's a telephone on the desk. The code is 352. Then enter the country code and number."

The small, unexpected kindnesses of strangers. He wanted to kiss her.

"Thanks."

Jenny answered on the second ring. "Hello?"

"Hi, sweetheart. It's your father."

"You remembered."

Remembered what?

A song played in the background as she said, "I was

hoping you could be here, but I wasn't really counting on it."

That's right. Her seventeenth birthday was the twenty-second. Was today the twenty-second? He'd promised to be home by then.

"I'm sorry, sweetheart. With all that's been going on here, I lost track of time."

He flashed back to Malie's half-dead face, and the stench thickened around him. Irony and guilt squeezed his head and throat. He'd risked his life to save a young Norwegian woman but forgotten his own daughter's birthday.

What kind of father am I?

"No, Dad, it's okay. I know you're busy. I'm glad you called."

"I should be there."

Remembering all the birthdays and holidays he'd missed, he felt himself being pulled into a disorienting maelstrom of pain, flashbacks, moral ambiguities, questions about why he was doing what he was doing, and the realization that he was more than seven thousand miles from home.

"Jenny, I just want you to know that when it comes to the important things, like the fact that I love you unconditionally, I'll always, always be there for you. No matter what happens."

"I know that, Dad."

"You do?"

He wanted to confess to her that he was a flawed man and knew it. Sometimes, maybe, he went too far to protect her. Sometimes he didn't understand why he did the things he did.

But he stopped himself. Wouldn't his honesty just confuse the seventeen-year-old, who was already flirting with cynicism as she struggled to find her way in her new life in Virginia?

"Dad, you sound tired. Are you okay?"

"I'm fine, sweetheart. How are you?"

School was okay, she said. She'd met a couple of girls her age that she liked.

"Good. I'm glad to hear it," he said, drifting back to the image of Malie's yellow-gray face, her angelic expression. Thinking: So many times we forget the most important things in life.

One day he would tell his daughter about the Norwegian girl and her rescue, but not now. Akil appeared in the doorway.

"The king wants to speak to you," he whispered.

Crocker took a deep breath and said, "I have to go, sweetheart. I wish you a very happy birthday. I love you. I'll be home soon."

He walked back to the waiting area, scolding himself for not speaking to his wife, too, and hoping she'd understand.

I'm going to be a better father and husband. I'm going to treat myself better, too.

The king of Norway sounded like a soccer coach exhorting his team after a late-season victory. "We shouldn't forget that Malie is just one of thousands of young women who are victimized like this every year. But this is an important accomplishment, a message to people all over the world that the good will prevail and..."

"Yes, Your Highness. I agree."

The king's words sounded hollow. For all Crocker knew he could have been some preacher or motivational speaker from down the street.

"Thank you, Your Highness. I'm glad we were successful. Yes, I'd be honored to visit your country. But I have to spend time with my family first."

The joy on the people's faces in the waiting room was real. Jakob, Mancini, the red-haired man from the embassy, the ambassadors of Norway and France, Klausen, Bahrami, Waleed, Davis, the nurse and doctor, even Jim Anders and Claude Mathieu were all celebrating, congratulating one another, happy and open, in a way that said We're all in this together.

A moment of truth. Yes, *we are all in this together.*

Then something dark intruded. What?

Amid the bright chatter, the ship drifted across the horizon of his conscious again.

Oh, yeah. The *Syrena.*

Figuring that this was as good a time as any to tie up the last loose end, he found Bahrami discussing the qualities of horse breeds with Waleed and pulled him aside.

"You think you can get me in to see the captured kidnappers?"

"Do you know anything about horses, Mr. Crocker?" the colonel asked back.

"Beautiful animals. But I need to talk to the kidnappers."

"You want to do this now?"

"That's correct."

"But why?"

"I continue to be concerned about the ship."

The colonel's eye glistened as he lifted a thick eyebrow. "You're an interesting fellow, Mr. Crocker. Are you always this focused and driven?"

"Most of the time, yes."

"And you're convinced that the ship is still relevant?"

"Haven't my instincts been accurate so far?"

The colonel's laughter sounded like hiccups. "I can't argue with that. Follow me."

Up they went to the dimly lit fourth-floor hallway, where they stopped at a door guarded by two sleepy Omani soldiers holding AK-47s. The colonel from the Internal Security Service spoke to them in Arabic, and the two soldiers saluted and stepped aside.

At the door Bahrami whispered, "I'm sticking my neck out for you, Mr. Crocker. And in return, I expect you to act within the bounds of reasonable behavior."

"I appreciate that, Colonel," the SEAL leader answered, wondering what he meant by "reasonable behavior." "I'll make it brief."

The hospital room was dark and smelled sharply of ammonia. A man's snores echoed off the walls. As soon as Crocker saw the kidnapper's profile in the moonlight through the window, his anger started to rise.

He leaned over and slapped the prisoner on the cheek. "Cyrus? Hey, asshole. Wake up."

Crocker switched on the light over the bed.

The young man stopped midsnore and opened his eyes. They were black and defiant, immediately expecting trouble.

"Cyrus, remember me? You tried to shoot me in the hotel suite."

Fear froze the skin around the man's eyes.

"Here's the situation," Crocker explained firmly. "Your

days of kidnapping girls—of doing much of anything—are over. But if you cooperate with me, I can help your family."

The prisoner's hoarse breathing quickened as he turned his head toward the wall.

"Cyrus. Look at me. Listen..."

When the wounded kidnapper slowly turned his head back, Crocker noticed that his right cheekbone had been broken and his nostrils were stuffed with cotton.

"I'm not going to lie to you. You're either going to hang, or spend the rest of your life in jail. That you can count on."

The corners of the young man's mouth curled into a kind of grim recognition.

Crocker continued, "As a man, a son, maybe even a father, your responsibility now is to your family."

"I have no family," the prisoner mumbled.

"What'd you say?"

"I have no family."

Crocker realized that he was at a certain disadvantage. Though Oman was an Islamic country, it maintained a deep respect for the rights of all of its citizens, even prisoners. In Pakistan, Saudi Arabia, or Iran, Cyrus would have had the truth beaten out of him. But not here. As long as he was in Omani custody, he couldn't be forced to talk.

"We all have families, Cyrus," Crocker said authoritatively. "We come from somewhere. People I know will find them. That's what happens in cases like this."

"Go to hell."

"Why should your relatives suffer for the things you've done? Like kidnapping innocent girls and torturing them."

Cyrus gritted his teeth.

Crocker's anger broke to the surface; he pushed it down again.

"Why should they suffer for you, Cyrus? Think about that."

The kidnapper responded in a grim, unsteady voice. "Our fates are, and always will be, in the hands of Allah."

"Doesn't Allah condemn torture and kidnapping? Doesn't he show mercy to those who show compassion to others?"

"You're an infidel. What do you know about Allah?" Cyrus spat back.

"I suspect that you have a wife somewhere. Maybe a young child."

"I have nothing!"

"Think about them."

"We are at war, you and me! That's all we need to know about one another."

"But now you're of more use to me than you are to your own side."

"We will win in the end. You'll see!" The kidnapper's eyes threatened to pop out of his head.

"You failed, Cyrus. Didn't you?"

This struck like a bullet.

"No."

"You were caught. Now Zaman would prefer that you were dead."

Sadness crept into the corners of the kidnapper's eyes. "What do you know, infidel?"

"Any promises he made to you before, to protect your family, don't mean anything now."

"Go away."

"Think of them. Think of the burden they'll have to bear. Their son, their father, their brother has put them in danger. He failed his cause."

The skin around Cyrus's mouth started to tremble. "*Imshi!*" (Leave me alone.)

Sensing a tiny opening, a moment of vulnerability, Crocker pressed on. "Tell me about the ship you arrived on and I'll make sure your family is given money and moved to a safe location."

Cyrus's dark eyes grew darker as he considered.

"The ship, Cyrus. Be smart."

His head shook slightly.

"I know it's being used for some sinister purpose. If you don't talk, my air force will blow it out of the water."

"No."

"Help your family."

"Kill me!" the prisoner snarled, turning toward the window. "Make me a martyr. *Mush mushim.*" (I don't care.)

Crocker couldn't see the kidnapper's face past his shoulder but sensed that the conversation was over.

"Cyrus, the next group of people you see won't be so reasonable. They'll start by breaking your toes and fingers, and pulling out your teeth."

"Allah will show mercy."

"The pain will be real. And your family will suffer. All you need to do is tell me about the ship."

As the American leaned closer, Cyrus turned with great energy and Crocker saw that his right hand held a pointed object aimed at his neck.

"*Allahu Akbar!*"

The SEAL countered fast, throwing his right elbow

and forehead into the bridge of the kidnapper's nose and using his left to block his hand.

Cyrus's nose snapped, and another punch to the neck loosened his grip on the weapon, which Crocker pulled free. A ballpoint pen that a careless doctor or nurse had left behind or dropped.

Crocker smashed the bloody terrorist powerfully in the mouth. "That's for trying to fuck with me, Cyrus!" Then he unloaded on his face again. "And that's for the girls you kidnapped and abused!"

Back in the hallway, Bahrami saw the blood on Crocker's hand and threw his arms up in disgust. "I asked you to be reasonable! This is an outrage, sir. Totally unacceptable!"

"He tried to stab me," Crocker explained, handing him the bloodied pen.

Fortunately, Cyrus's colleague down the hall wasn't as well informed about the protections of Omani law. This young man, who was recovering from a self-inflicted gunshot wound to the right foot, a shattered collarbone, and a dislocated shoulder, claimed he was a poor former Pakistani policeman who had been hired by Cyrus in Karachi to provide security for Sheik Rastani.

He gave up the following to Bahrami with very little persuasion: One, Sheik Rastani had not been a passenger on the ship; he had met them when they docked in Muscat. Two, Cyrus deferred to an older, serious man with a thick black beard who rarely left his cabin and seemed to be the leader. He didn't know the man's name or nationality. Nor was he able to understand what the man was saying, because he didn't speak Arabic, only his native Urdu.

Three, the ship was run by a small crew of Middle Eastern men and Filipinos. Also on board were a half-dozen men who exercised on deck and prayed often, kept to themselves, and could be some sort of commandos. Four, he had been hired to accompany Sheik Rastani from Muscat to Kuwait. From there, he was supposed to fly back to Karachi.

Five, he said he wasn't aware that Brigitte and Malie were on board until they disembarked in Muscat. Six, he claimed that he had taken the job to help his wife, who was suffering from cancer of the bladder.

The question Crocker faced: What to do now?

It was nearly two o'clock in the morning. The celebration on the third floor seemed to have ended. Chief Warrant Officer Crocker found Akil and Davis helping the nurses clean up empty wine bottles and cans of soda.

"Where'd everyone go?" Crocker asked.

"Klausen and Anders went with the Norwegian ambassador to look in on Malie. The others scattered."

"Where is she?"

"The critical care ward on four."

Ironically, the kidnappers and their former victim were recuperating on the same floor.

"You know the room number?"

"I'll show you," volunteered the African nurse with the scars.

The half-dozen men gathered in front of the door reminded him of excited teenagers stealing looks at pictures in *Playboy*. They were taking turns peering through the six-inch-square window in the door.

"Crocker, you want to look?" Mikael Klausen asked.

The room was dimly lit and bigger than the others,

the walls a dirty yellowish color. A nurse and a doctor blocked his view of the bed. When they moved away, Crocker saw Malie sitting up, wide awake.

Her skin gave off a pink healthy glow, and her blue eyes sparkled. Seeing his eyes through the little window, she smiled as though nothing out of the ordinary had happened. Her composed serenity took Crocker's breath away.

"She looks well, doesn't she?" Klausen asked.

Crocker took a second look to make sure. "I'd heard that Norwegians were hearty people, but I never expected a recovery as fast as this," he remarked.

"The doctor thinks that in another day or two she'll be able to return to Oslo," Klausen said proudly.

Seeing her like this suffused the American with renewed energy. "Before you men disperse, there's something important we need to discuss."

"What?"

Klausen, Anders, the Norwegian ambassador, Akil, Davis, and Bahrami followed him to the nurses' station in the middle of the hall.

"Here's the situation..." It took great mental concentration for Crocker to recount what he had learned from the former Pakistani policeman and bend his mind around the reasons why the ship posed an impending threat. Exhaustion, pain, and a sense of dislocation had taken their toll.

The Norwegians weren't interested. They'd gotten what they wanted and were pulling away from the group, which was disappointing but understandable. But the American and Omani participants immediately grasped the threat the ship might pose to commerce in the Persian

Gulf, which accounted for roughly 25 percent of the world's crude-oil supply.

Saudi Arabia, the world's largest oil producer, was particularly important. One of al-Qaeda's long-standing goals was the overthrow of the Saudi royal family, who controlled the holy mosque in Mecca.

Jim Anders was struck by the new information about the commandos aboard the ship and their bearded leader. He and Bahrami agreed that in the little time they had before the *Syrena* either disappeared from sight or completed its mission, they needed to establish its current location and either warn the Saudis or secure the necessary equipment and permissions to board the vessel and inspect it.

Bahrami offered to talk to his superiors, a critical step because any operation launched from Omani soil would require their approval.

"First we need to establish the position of the ship."

Crocker asked Akil and Davis to visit the port dispatch officer and solicit his help.

"Will do."

"If he can't pinpoint the *Syrena*'s current location, ask him who can."

"We'll find out, boss, one way or another."

"Good."

That's when Anders grabbed Crocker by the shoulder. "I can't let you go active without consulting you-know-who."

"Where is Donaldson, anyway?"

"He went back to the Sheraton, about half a mile away."

"You got wheels?"

"Yeah, I have a vehicle downstairs."
"Then let's go see him."
"Mr. Donaldson is probably asleep."
Crocker just smiled.

CHAPTER TWENTY

Don't wait! The time will never be just right.

—Napoleon Hill

FOUR AND a half hours later, the first delicate flicks of sunlight danced off the water. The heavy churning of engines pounded his head.

Crocker peered out the side window of the British-built Super Lynx helicopter to the Persian Gulf below. Sun-baked Iran to the north, the Saudi desert to the south, the two political and Islamic rivals separated by the wide ribbon of water.

Past the tail rotor, the horizon was turning rich deep gold. The land, air, and water were all serene. But no sign of the ship.

The SEAL Team Six assault leader had gotten authorization from the CIA, his CO in Virginia, and Oman's ISS to go on a last-minute reconnaissance mission. He and his men had orders to locate the *Syrena* and follow it until it reached Iranian waters. Crocker had argued for, and failed to win, approval to board and search the ship.

He and his men were doing this by the seat of their pants—no plan, no rest, no real prep. They didn't even have a detailed description of the *Syrena*, except that it was a small tanker of Yemeni registry with an orange-red hull and a white bridge.

Crocker half listened to the Omani copilot telling Akil about a boatload of Afghan opium smugglers they had battled a week ago. How the leader had bled to death on the same bench where Akil and Ritchie were sitting now.

Davis and Mancini sat across from them. All four men looked determined and alert.

Crocker, meanwhile, was trying to stay focused. The combination of pain medicine for his knee and shoulder, fear, and lack of sleep brought back strange memories. Like sitting in a matinee with his father and uncle when he was six, watching a cowboy riding into the sunset, a crooner on the soundtrack singing:

Saddle your blues to a wild mustang
And gallop your blues away.

The helicopter radio spit out an urgent stream of Arabic as Crocker sorted through random childhood images. Helping his mother fold laundry. Making rifles out of sticks with his friends. Chasing through the woods, ambushing imaginary bad guys—Indians, Russians, Chinese.

Akil leaned toward his ear. "Boss, according to the latest satellite intel, the *Syrena* has turned and is headed toward the south shore of the Gulf."

Mention of the *Syrena*'s change of direction hit him

like a bucket of cold water. "What? I thought it was going to Bushehr, in Iran."

"The ship made a sharp turn and is approaching Ras Tanura."

Crocker jolted to attention. Ras Tanura was the world's most important oil export terminal. Something like 80 percent of the nine million barrels a day pumped from Saudi oil fields passed through Ras Tanura, where it was loaded onto supertankers bound for the West.

An attack on the critical oil loading station could destabilize the world economy and potentially topple the Saudi regime.

"Why the fuck is a chemical tanker headed for an oil export terminal?"

"Apparently it issued a distress signal and is flying an orange flag."

"And the Saudis let it through their security perimeter?"

"Appears so. Something to do with faulty electronics and possible engine failure."

Crocker didn't like it at all. "Tell the copilot to get on the horn. Alert the Saudis. And tell the Omanis we need permission to board."

"Yes, sir."

"This is an emergency, Akil. Code red!"

"Understood."

Faulty electronics, my ass.

He had a feeling that this might become more than a reconnaissance mission. Now he huddled with his men and outlined the situation.

"I thought you said we were simply going to observe the ship," Davis muttered.

"We just received updated information. What we're doing here is rapid assessment and response."

The men looked excited. They lived for ops like this.

"Like riding a bucking bronco," Ritchie remarked.

"Whether the men on board resist or surrender, we've got to gain control of the bridge and stop this sucker before it reaches Ras Tanura."

Mancini said, "I can do that."

"Are we dropping in the water?" Davis asked.

"I won't know until we get close."

"And see what the bastards throw at us."

"Basically, we're going to improvise," Crocker said. "What have we got to go in with?"

Mancini, always the finagler, had managed to smuggle aboard a couple of MP5 series submachine guns, a half-dozen nine-millimeter handguns, about a thousand rounds of nine-millimeter hollow-point, a few KA-BAR knives, a dozen frag grenades, waterproof weapons bags, and some waterproof utility pouches. All compliments of a friend of his in the military attaché's office.

"No wet suits or fins?" Davis asked.

"The water's warm. We'll manage. Let's find out what the Omanis have on this bird."

The men held on as the copter banked left, then scrambled through the fuselage looking in the weapons bays for anything they could use, turning up four more submachine guns, a couple of grenade launchers, an inflatable raft, flares.

Crocker spotted the Saudi coast out the left window, a glowing yellow ribbon.

"Boss! Boss!" Akil shouted from near the cockpit. "Look!"

Pressing his face to the glass he saw a weathered-looking tanker approximately 350 feet in length. Orange-red hull with a matching red stack; white bridge. To anyone else it would have appeared to be an innocuous, smallish, rusting tanker puttering up the coast.

The men pressed their faces against the side window for a better look.

Crocker rushed to join Akil up front. "Tell the pilot to bring this baby right over the bridge."

"Ten-four."

A lot of arguing back and forth in Arabic. Crocker asked, "What's the problem?"

"We've entered Saudi airspace. He's waiting for permission."

"Screw that. No time."

The pilot was a stubborn-looking fellow with a big bald circle on the top of his head and fierce dark eyes. As Akil argued with him and the mustached copilot, the helicopter drew closer to the ship.

"Tell him we don't have time for permission. We've got to act now to prevent a catastrophe."

Akil: "I have."

From approximately three hundred feet above and fifty feet to the side, Crocker made out men on the bridge waving up at the helicopter and pointing at the orange and black distress flag. A number of them wore black beards.

"What do you think?" Akil asked.

"They don't look like sailors to me."

"Me either."

"Tell the pilot to take it closer."

"He won't."

"Why not?"

"He's waiting on orders."

"Fuck the orders!"

Leaning past the back of the pilot's seat, he grabbed the man's shoulder and pointed. "Down! Down, man. Take it closer!"

"No!"

"Yes, goddammit. The ship's headed for Ras Tanura. Do you know what that means?"

The pilot shouted something to the copilot, then steered the metal bird lower until they were about 150 feet over the bridge.

"Lower! Lower! You can do it. Go ahead!"

The pilot shook his head vigorously.

"Lower, my friend."

"La!" (No!)

"Yalla! Yalla!" (Let's go! Let's go!)

"Akl laa!" (No way!)

"You see that ship? It's going to hit the oil terminal if we don't stop it. Big explosion. *BANG!* Your sultan will be pissed."

"He can't understand you, boss."

"Translate."

Akil did. "He says he's the commander of this aircraft, and you're insulting him."

Pissed off, Crocker started squeezing through the space between the seats. "Move aside. I'll fly this fucking thing myself!" He'd been trained, along with a handful of other ST-6 operators, to fly helicopters by the pilots of Special Operations Aviation Regiment TF-160, the best in the business.

The Omani pilot started to reach for a pistol on the console. Crocker slapped his forearm and the pistol hit the instrument panel, then clattered across the metal floor.

The pilot flew into a rage, shouting insults in Arabic, then steering the bird away from the ship. As Akil tried shouting over him, Crocker retrieved the MK23 .45-caliber automatic from the floor.

Another garbled voice came over the radio, a stream of excited Arabic that Crocker couldn't begin to translate in the deafening clamor. Running out of options, he pointed the pistol at the pilot's head.

"Lower this motherfucker! That's my fucking order!"

The pilot's voice slid up an octave. *"Akl laa!"*

Akil: "He says shoot him if you want to, but this is as far as he'll go."

Crocker pulled back the trigger. "Then I'll have to shoot him!"

Cursing under his breath, the pilot lowered the bird and banked it over the ship. As the Super Lynx closed within fifty feet, the men on the bridge stopped waving and started running for cover. Within seconds a hail of automatic-weapon fire started coming their way and slamming into the helicopter's metal belly.

"We're getting hit!" Akil shouted.

"We're taking fire!"

"Hold steady!" Crocker shouted.

The pilot looked like he was about to be sick.

"Tell him to bank right and take it down farther."

"He says that's impossible!"

Crocker handed the gun to Akil. "Stay here and shoot him in the head if you have to. We're going in!"

He joined the other three SEALs at the side door. They were ready to go.

"Boss! Boss! What's the order?" Davis shouted.

"You got the weapons in the waterproof bags?"

"Aye, aye!"

"Line up. Prepare to jump."

"Ready, boss!"

"Stop the ship!"

Crocker slid the helicopter door open. The dark blue water of the Persian Gulf waited twenty-five feet below.

"All clear!" he shouted.

"All clear!" the others echoed.

"Eyes on the horizon! Arms crossed over your chests!" This would prevent them from breaking their necks when they hit the water.

They jumped one after the other and hit the surface hard. A moment of knifing into the warm liquid, then gaining buoyancy and coming up slightly dazed. The current quickly pulled them within ten feet of the rusted red hull, which was slipping past.

Bullets sprayed the water. The rotor wash caused by the helicopter slapped Crocker's face.

The silver Super Lynx dove over the deck, drawing some fire away.

Thanks!

Through the spray, half-light, and automatic-weapon fire, Crocker saw Ritchie reach the ship's fire hose and start pulling himself up. Mancini followed behind him, hanging on and managing to extract a grenade from his pack.

"No, Mancini! Don't!" Crocker shouted from the water.

Mancini threw one, then another.

Jesus Christ!

Panicked shouts in Arabic echoed off the deck, followed by two explosions. The ship kept sliding through the water, and the shooting stopped for a moment.

The helicopter made another pass through the smoke, then climbed and banked.

"Boss, here. Grab onto my hand!"

"I got it." Out of breath, salt water in his mouth and nostrils. In Mancini's face, "This is a tanker! Don't throw any more fucking grenades, you maniac. The whole god-damn ship can blow!"

"They were smoke grenades, boss, for cover. I made sure to aim them at the bridge."

"No more, you understand? Too fucking hazardous. We don't know what kind of cargo it's carrying."

"Roger!"

Crocker figured the tanks in the hold were fully loaded, since the ship rode low in the water. It was a mere eight or nine feet to the cargo deck.

There the strong smell of kerosene met them. A small fire had broken out on the bridge.

A hail of bullets ricocheted off the metal pumps and ripped into the ballast pipes. The SEALs dove behind any cover they could find—valves, metal flanges, railings.

Crocker sent Mancini to inspect the bow. Then he and the others retrieved their weapons from the waterproof bags and started returning fire.

"Don't waste ammunition. Our supply is limited."

One hairy-chested terrorist in a soiled white T-shirt charged down the stairs firing an AK-47—a spray-and-pray maneuver, the kind amateurs often resorted to. Ritchie aimed and caught him in the throat, and the man spun and tumbled down hard, like a rag doll losing parts.

Mancini was back, panting, his face beet red. "I spotted explosives all up and down the outlet pipes on the hold. This baby's rigged to blow!"

Figure about ten thousand tons of some highly volatile substance. Kerosene? Gasoline? Jet fuel?

Whatever the amount, it would create an enormous bomb. Make the passenger jets from 9/11 look like firecrackers.

"We gotta steer it away from the loading station!"

"I got that covered, boss," Mancini countered. "But we got to take control of the bridge first."

"Roger that."

Enclosed by windows, the bridge sparkled like a crown atop the five-story white superstructure adjacent to the ship's stern. Rising twelve feet above it was a tall white communications tower, radar tracker, and emergency beacon.

Crocker said, "Davis and I will attack from the starboard side. Mancini and Ritchie take the port."

"Now?" Ritchie asked, burning with intensity.

Crocker looked behind him to see the Ras Tanura oil terminal playing hide-and-seek beyond the arched metal. Turning back toward the bridge, he looked at his men and said, "Move!"

Ritchie took off like a rocket with Mancini behind him, ducking, zigzagging, and firing all at once.

Crocker slapped Davis's arm. "Follow me!"

With bullets smashing and ricocheting around them, Crocker ducked under the deck lines that ran fore and aft down the middle of the ship. They provided some cover. Still, the terrorists firing from three decks above had a definite advantage.

How many of them are there? Crocker asked himself,

as Davis shouted near his shoulder: "Boss, watch out! Get down!"

Crocker turned to see two bearded men emerge from a stairway past the first hold, approximately forty feet behind them, in the direction of the bow. Seeing the Americans, the two terrorists pointed their weapons and opened fire.

A paunchy man with longish thinning black hair and a thick stubble appeared behind the two shooters, accompanied by a younger man. The overweight one looked vaguely familiar.

"Isn't that AZ?" Davis asked, his urgent breath in Crocker's face.

"Which one?"

"The pudgy barefoot guy in the black pants."

Crocker quickly compared the broad face and long nose to the image in his head.

"You might be right!"

"It's him, boss. I'd put big money on it."

"Where the fuck are they going?" It was difficult to see because of the unending volley of incoming bullets. Even raising their heads a fraction invited instant death. Squirming to his right, Crocker found a crack between the metal railing and the bulkhead, and looked in the direction of the bow.

Here he saw a portable ladder unwinding down the starboard side of the ship, then two bodies descending. Below them he made out the top of a ten-foot launch bobbing in the water. Trapezoidal, with twin outboards in back.

A last terrific volley, then the firing let up. Crocker raised his head in time to catch the last two men scurrying over the side.

Davis: "Where the fuck did they go?"

"They got into a boat. Follow me!"

But the second they left the safety of the overhang, they were stopped by ferocious firing from the bridge behind them. Pinned again, chins and stomachs to the deck, protected only by a metal outlet valve and pump.

He heard a motor start up below. The launch.

Amid the terrible clatter of incoming fire, Crocker looked in the sky for help from the helicopter, but it was nowhere in sight.

Fuck'n asshole pilot!

Zaman was escaping! The American felt an ache that traveled all the way into his bones.

I can't let it happen. Not again.

"Cover me!" Crocker shouted desperately, knowing he had to go for broke.

"Boss, hold up!"

But he was already gone, springing from the deck, turning and running approximately thirty feet toward the bow, then veering to the starboard side of the ship. He climbed to the spot where the ladder was attached and, glimpsing the launch below pulling away from the hull, threw himself off.

All in!

MP5 in his right hand, KA-BAR in his left, he flew like a missile.

The four terrorists in the launch didn't see him coming. He hit the tallest one full-on, driving into the man's chest so that his knees gave way and he crumpled backward. Crocker heard the terrorist's ribs crack when his back hit the side of the craft, which simultaneously helped soften the American's landing and jolted the boat enough that the other three lost their footing, stumbled, and reached for the sides.

This gave Crocker the momentary advantage he needed. Filled with purpose and fury, he grabbed the man closest to him and snapped his neck with a wicked twist. As another terrorist reached for his AK-47, Crocker plunged the KA-BAR into his gut and raked it up to his sternum.

A terrible muffled scream sounded as insides spilled out and the man went down.

The SEAL team leader took a deep breath.

As he exhaled, he felt a sharp pain at the back of his calf. Then the tall man behind him—the one he had slammed into when he dove into the boat—threw a loaded magazine that hit the side of the launch and fell into the water.

The SEAL took two quick steps toward him and brought his boot down hard on the man's throat.

Now it was just Crocker and Zaman in the launch—Crocker near the stern, Zaman at the bow. Two bodies between them pouring out blood.

The al-Qaeda leader reached down for an AK-47 near his feet. But the American was quicker, kicking it away despite the pain in his calf.

When he looked up, their eyes locked—enemy faced mortal enemy; religious fervor confronted fierce determination.

"Where's your burka?" Crocker asked.

Sneering, Zaman glanced at the AK-47 behind him, then back at Crocker. He had something clenched in his right fist.

I fucking dare you, Crocker's eyes shouted.

The launch continued to drift away from the ship. Blood from the KA-BAR dripped down the American's right arm.

"You're mine now, Zaman."

"No, I'm not." The voice came back in clear British-accented English. Under the circumstances it was eerily assured.

Adrenaline racing through him, Crocker took a step closer, as Zaman reached for whatever he had in his right fist.

The American heard a distinctive metallic click and stopped. Zaman had pulled the pin to a grenade, which he held to his chest. He smiled like the devil, without doubt or fear.

"We meet the Messenger together. *Allahu Akbar*."

Fuck that!

With no time to think, Crocker sprung over the side and hit the water just as the grenade went off. He felt a piece of hot metal rip into the skin near his ankle and heard a muffled roar as he sank into the Gulf.

Even in the bitter smoke and tumult, his heart rejoiced.

CHAPTER TWENTY-ONE

Victory is reserved for those who are willing to pay its price.

—Sun Tzu

A PART of him wanted him to stop. It kept telling Crocker that he could relax now that Abu Rasul Zaman was dead. Other people would deal with the ship. His body had taken a beating since he'd arrived in Muscat. He'd basically had the shit kicked out of him—having been punched, shot at, burned, shot up with painkillers, deprived of sleep. He needed a break.

But he continued moving automatically—tying the shredded wreck of the launch to the side of the *Syrena*, slinging the MP5 over his shoulder as he climbed the ladder.

The SEAL team leader half expected to be greeted by Saudi troops or U.S. Rangers, but instead stood alone on the deck, the sun starting to heat up behind him, bursts of automatic-weapon fire coming from the bridge.

I guess we'll have to stop this bad boy ourselves.

Why not? He and his men were once again at the pointy end of the spear. They'd been trained to do the undoable. But the challenge they faced this time seemed unreal, given the size of the vessel, the fact that it was loaded with kerosene and rigged with explosives. Fire burning on the third deck, sent a plume of black smoke into the early-morning sky. No one had arrived to help.

Hadn't anyone else taken notice? Were he and his men the only ones who appreciated the danger the ship presented? What had happened to the Omani helicopter? Where were the Saudi patrols, the satellite cameras, the billions spent in the United States, Great Britain, France, on security?

Turning and looking behind him, he saw the Ras Tanura oil-loading platform past the ship's bow, no more than half a mile away. If the ship did manage to reach the platform and explode, the entire industrialized world would feel the repercussions. Gasoline and heating-oil prices would skyrocket, affecting businesses and economies. Presidents, prime ministers, and generals would pay attention then.

But where were they now? Sleeping? Making pronouncements? Sitting in meetings discussing policy?

He heard a whisper from near the bottom of the cabin structure. "Boss. Boss, over here."

And recognized the voice. "Davis, is that you?"

"Fifteen feet in front of you. Ten o'clock."

Shielding his eyes from the glare of the morning sun, he spotted a figure seated in the shadows, his back against the dirty white metal wall. It was Davis, cradling his MP5 and trying to look like he was okay. But when Crocker stepped closer, he saw the intense anguish in Davis's blue eyes. A bullet had torn through his forearm and fractured his ulna. Davis had used his shirt as a tourniquet, which he'd tied just below his shoulder. His white undershirt was dark with blood.

"We've got to get you out of here," Crocker said, before remembering that they had deployed without the rescue or contingency plan they were accustomed to spelling out in meticulous detail. They hadn't even carried a first-aid kit or blowout patch to put over a big wound like this.

Davis said grimly, "Looks like you're going up alone."

There was no time to try to stop the ship via the engine room.

"Guess so," Crocker answered, hearing gunfire coming from the other side of the superstructure and hoping it was a sign that Ritchie and Mancini were making progress.

He admired the younger Davis's warrior spirit, and hated leaving him.

Davis grimaced and asked, "Hey, boss, was that man we saw really AZ?"

"He's dead now," Crocker answered.

"Good work."

Crocker took the narrow metal steps two at a time, feeling the burden of responsibility to his men—all brave and willing to give their lives.

Volleys of automatic-weapon fire echoed through the stairway. Spotting a still body on the floor of the passageway of deck two, he gritted his teeth and prayed that it wasn't Ritchie or Mancini. Taking a step closer, he saw a bearded face and expectant eyes—waiting for a dozen beautiful virgins, no doubt.

Acrid gray smoke poured out of a cabin behind the corpse. He heard someone calling out in Arabic from a higher deck.

Shielding his eyes, Crocker stepped inside the cabin and saw that it had been a lounge of some sort. A game console was in one corner, a small flat-screen TV on the far wall, a couple of old leather armchairs. There was also a box of nine-millimeter ammunition, shells scattered across the floor, and shards of glass everywhere.

All he could hear was the crackle of something burning inside, so he backed out quickly and hurried up to deck three.

The balcony there was a mess: pools of blood, part of an arm with a hand attached, flames shooting out of the cabins, walls blackened and pitted from an explosion.

The smoke blinded him and burned his throat. The metal under his feet was so hot that the soles of his boots started to melt.

Shielding his eyes with his arm, he was halfway up to deck four when he was deafened for a moment by an explosion. Then, without warning, someone running down the smoke-filled stairway crashed into him chest to chest, as had happened to him one of the few times he'd played rugby.

Crocker went down hard and quickly tried to pull himself up. Got partway when he blacked out, the wind knocked out of him.

He came to seconds later and reached for his weapon, which he couldn't locate. His hands were seared by the hot metal.

Fuck!

He was getting to his feet unsteadily when the other man hurled himself on top of him. Had him in a headlock before Crocker could react.

The two men grappled in the narrow smoky stairway.

Impossible to see and difficult—painful, even—to breathe.

The man squeezed Crocker's throat with one arm and reached for something with his other hand. A knife, most likely.

The American had no room to maneuver, and the metal through the back of his shirt was hot. His right arm pinned against the wall, his left grabbed the terrorist's hair and twisted his head hard.

The man growled and swore in Arabic.

"Fuck you, too!"

He brought his knee up into the terrorist's crotch. And again. And one more time, with vigor, until the bearded man groaned and loosened his lock on Crocker's neck.

He pulled free. But a big intake of smoke-filled air clouded his head, and immediately the terrorist swung his right arm and Crocker felt a burning sensation travel along the top of his bicep.

Motherfucker!

The pain from the cut brought a tremendous surge of energy, which Crocker directed into his free left hand, which moved up the man's chest to his beard. Grasping the mesh of whiskers, with all the force he could muster he shoved the man's head back until it smashed into the wall of the stairway with the dull echo of a hammer.

The man struggled to raise his knife.

Crocker bashed his head into the metal wall one more time, harder. Then a third, until he heard the skull crack and the knife clatter down the metal stairs. He felt the fight drain out of him.

Round one. Or two. Or three, four, or five. He'd lost count.

His head spinning from the combat and the smoke, Crocker kicked the groaning man in the chest, then stepped over him and relieved him of the nine-millimeter pistol stuck in his belt. Crocker's own MP5 had slid down the stairs when the men collided. There was no time to look for it now.

Pushing through the dense smoke and stepping over another body, he arrived on the top deck—the bridge. His lungs and chest burning. Blood from the cut across his bicep spilling down his arm.

He tore off a piece of his shirt and made a field tourniquet, tightening it around the top of his arm until the bleeding stopped. He figured he had a couple of minutes at best before he passed out from the smoke or loss of blood.

Righting himself against a metal doorway, he seared his left palm again.

Men were grunting and struggling nearby. Through the smoke he recognized the back of Mancini's square head. Then the side of a stubble-covered face, the whites of someone's eyes.

In a little oval window of visibility, he saw Mancini and a terrorist locked nose to nose, knife blades glistening, eyes bulging. Mancini shoved the terrorist against a dark blue instrument panel. Then his feet slipped out from under him and the two men fell.

Knives clattered across the floor.

Crocker lost the two men in the smoke.

"Mancini? Where are you?" His heart beating desperately.

"Watch out, boss!"

Holding his KA-BAR knife ready, Crocker bent at the

waist, trying to see through the thick murk. He saw someone raise a pistol, then a terrified look on Mancini's face.

He dove for what he hoped was the terrorist's arm, held it, and twisted it right. Two shots from the pistol reverberated in the half-open space and numbed his hearing.

Teeth sunk into his left shoulder.

Fucking savage!

"Manny, you all right?" All the while clubbing the side of the man's head with his fist. Then he stumbled over a pair of legs and fell. Landed on his bum shoulder.

Fuck!

A stab of pain shot from his arm to the base of his head. From his vantage on the floor of the bridge, he saw a knife blade drag across a man's throat. The thin ribbon of red grew wider.

"Manny, fuck—"

He held his breath and readied himself. His heart pounded; his arm, shoulder, and eyes burned.

"Boss, you still here?" the Italian American whispered.

Huge relief. "Hey, Mancini. How about you help me the fuck up?"

The gunfire had stopped. Both men were breathing hard, wheezing from the smoke.

"That was fun."

"You see Ritchie?"

"He went inside to try to get the radio to work. Call for—"

A whooping sound.

"What the hell is that?"

Up ahead, past the bow, they saw two Saudi navy patrol boats approaching with wailing sirens.

"I'll look for Ritchie," Crocker said. "You try turning this piece of shit around."

"Sure, boss." Then, pointing at the patrol boats, "What about them?"

"What about 'em?" Crocker retorted, thinking that the Saudis had arrived with too little and were way too late.

As he pivoted to his right, an explosion went off in one of the cabins, throwing both him and Mancini to the floor.

"I'm getting tired of this shit," the Italian American groaned from near the wheel.

Crocker's ears were still ringing. "What'd you say?"

"Ears are fucked, right knee is screwed to shit again, but I'll manage."

Crocker saw something, or someone, emerging from the smoke-filled cabin and reached for his knife.

"Three o'clock!"

Mancini aimed his pistol and was about to pull the trigger when Crocker recognized the Nike footwear Ritchie favored. "Ritchie, that you?"

The dark-haired SEAL removed the blanket he'd thrown over his head and squinted. "Boss?"

"What'd you find?"

"Radio's for shit. Some of the explosives are on a timer, so unless we want to get blown to pieces, we'd better abandon this shitbox. Like, now!"

Crocker turned to Mancini, who had his nose inches from the controls. Through the shifting smoke he could make out a professional navigator, a radar screen, charts, assorted gauges.

"You hear that, Mancini?"

"I need a minute," the thickly built SEAL said, grasping the ship's wheel.

"You know what you're doing?"

"I don't know this vessel specifically, but I haven't me one yet that I couldn't figure out."

Crocker took some solace in the fact that the Italia American was one of the leading VBSS experts in Nava Special Warfare. His training had included practice i taking down ship bridges and engine rooms in everythin from cruise ships to destroyers and supertankers.

Ritchie wasn't happy. "No time for figuring shit out right, boss?"

Crocker felt himself fading in and out of conscious ness, and begged his mind to hang on for another minut or two.

"Motherfucker's gonna blow any second!"

"What?"

"You hear me, boss? We'd better bail!"

"No..."

"No, what? Boss, can you hear me?"

Ritchie was holding him up.

"Manny...Rich..."

"Boss, what are you trying to say?"

"Go down to the main deck. Get Davis. You need to help him to the launch. It's tied up midship. We'll meet you on the starboard side."

"You sure you don't need help?"

"Quickly!"

As he spoke, he felt the ship shifting under his feet.

He looked through the smoke to see Mancini smiling like a kid who'd just discovered how a new toy works. "It's like steering a big semi, but smoother. Really nice."

"You got it turning?"

"Look." The Italian American's whole body was

shrouded in gray-black smoke, which curled around his neck. Past his shoulders, through the windows, Crocker saw that the ship was veering northward.

"Excellent, Manny! Nice fucking work."

"The Saudis sure seemed surprised."

"Where?"

Mancini pointed toward the port bow, where the two Saudi patrol boats appeared as the ship swung right. They sounded their sirens and fired flares.

"Lot of good the flares will do."

"Except possibly set this big sardine can on fire."

Crocker started to cough. His head wobbled and his lungs hurt.

He felt Mancini lifting him up. "Boss. Lean on me, boss. Like the Bill Withers song." Mancini started humming in his ear. Everything felt sticky and hot.

"Stop fucking around," Crocker said with a groan. "Keep an eye out for terrorists. Abandon ship!"

He blacked out as Mancini started to explain how he'd aced a piloting course at the New York Maritime College the team had sent him to a few years back.

Next thing Crocker remembered was standing on the deck and seeing an endless expanse of water in front of the bow.

That means we've succeeded. Right?

He was leaning against Mancini's shoulder. "What happened? Where are we?"

"Watch the cables."

"Davis. Where's Davis? I need to treat his wound."

"Ritchie's got him."

Good...

He felt warm salt water all around him and opened his

eyes. Mancini had an arm around his chest. He started kicking, trying to swim.

"Relax, boss. Stop struggling."

"I'm good." His shoulder and arm burned like hell from the salt.

"Boss, I got you."

"Where's the launch?" His vision started to blur.

"The launch sunk."

"What?"

"There's a Saudi boat here. We're close..."

He remembered treading water, then blinked and saw a ship in the distance, steaming away. He blinked again and was seated on a deck. Saudi men in uniform scurried around him. One of them handed him a blanket.

"Is that the *Syrena?*" he asked pointing at the distant ship with its stern toward them.

Ritchie: "Yes, boss. That's it."

He counted his men: Ritchie, Mancini, Davis.

Where was the fourth? Where was Akil?

The next time he opened his eyes, he was shaken by a huge explosion. The *Syrena* had been replaced by a tremendous ball of orange flames. The Saudi boat rocked; a heavy spray of water hit him in the face.

"What the fuck was that?" he asked, holding on to a metal flange.

"The tanker, boss. The tanker blew."

"The *Syrena?* You sure?"

"Gone."

"Really?"

"It's all good, boss."

"Where's Akil?"

"We left him on the helicopter, remember?"

"That's right."

"Mission accomplished!"

It hurt to smile. "Mission accomplished..."

He sighed, and relaxed.

He looked up to see Jim Anders in his light blue suit grinning down at him, sunlight forming a halo around his head.

"Crocker," he said. "Congratulations."

Crocker squinted into the sunlight that streamed past the curtains, not sure whether what he was experiencing was a dream or reality.

Anders stepped closer. "You wanted Zaman and you got him. And in the process stopped a major terrorist attack."

Crocker's lungs hurt when he took a deep breath. "Where am I?"

"You're back in Muscat."

He pulled himself up carefully, pain and stiffness radiating from all areas of his body. "How's Davis? Where are my men?"

"Davis is recuperating. The rest of your team is resting at a nearby hotel."

"Is he okay?"

"Davis? Yeah, the doctors patched him up and say he'll be out of here by the end of the week."

"Good. And he's spoken to his wife?"

"Yes. The baby arrived early. It's a girl."

Crocker grinned. "A girl. That's funny."

"Why?"

"It's not important."

Anders kept smiling as though he had more to say.

"I've got to give you credit, Crocker. You were right all along."

"About what?"

"The connection between Zaman and Cyrus."

"Oh, that." Crocker wanted to sleep.

"Zaman was using the kidnapping operation to fund his terrorist activities. Sheik Rastani was one of his clients. Our people in Marseille have uncovered more evidence linking Cyrus and Zaman. The FBI and Interpol are tracking down additional girls."

"I'm glad."

"You saw the connection clearly. We weren't so sure."

Crocker had to will his eyes to stay open. "When you're on the ground, in the middle of the shit, you learn to trust your instincts. They're always way ahead of your rational mind."

"But policy decisions have to be justified."

Crocker wanted to say, "Try it sometime." But he had already sunk back on the bed and was fast asleep.

Two days later, he was dreaming of being tossed back and forth by two large men dressed in gorilla suits. One of them sounded like Mancini. The sailing through the air made him giggle.

"Stop, you guys! Stop!"

He was laughing so hard he thought he was going to piss his pants.

"That's an order! I can't—"

He woke up in the window seat of a passenger jet, smiling. A stewardess with bright eyes leaned toward him and asked him to bring his seat to the upright position.

"Where are we?" he asked, looking out the window.

Saw that the airplane was passing through billowy white clouds that reminded him of smoke.

For a few seconds he was back on the bridge of the *Syrena,* in the chaos and grunting bodies, trying to locate Mancini's face.

"Ladies and gentlemen, we're beginning our approach to Dulles Airport," the voice over the PA said. "The captain is expecting some minor turbulence."

He relaxed and, feeling pressure in his bladder, knew what he had to do.

The woman in the business suit in the aisle seat looked annoyed when he asked to get by her. He recalled that earlier in the flight she had asked him if he was a boxer.

He'd answered, "No, ma'am."

"Then what happened to your face?"

"I fell off a horse."

Confronting his bruised face in the bathroom mirror, he remembered the last two days in Muscat, mostly spent in the hospital, where he'd been stitched up and treated for smoke inhalation. Then the reunion with his men in Davis's room, the debriefing from Lou Donaldson, the congratulations from the U.S. ambassador, and, finally, a medal awarded by the sultan of Oman himself.

The Legion of Royal Merit, or something like that. Crocker had stashed it in his luggage. Planned to show it to Jenny when he got home.

The two days since the mission in the Persian Gulf had been a blur of sleep, dreams, and pieces of memories.

All he really cared about was that he and the members of his team had completed their mission and were returning home alive.

He longed to see Holly and Jenny again, to spend time

in their company and rest. Maybe take them for a drive into the Shenandoah. Hike. Camp. Maybe book a couple of nights at a nice hotel. Enjoy some good meals. Feed his soul with live music. Work out.

Sonny Rollins's strong, confident version of "My One and Only Love" played in his head.

Crocker knew himself well enough to understand that in a week or two, he'd start getting antsy and would be ready for another dangerous mission somewhere in the world.

Returning to his seat, he leafed through the front section of the *New York Times*. Headline stories about political haggling on Capitol Hill, inflation in China, volatility on the stock market, a boy from Korea who had become a millionaire at nineteen.

But no mention of the kidnapped girls, or the dramatic end of the *Syrena* in the Persian Gulf.

Crocker decided it was better that way.

The last weeks had underlined several important truths. One, all those dedicated to fostering and preserving individual freedom were in this fight together. Two, the world was becoming increasingly complex and interdependent—which meant that the dangers to free people everywhere were growing exponentially. Three, his men hadn't let him down and never would.

Once again, they'd lived up to the promise they'd made when they received their tridents and became SEALs—to "never quit," to "persevere and thrive under adversity," and to "be physically harder and mentally stronger" than their enemies.

Arguably the world's most lethal, versatile, and highly trained warriors, Crocker and his men had succeeded in defeating the terrorists this time, with the help of dedicated Omanis and Norwegians. But barely.

Maybe next time they wouldn't be so lucky.

Crocker knew that possibility wouldn't diminish his enthusiasm for doing what he was driven to do. He also understood that to stay ahead of freedom's enemies, he and his team would have to get smarter and be more proactive.

He'd make sure they did.

ACKNOWLEDGMENTS

Don and Ralph would like to thank their great editor, John Parsley, as well as William Boggess, Chris Jerome, Miriam Parker, Ruth Tross, and the talented designers and other professionals at Mulholland Books / Little, Brown. They also want to express their appreciation to their outstanding agent, Heather Mitchell. Don also thanks his fellow Navy SEAL teammates who inspired this book. Finally, Ralph wants to salute the brave Navy SEALs past and present, and acknowledge his wife, Jessica, and children, John, Michael, Francesca, and Alessandra.

ABOUT THE AUTHORS

Don Mann (CWO3, USN) has for the past thirty years been associated with the Navy SEALs as a platoon member, assault team member, boat crew leader, and advanced training officer, and more recently he has been program director preparing civilians to go to BUD/S (SEAL Training). Until 1998 he was on active duty with SEAL Team Six. Since his retirement, he has deployed to the Middle East on numerous occasions in support of the war against terrorism. Many of the active-duty members of SEAL Team Six are the same men he taught how to shoot, conduct ship and aircraft takedowns, and operate in urban, arctic, desert, and river and jungle warfare, as well as close quarters battle and military operations in urban terrain. He has suffered a broken back, two pulmonary embolisms, and multiple other broken bones in training or service. He has twice survived being captured during operations.

Ralph Pezzullo is a *New York Times* bestselling author and award-winning playwright and screenwriter. His books include *Jawbreaker* (with CIA operative Gary Berntsen), *At the Fall of Somoza, Plunging Into Haiti* (winner of the Douglas Dillon Award for American Diplomacy), *The Walk-In, Most Evil* (with Steve Hodel), *Eve Missing,* and *Blood of My Blood*. His film adaptation of *Recoil* by Jim Thompson, directed by James Foley, is scheduled to reach theaters next year.

...AND THEIR NEXT NOVEL

In December 2012 Mulholland Books will publish *SEAL Team Six: Hunt the Scorpion,* the sequel to *SEAL Team Six: Hunt the Wolf.* Following is an excerpt from the novel's opening pages.

"Act in the valley so that you need not fear those who stand on the hill."

—Danish proverb

CHIEF WARRANT Officer Tom Crocker of SEAL Team Six looked up at the moon rising ominously over the mud-walled compound, which was roughly two hundred feet in front of him. Then turned to Davis, the blond-haired comm man to his right, and asked, "Any news?"

"The drone is on its way."

"How much longer?"

"Ten minutes max."

"Ten additional minutes?"

"That's what HQ said."

The SEAL Team Six assault leader looked down at his watch. It was 2202 hours local time, which meant that they'd been waiting for nearly an hour behind the dry scrubs that grew around an outcropping of rocks on a hill in southern Yemen.

It was a minor miracle they hadn't been discovered. They sat smack in the middle of al-Qaeda territory, only a dozen miles south of the city of Jaar, which had been seized by the terrorists in March 2011. The lights of a little Yemeni village sparkled in the distance to Crocker's right.

This was supposed to be a simple insert and destroy. The target: a Sunni mullah named Ahmed, formerly a citizen of the UK, currently a vocal leader of al-Qaeda in south Yemen.

Because of U.S. political considerations, the target had to be ID'd first, which involved an elaborate trail of digital connections that began with the SEAL team on the ground and ended in a trailer in the parking lot of CIA headquarters, where an officer from CIA Directorate of Operations (DO) had to peer into a video monitor, connected by satellite feed to a camera on the tardy drone, and confirm that the image on the screen likely corresponded to the intended target. Then, and only then, could he give the order to Crocker and his team to take the target out.

How was the officer in Langley supposed to establish the mullah Ahmed's identity with any degree of certainty when he was probably bearded and wearing a black turban like all the other al-Qaeda terrorists? Why was the Agency being so careful?

These were questions of DC bureaucratic politics Crocker had learned to avoid, as much as they seemed to want to drive him crazy.

Instead of complaining, which he knew would do no good, he focused on applying his extensive training, experience, expertise, and instincts to the mission at hand.

Surveying the area around him through AN/PVS helmet-mounted night-vision goggles, he confirmed that all the pieces of the op were in place. Ritchie (his explosives expert and breacher) and Mancini (equipment and weapons) were in position outside the back of the compound. They were ready to detonate the explosives that would initiate the assault and cover anybody retreating out the back. Akil (maps and logistics), Davis (comms), and Calvin (the Asian-American SEAL sniper he had brought with him) hugged the ground to Crocker's immediate right.

The four of them were positioned on a hill that looked directly into the front of the compound, which was approximately one hundred feet wide. Contained three structures—a main house and two smaller sheds or garages. The second and third stories of the house were visible above the ten-foot-high wall. Low yellow lights shone in some of the windows, creating an eerie effect.

"This is Tango two-five. You guys fall asleep? What's the good word?" Ritchie's voice came through the earphones built into Crocker's helmet.

"We're still waiting for the order."

"Manny's getting hungry. He's looking at me funny. What's taking so long?"

"We're waiting for the drone. Stand by."

Crocker understood their frustration. He and his men liked to strike fast and extract. Cooling their heels in enemy territory only invited trouble.

He hoped that once they got the go-ahead, they could overwhelm the compound quickly and finish the job. First, a big explosion along the back wall, then Akil would run forward and attach C5 to the front gate. Blow it in. Then they'd rush in taking preplanned routes and getting into firing positions. Should the terrorists show themselves in any of the compound windows, Cal would pick them off.

Once the mullah was down, Mancini and Ritchie could cover their retreat to the helicopter extraction point, which was approximately half a mile behind them.

His team was also prepared for other contingencies, should they occur.

Approximately eight feet ahead and three feet to his right, Cal was completing the set up of the MK 11 Mod 0 sniper weapons system, which consisted of an MK 11 precision semiautomatic rifle, a twenty-round magazine box, QD scope rings, a Leupold Vari-X Mil-dot riflescope, a Harris swivel-base bipod on a Knight's mount, and a QD sound suppressor. The weapon fired a 7.62 NATO round with a muzzle velocity of 2,951.5 feet per second and an effective range of 1,500 yards.

Cal—who looked Polynesian but claimed to be a mixture of Japanese, German, and Irish—carefully adjusted the Leupold scope to factor in the wind blowing from the southeast. Four clicks moved the point of impact one inch at approximately one hundred yards.

Crocker had relied on Cal in similar circumstances before and knew him to be a deadly shot. He was also an avid conspiracy-theorist, hunter, and Texas Hold-'em enthusiast in his spare time. A somewhat odd but friendly fellow who claimed to have won over half a million dollars playing poker. Unmarried, unattached. Almost never spoke about his personal life. His eyes and mouth upturned in a seemingly perpetual smile.

Having adjusted his weapon, Cal turned and flashed a thumbs-up sign.

"See anything?" Crocker asked.

"Got one of the camel-jockeys in my crosshairs through the upstairs window. Can I take the shot?"

"Any minute now."

"I'm ready. More than ready."

"Hold on."

"I'll make this easy. Pop. Pop. One dead mullah. We go home. Listen to some music."

"Negative, Cal. We're waiting for the drone."

Crocker glanced at his watch. More than ten minutes had passed since the last time he looked. He sat in a crouch behind a car-size rock listening for the hum of an approaching drone. But all he heard was the low whistle of the wind over the mostly barren hills and goats braying in the distance.

He turned to Davis and asked, "What the fuck is taking so long?"

"Apparently the Predator got lost."

"What?"

"The Predator got lost."

"How does a drone get lost?"

"Some doofus entered the wrong coordinates into the computer."

"Fuck that."

"Human error dinks us one more time."

Crocker started to think about all the SEALs he knew who had lost their lives because of bad intelligence or some careless screw-up—a helicopter full of them in southern Afghanistan, at least a half a dozen outside of Fallujah, Iraq. He stopped.

Akil, the tall, barrel-chested Egyptian-American maps and logistics expert, leaned in and said, "I think we ought to set off the explosions now."

Crocker wanted to bark: *Don't think, just follow instructions.*

But he was a better, more restrained leader than that. He valued and welcomed the input of his men. Six disciplined, combat-tested brains were better than one.

He said, "First, we'll find out if the drone can see through the windows up front using its infrared. Apparently it's also equipped with some new camera gizmo that can deploy inside buildings."

"Sweet."

"But don't ask me how it works."

"I won't. You still haven't figured out how to change the oil in your car."

Akil was referring to a recent mishap Crocker had at home, in which he had failed to fully tighten a gasket after an oil change on his wife's Subaru Outback, which caused her engine to lock up on the highway.

Again, he heard Ritchie's voice through his earphones, "Tango two-five here. Looks like we got something moving in from the southwest."

Crocker's calves and knees were starting to ache. "What?"

"Appears to be a vehicle."

"Only one?"

"I'm gonna say one, yes."

"What do you see exactly?"

"Two headlights approaching, slowly winding down out of the hills to our right. Your left. Direction northwest."

"Roger, Tango. Heads down. Weapons ready."

"Roger and out."

He turned to Davis manning the radio and said, "Tell HQ we've got a vehicle approaching."

"Yes, sir."

From somewhere in the hills beyond the compound, he heard an engine. Then the grind of tires on a dirt road. Saw what looked like a light-colored extended-cab pickup swing into the half light.

Crocker readied his MP5, then spoke into his headset: "Tango two-five. Report a white truck. Looks to be at least two individuals inside. Approaching the compound."

"Correct that. I see three, sir. Two in the cab. One in back."

"Three then."

"Roger."

Crocker watched the gate to the compound open. A bearded man wearing a black turban waved the battered Toyota pickup in. He made out a man with a long beard sitting in back with an AK-47 held between his knees.

He saw Cal to his right, peering through the scope of the MK 11 Mod 0 sniper system, ready to take a shot. Felt a rush of excitement.

God, he wanted to give the order now. Now was the time to attack—while the gate was open. But his discipline held him back.

He heard Davis's urgent voice to his right. "Boss. Boss?"

"What? You spot the Predator?"

"No, headquarters says abort."

"Abort, now?" He thought it had to be a joke.

"Abort. That's correct."

"What do they mean abort? Tell 'em we've got the terrorists in our sights."

"I did already. They want us to pull back to the extraction site."

"Now?"

"Yes."

Feeling like the wind had been kicked out of him, he asked, "Why?"

"No reason given. It's a simple abort."

Twenty-two minutes later, Crocker and his team were strapping themselves onto the benches of a Blackhawk helicopter and cradling their weapons as it lifted off the desert ground.

Ritchie, his dark eyes blazing, sat to Crocker's right.

"Boss?"

"Yeah." Shouting over the helo's engines.

"What just happened?"

"Beats the shit out of me."

"Were we at the wrong compound?"

"Not as far as I know."

"SOS [same old shit], huh, boss?"

"Yeah, SOS."

"Crazy-ass way to fight a war."

This wasn't the first time this had happened. They'd spent the last five weeks on the Arabian penninsula training, collecting intel, practicing for different ops, then being told to abort at the last minute. Adding to their annoyed state of mind was the fact that they missed their families and needed a break from the 24-7 pressure of being deployed.

Davis's wife had a young baby and was expecting another. Ritchie's new girlfriend was threatening to start dating other men if he didn't come home soon. Crocker's wife wanted some relief in dealing with his daughter, her stepdaughter, who had been living with them for a year. Mancini's wife was looking after his younger, wheelchair-bound brother, who was suffering through the final stages of pancreatic cancer and about to die. Akil's Egyptian-born father's jewelry repair business was losing money.

Every one of them had myriad problems and concerns outside their jobs.

As Crocker unbuckled his helmet the copilot, wearing a camouflage flight suit and helmet, walked over and tapped him on the shoulder.

"Sir?"

"Yeah." Holding on as the copter banked sharply.

"You Chief Warrant Officer Tom Crocker?"

"That's correct."

"Orders to fly you and your men to USS *Carl Vinson* in the Gulf of Aden."

"What for?"

"We're operating on a need-to-know basis here, sir. Those are my orders."

"Received. Thanks."

Fifteen minutes later, safely landed on the deck of the USS *Carl Vinson,* an LSO (landing signaling officer) handed Crocker a bottle of water with the ship's seal stenciled on it underneath the Latin motto *Vis per mare*—"Strength through the sea."

She was strong all right. A metal beast measuring 1,092 feet long with a capacity to hold up to ninety fixed-wing aircraft and helicopters. It carried a crew of over six thousand, including airmen. One of a fleet of ten Nimitz class supercarriers—the largest, most lethal warships on the planet.

The last time Crocker stood on the deck of the *Carl Vinson* was the night of May 5, 2011, when he and his team watched the corpse of Osama bin Laden being disposed into the ocean.

As much as they wanted to kick and piss on that piece of shit terrorist, they weren't permitted to. But they did cheer as his white-shrouded body was slipped overboard and devoured by sharks.

It seemed like a lifetime ago now. Since the death of the notorious al-Qaeda leader, Crocker and his team had been running ops almost nonstop. Over fifty in the past year to places like Pakistan, Afghanistan, Yemen, Sudan, and Somalia.

Crocker managed to squeeze a few racing events in between. Like the 135-mile, six-stage marathon across the Sahara Desert in Morocco (called the Marathon des Sables) that they were scheduled to compete in next week. He and his men had been trying to build up to it with at least sixty miles a week, plus a long thirty-mile run on their day off.

Which explained why both his Achilles tendons were tight and his knee and lower back were barking. Crocker was used to dealing with pain. He thought of it as weakness leaving his body. But he and his team had been shedding quite a bit of weight lately.

The lean, white-shirted LSO led him briskly along the flight deck, passing one of the steam catapults (known as a "Fat Cat") that was capable of accelerating a thirty-seven-ton jet from zero to 180 miles per hour in less than three seconds.

The marvels of technology. As much as Crocker admired engineers and scientists, they still hadn't invented anything that could replace the versatility and ingenuity of men on the ground.

He and his men were arguably the most highly-trained, battle-tested, and lethal fighting force in the world, prepared to deal with anything—sea, air, or land. Raids behind enemy lines, commandeering ships or airliners, rescuing hostages, assassinations, sensitive intel-gathering ops—all in a day's work.

A wise man named Friedrich Nietzsche once said, "Many stumble in the pursuit of the path they have chosen; few in pursuit of the goal."

Crocker had committed those words to memory. They were his mantra. Don't worry about the fuck-ups and bumps in the road; focus on your goal.

The goal was to protect his countrymen from people who wanted to destroy their way of life, take away their freedoms, shred the Constitution and Bill of Rights.

That wasn't going to happen as long as Tom Crocker was alive. No way. He hadn't earned his reputation as "Chief Warrant Officer Manslaughter" for nothing. People would *ooh* and *aah* over high-tech drones, listening systems, heat imaging. But when really nasty, difficult shit needed getting done, it was sheepdogs like him and his men who had to step in and protect the sheep from the wolves.

Crocker followed the LSO down steep metal steps, through a tight corridor that led to the captain's quarters. Photos of the ship's namesake, Congressman Carl Vinson—the only man to serve more than fifty years in the U.S. House of Representatives—lined the walls. Another bald-headed, sharp-eyed man in a suit standing in front of a mansion with columns.

All Crocker wanted when he grew old was a shack in the woods, his wife—hopefully—and a means of getting food.

He'd been up for twenty-four hours and would have preferred something with a little kick, like black coffee, Red Bull, or a can of Diet Mountain Dew. But water was better than nothing, especially with the taste of the desert still in his mouth.

The LSO stopped and opened the door to a state-of-the-art conference room. The ship's captain—an energetic man with a lantern jaw and short-cropped gray hair—stood and squeezed Crocker's hand.

"Welcome aboard, Warrant. Glad you could make it."

"It's good to be back, sir."

"Take a seat and we'll drop the disco ball."

Crocker, still dressed in his desert cammies, barely got out a question—"Sir, what's going on?"—before the lights dimmed and a panel of four large color LED monitors descended from the ceiling and lit up. On one of them he recognized the gaunt face of his CO back at SEAL headquarters in Virginia.

Which caused him to sit up at attention. Instinctively, he started to wonder what he had done wrong.

"Crocker, is that you?" His CO, Captain Alan Sutter, squinting through wire-framed glasses.

"Affirmative, sir." Focused on the bump where the captain's nose had been smashed during Operation Urgent Fury in Grenada, 1983, when his chute had failed to open and he crashed into a tree. Lost a mouthful of teeth, too.

"Can you hear me?"

"See and hear you clear as day, sir." His CO was damn lucky to be alive. So was he.

"Good."

"How are things back at headquarters?"

His CO didn't answer, cutting the small talk. "A critical situation has come up. Somewhat of a strategic emergency. Demands a swift response."

"My men and I are ready, sir, to do whatever's needed."

"We need someone we can trust with a very difficult scenario who's deployed in the area," Captain Sutter continued.

Crocker was going to say "difficult is my call sign," but bravado didn't sit well in the teams. Operators were expected to be humble, do their jobs, and limit the chest pounding.

"I appreciate that, sir," Crocker said instead, fighting through his exhaustion. He wasn't twenty years old anymore, but in his mid-forties. And even though he was in incredible shape, his body needed time to recover.

He could probably forget about resting tonight.

From the video monitor, his CO continued, "Involves a pirated cargo ship off the Somali coast."

The word "pirated" intrigued Crocker further. He'd heard stories of local gangs stopping cargo ships and even supertankers off the coast of East Africa and the Malacca Straits in Indonesia.

An aide slipped a pad and pencil in front of him, and Crocker took notes as his CO and two officers from the CIA CTC (Counter Terrorism Center) related the ship's position and various details, including info gleaned from the ship's emergency signal and satellite surveillance.

Crocker wondered why a cargo ship of Australian registry was getting so much attention when his CO mentioned that the ship was transporting "sensitive nuclear material" from Melbourne, Australia, to Marseilles, France.

Among Crocker's various duties, he happened to be the WMD officer at SEAL Team Six. "You referring to yellowcake, sir, or something else?" he asked. Yellowcake was uranium ore concentrate. Once it was enriched in a process that involved turning it into a gas called uranium hexafluoride, it could be used to fuel nuclear bombs.

"The exact nature of the material is classified. It's not dangerous in its current state. But it's important. Very goddamn important."

"I understand, sir."

"The White House wants this handled immediately."

"Yes, sir."

"Get your men geared up and ready to deploy."

"You can count on us, sir."

"There's no time to fly in another team or the cigarette boats. You think you and your men can handle this situation alone?"

"Absolutely. We'll take care of it, sir, as long as someone can get us there."

Typically pirates operating off the coast of Somalia held ships and their crew hostage while they negotiated five- and six-figure ransoms. So Crocker asked, "Have there been any communications from the pirates, sir? Have they made any demands?"

"None so far."

Strange, he thought.

"Approximate number of pirates?"

"Expect six to ten. Secure the sensitive material because the White House would like to use it as evidence."

Evidence of what?

"Deploy as quickly as you can," his CO said.

"Yes, sir."

As soon as the room's lights illuminated, the supercarrier's operations officer appeared at Crocker's side. A big man with a shaved head dressed in a khaki uniform.

He said, "Give me a list of what you need and I'll turn this carrier upside down to find it."

Crocker thought quickly and answered, "A helicopter that can get us there fast, two Zodiacs with twin outboards, wet suits and skin suits, fins, Dräger LAR V rebreathers, twelve frag grenades, a telescopic pole and caving ladder if you have one, flares, tie-ties, comms, SMGs and pistols."

The op officer scribbled everything down. "That all?"

"A cutlass and eye-patch if you can find them."

"What?"

"It's a joke."

"I should find most of this in one of the conex boxes from the last SEAL platoon on board."

"Works for me."

"Be on the flight deck in fifteen minutes with your men."

"Yes, sir."

Crocker was thinking about his wife, Holly, as a tall Navy officer led him through a maze of corridors past a gym, commissary, and barbershop. She worked for State Department Security and was about to deploy overseas any day, too. He wanted to call her, but there was no time.

He entered the ship's mess, where he found his men feasting on Szechuan chicken and lo mein noodles. Moving to a corner table out of earshot of other diners, he briefed his team as more aides arrived with nautical charts and satellite photos.

According to the latest intel, an unmarked assault boat appeared to be towing the MSC *Contessa* to the coast of Somalia, which was highly unusual. What were primitive pirates doing with a launch that was powerful enough to tow a forty-thousand-ton ship?

Crocker and his men would soon find out.

Still chewing a mouthful of chicken, he helped his men carry their gear and weapons up past the ship's hangars to the flight deck. There they were greeted by a fresh ocean breeze. A welcome relief from the stale air and compressed feeling below.

Crocker didn't like the confined feeling of ships, particularly the submarines he and his men had deployed from a dozen or so times over the years. Sardine cans filled with pasty-faced men. He especially disliked the Swimmer Delivery Vehicles (SDVs), which were basically mini-subs.

He covered his ears as an F-18 Super Hornet approached the *Vinson*'s flight deck, its engines screaming, its tail hook deployed. The F-18 hit the deck, sending up a tremendous shower of sparks into the night sky. But the fighter jet was slightly off track, so it missed the ship's arrest wire and quickly zoomed up to full throttle and took off again with a roar.

Crocker noted that the sky was cloudy and the sea choppy, which caused the carrier to rock side to side.

"That can't be easy," Akil remarked.

"Flying in at a hundred and seventy-five miles per hour and trying to hit a wire. You try it some time."

"No thanks."

The LSO who was escorting them shouted into Crocker's ear. "Be careful where you walk. A year ago one of our maintainers got his cranial sucked right out of his head when he stood too close to the intake of an A-6E."

"Good to know."

Right under the ship's superstructure—known as the island—they met the pilots and copilots of the two MH-60 Knighthawk helicopters that had been tasked with flying them in. Each helo was equipped with M240 machine guns and Hellfire missiles.

The four stood in a huddle studying weather charts as Crocker's men loaded their gear. One of the pilots—a lanky-haired man with gray eyes and a Fu Manchu mustache—turned to Crocker and said, "Expect the flight to be a little rough. We got some weather blowing in from the south."

"What have you got in terms of in-flight entertainment?"

"If you watch carefully you might be able to see a pelican taking a crap."

"Just get us close. We'll be fine."

"You planning to fast-rope onto the deck?"

"No, I think I'd rather take the bastards by surprise," Crocker answered.

"How far away you want us to drop you?"

"You'll need to approach lights out. Drop us about a mile behind the stern so we can't be seen."

The lead pilot nodded. "We can do that."

"Then what are we waiting for?"